To love Veronica Bee

It's **POP** fiction – book includes on-line games, animation, artwork, multimedia, music and more...

Sarah Boland

POP Fiction Press

Sarah Boland was born in Melbourne, Australia. She writes for young adults, and in 2001 conceived the Pop Fiction Youth e-Literature event. Sarah tours the event to schools, universities and libraries.

Pop Fiction is more than just reading. It's about young people using multimedia to make art that's related to a selected book. They can use the story's characters, plot, themes, issues, symbols, even important words to create their own Pop Fiction creations. After making their Pop Fiction they get to star on the Pop Fiction website.

Even if you aren't a Pop Fiction star, you can still check out the Pop Fiction site and play on-line games, watch animation, check out artwork, interact with multimedia, listen to music, meet young and emerging artists and multimedia makers, plus heaps more!

To love Veronica Bee is the first novel to be adapted into Pop Fiction. Everything on www.bumble.com.au is made by young people. They have read the book *To love Veronica Bee*, developed ideas for their artwork and/or multimedia, created their masterpiece and then posted it onto the website. Some of the artwork and multimedia is dead-set wicked, some of it makes you laugh hard enough to spray milk out of your nose (that's what John Barton said happened to him), some stuff is kinda related to the book and other stuff is really *really* related to the book – one thing is for sure though, its all gets posted for everyone to experience!

Go to **www.bumble.com.au** to find out more about Pop Fiction

If you'd like Pop Fiction to come to you, contact **popfiction@bumble.com.au**

For Mum,
Pouk
and Pop

First published in 2004
by
Pop Fiction Press
PO Box 112 Malvern VIC 3144 Australia
Fax: (61 3) 9504 8442
Email: popfiction@bumble.com.au
Web: www.bumble.com.au
1 3 5 7 9 10 8 6 4 2
National Library of Australia Cataloguing-in-Publication entry:

Boland, Sarah, 1972- .
To love Veronica Bee.
ISBN 0 646 43410 1.
I. Title.
A823.4
Cover illustration by Rachel Ehrat
Cover design by Dave Jones
Photography by Chris Baikie
Edited by Deb Doyle
Typeset in 10.5/13pt Palatino
Layout by Graphic Byte
Printed in Australia by Griffin Press

Acknowledgements
Due to the nature of Pop Fiction and its expanding community,
book and website thank-yous are available on-line at www.bumble.com.au

CONTENTS

There's no way I'm going to love Veronica Bee.
Not for the next year, ANYWAY!!!!!!!!!!!!!!!!!!!!X#*+@Y???!!!

1

'*Veronica*! *Veronica*!'

Raleigh Berry was running two metres in front of me. We raced around the bend of the track, into the home straight. I could see the Year 7's standing in the shade of the gum trees, and hear Susie screaming louder than everyone else. Fair enough: it was okay with me if Susie wanted to make a fuss – we were best friends and 'competition freaks': always trying to win the trophy when we were competing in weekend horse shows . . . but the rest of the class?

Lifting my knees, I closed the gap between first and second place. I'd never beaten Raleigh – her legs were twice as long as mine – but I was furious about *everything*, so I ran like Cathy Freeman. I was – *Atta girl*, I told myself – gaining even more speed and now shoulder to shoulder with Raleigh. I could see the side of her face and her cheek shuddered as her shoes struck the ground.

'*Veronica*! *Veronica*!'

Neil Wright ran to the side of the track. He slapped his hands against the school banner, and yelled my name. Two weeks earlier, he and I had a punch-up in the quadrangle after he'd caught me trying on his football jacket. And Craig Berton: there he was – waving his End-of-Year Break-up Carnival itinerary in the air like he'd just seen a spaceship! At lunchtime, as we'd been putting the high-jump mat away, he'd shoved me after I'd kicked him for calling me 'Four-Eyes' *again*. And as for the 'cricket-pitch chicks', who during lunch had hung out at the back of the cricket nets kissing the Year 10's, they were cheering like they were my best friends.

I'd just turned 13, so that meant I wasn't born yesterday. Arching my chest forward – an inch in front of Raleigh – I sprinted across the finish line, past my Year 7 fan club, over the embankment, through the quadrangle, and into the girls' toilet block. I pushed open a cubicle door. *Heuuurrrgh*: chunks of grated carrot from my packed lunch splashed into the toilet bowl.

If I'd really had my way, I'd have sprinted across the finish line, past my *real-life genuine* fan club, waved and blown kisses over my shoulder, and continued past the toilet block, down the tan-bark track to the edge of the creek.

And I'd have laughed and rolled around among the clover, and have thought about how *cool bananas* my life was – it rocked!

And that's when I'd have seen the four-leaf clover. And I'd have plucked it from its stem and kissed it. And thought that I, Veronica Bee, was truly lucky – so *lucky* that if I came up with a Top Ten wish list, I'd be granted every one of those wishes. That's how *cool bananas* my life should've been.

I slumped back against the wall. My stomach tightened to a knot. My eyelids flickered over my eyeballs. Not one, not two, but all the Year 7 kids had cheered me on. '*Hah!*' Even though I was a better athlete than most of the other students, I was always the last one to be chosen from the line-up to be a captain or selected player for the team.

'*Veronica*! *Veronica!*' . . . They'd cheered for me!

Then, like a punch in the face, reality hit. I looked down at my worn-out runners . . . my long, white socks pulled up to my knees. I flicked the elastic of my bloomers, tweaked the plaits of my browny-blonde hair, took off my glasses, and folded the arms of the glasses over the lenses. They'd cheered for me because they didn't want to cheer for Raleigh Berry. Her teeth stuck out like a porcupine's spikes, and food was usually stuck in between them.

Heuuurrrgh.

Squatting onto my heels, I reached into my sock for a tissue. That's where I kept them: between my socks and the skin of one of my calves. But as I wiped my face, this 'tissue' paper scratched. It wasn't a tissue, it was the letter that Mum had handed me that morning as I was running out the door to catch the bus. I'd forgotten about the letter; in fact, I was trying to forget I even *had* a mother.

Dearest Veronica,

Your Mother loves you. Please don't make this any harder on yourself. I know you're not ecstatic about the family's move to Kew. I know how much you love Yarra Valley and that Susie lives just over the hill and that Ebony and Major trot around in the paddock outside your bedroom window.

Living in the city will mean that some things will change. I'm not pretending that they won't. But we are only moving a one-hour car drive closer to Melbourne, so all the things that are dear to you will not be taken away. You can still see Susie on the weekends and go riding together. And of course Susie can come and stay.

Think of all the exciting things. The new friends you will make at Lagilla Convent. I spoke to Sister Therese Cecilia yesterday and she's extremely excited to have another girl from our family attend. Firstly your grandmother, your mother, Auntie Lisa, Penny and now you - my very own Bumble-bee, following in the footsteps of her family tree. Besides, you were never that keen on the boys at Yarra Valley High. And just think, you won't have to catch a bus back and forth each day to Lagilla as Penny has done for the past six years.

You can still be a Veterinarian Equine Specialist and a champion horse rider. You never know, moving to the city may open new horizons. As promised the first year is a trial year and if the family decides to return to Yarra Valley, so be it. I miss my Bumble-bee and her beautiful smile.

Please try to love Veronica Bee.
All my love, Mum

Gritting my teeth, I tore off the last part of the letter in which my mother promised that the first year would be a trial year – that was the important evidence. Then I ripped the rest into smaller pieces and tossed them into the toilet bowl. The flush water sucked and gurgled the shredded bits.

As I shuffled out of the cubicle, the floor felt weird: it sank like a wet sponge. I tucked the saved bit of the letter into my sock, and then stared at my reflection in the mirror hung above the hand basin. I looked god-awful: bright-orange drool was smeared across my chin, and my green eyes looked yellow.

I crouched down and splashed cold water on my face. Surely there was some way of escaping – some side door I could sneak out of, or trapdoor I could fall through. Even being sucked into a black hole was better than this. I looked around; craned my neck; chewed on my lower lip. I held onto the basin, and balanced myself as the ground shifted – well, it felt like it shifted.

Maybe I could be rescued – and not like Cinderella, who was rescued by a prince. I could use 'wish one', and be rescued by a beautiful pearl-coloured unicorn with a silver mane and tail! And my unicorn would gallop towards me: across the quadrangle, straight for the toilet block. His humungous hooves would *kl-kl-klop* on the concrete. And his huge body would fly, as he'd jump over the seat where Susie and I sit and eat our lunch every day.

And then he'd skid . . . and rear up on his hind legs . . . and stretch his nose above his ears . . . and neigh: '*Her-hon-hi-haaaa*! *Ver-on-i-caaaa Bee*! *I've come to rescue thee!*' And then he'd bend down onto one knee . . . and I'd grab a fistful of his silky, silver mane . . . and swing my right leg over his big, powerful shoulder . . . and *gallop* away.

'VerOOOnica, are you *hiiiiding* in the toilet block?'

I ducked into the nearest cubicle; the toilet door banged against the metal lock. Only one student at Yarra Valley High spoke with an English accent. 'No,' I said. 'I'm not here; I'm invisible.' I shifted the lock into place, trying not to make a noise.

Susie's runners squeaked across the toilet floor. 'Open uUUp,' she said. The door shook. 'VeeEEee,' Even though Susie had lived in Australia since age eight, she spoke differently from everyone else at our school: her accent made her voice rise in the middle of her sentences, and she had a way of making some of the words sound a lot longer than how everyone else pronounced them. 'Ooopen uUUp.' The door pushed against the lock.

'What?' I asked. I pressed my shoulder against the door.

Susie reached under – the gap between the hanging door and the floor – and tapped me on the ankle. 'Doi!'

'Argh!' I screamed, and jumped back. 'Don't do that!'

She lay down on her back, poked her head under the door into my cubicle and smiled up at me. 'What?'

'*That*,' I replied, as firmly as I could.

'It's just me, you dick.' She blinked about 10 more times than she had to. 'I'm on my own,' she stated. 'What's up? You beat Raleigh Berry.'

I crossed my arms. 'If you're with one of those other *two-faced losers*,' I began, 'I'm not coming out.'

'VerOOOnica.' Susie wriggled under the toilet door then raised herself to stand beside me. 'Come on: Raleigh's –'

'So what?' I interrupted. 'I don't care.' I turned away and tucked the loose wisps of hair behind my ears.

Susie slammed down the toilet lid and stepped up on the toilet. '*Ha-hah*: first place!' she squealed. 'I'd like to present *thee*: Miss Bee – faster than a racehorse!'

'Cut it out.'

'No way,' she said. 'Come on: Raleigh's always beating us.' She jumped down off the toilet, threw open the door of the cubicle, yanked on my arm and dragged me outside.

'*Suze*, stop it!' I told her.

'No,' she said. 'And *suffer*!' She waved her arms above her head like she was in the front row at a concert. '*Suffer in your smelly-tuna breath, Raleigh Berry, you stupid dickhead*!'

I pressed my right hand over my mouth to stop myself from laughing. Even though, half way through the year, the cricket-pitch chicks had invited Susie to hang out with them, she'd said no. I thought she'd say yes, because the cricket-pitch chicks hung out with the guys from Year 10 and Suze had the hots for them. And *they* had the hots for Suze – like, when we waited for the bus after school, the Year 10 guys waved her over to chat with them. I'm not stupid. I know it's 'cause Suze is the tallest girl in Year 7, the best looking and her boobs are as big as the girls in Year 10. But even though Suze and me *were* different, we were as horse crazy as the other. And we both *hated* Raleigh Berry – she went to the same pony club, and hung around Suze and me like a bad smell.

I pushed Suzie back against the wall. '*Stop it*!' I demanded, but swallowed a giggle.

The shrill electric bell rang out. Susie grabbed my hand and dragged me across the quadrangle.

'Don't, Suze!' I pulled back. I had to shout to be heard above the other students coming back from the oval. 'Where are we going?'

'You'll see, *Nosey*.'

'But what about final-year assembly?' I asked, and pointed over my shoulder to where the music room was, where we were meant to go.'

Well, yes,' she answered. 'But first – um . . .' Then her eyes lit up like she'd been struck by a sudden brainwave. 'Mrs Thomson wants us to *laminate* the photos for the archive before we go back to class – yes!'

'The *what*?' I didn't understand: I'd often helped out Mrs Thomson in the library, but never on the last day of school. '*Photos*?'

'Yes – come on.'

'But, Suze!' But then I thought twice: *Maybe . . .* I fantasised, *Maybe it'll take us a* whole year *and I'll* have *to stay at Yarra Valley.* 'How many photos? Did she say?'

9

'Doi! I don't know. Hurry up. And stop your whingeing: she said it wouldn't take us more than 10 minutes.'

'*Oh,*' I groaned. So much for it taking us a *whole* year.

'Quick – come on.'

'*Suuuze*, I can't believe this is happening. This is like . . . god-awful. Would you stop laughing? I'm *not* trying to be funny!' I punched her arm. 'What's so funny?'

She kept laughing. '*This is terrible,*' she said. '"*God-awful!*" *Like a bomb going off!*'

I wasn't impressed. 'And I thought you were my friend!' I ran ahead, sprinting up the stairs to the library entrance. 'Rotten egg!' I yelled back.

'Vee, wait up! I didn't mean to laugh – it's just . . . I *will* miss you – truly! I love you like 10,000 John Landies!'

I turned on the top step. 'Oh yeah, right,' I said. 'And like I'm meant to think that's good.'

Mrs Thompson gave us a pile of photos. Our job was to laminate them so they'd be protected from people's fingerprints.

Susie wasn't a very good laminator. She swung back on her chair, happy to watch me instead. 'Do you think you'll move back?' she asked.

'Yes,' I said. I smoothed a bubble of air from the corner of the photo I was working on.

'You're such a perfectionist,' she said.

'I am not.' I imitated Susie running her fingers through her permed blonde hair. 'Says *you*, Miss Shirley Temple, and her perfect, *perfect* hair.'

'Really!' Susie smiled.

I was sorry I'd said it. I cut a square of laminate. The clear film peeled away smoothly from its backing.

'Hey!' Susie said, holding up a black marker pen. 'Dare you to draw a moustache.'

'No.' I pushed her hand away.

'Go on,' she insisted.

'No.'

'Can I draw one on you, then?'

'*Stop* it, Suze!'

Mrs Thomson looked up from her desk. We pretended to be smoothing out bubbles of air from between the laminate and a photo.

'*Psst*!' Susie tapped the marker pen against my wrist and then nudged my ankle. 'Who am I going to ride with when you're gone?' she asked, in a whisper.

'Raleigh Berry,' I whispered back.

We burst out laughing, and had to duck behind the nearest bookshelf. Susie bit down on her fist, hard. I couldn't look her in the face. I hugged my knees to my chest. When we finally stopped laughing, I stood up. 'There's only one photo left,' I announced.

Susie looked at her watch and then crossed her legs. She was showing no sign of getting up. 'Do you really think you'll move back?' she asked.

I rolled my eyes. How many times had she asked me that and I'd said the same thing? 'Yes,' I said, again.

'Will we still ride in the Olympics together?'

'Yes.' I hooked my little finger around hers. 'I promise. We'll ride for Australia. We'll win gold.'

Susie was a lot happier after that. We finished laminating the photos. Mrs Thompson thanked us as I placed the finished pile on her desk.

'All the best, Veronica,' she said. She stood up from her chair, and, turning to Susie, began, 'Veronica is a *wonderful* helper in the library. The returned books will start piling up in the drop box now that she's leaving: how about Susie helps –'

'Noooo!' Susie cut in. 'No. No. No. Noooo.' She bolted out the library door.

I straightened the photos, fiddling with a pen, and looked over at the photocopier. I wasn't sure whether I was about to laugh or cry – or maybe do both at the same time. 'Thanks,' I said. 'I liked helping out in the library.' I held my breath until I'd made it through the door safely. My eyes watered, and my throat choked up like a frog was stuck in it.

Susie pounced as I came around the corner. 'Come on,' she said. 'We'll miss the last bit of assembly.'

I walked into the music room.

'Surprise!'

I blinked twice. The desks were pushed together to make one huge table. Chips, lollies, biscuits, 'hundreds and thousands' sandwiches, fairy cakes, sausage rolls and party pies were stacked high on top of paper plates. The Year 7's stood at the back of the room, holding a banner above their heads.

My mouth popped. I'd thought no one cared. I turned to Susie. She winked back, and smiled as if she were clever.

'*Speech! Speech!*' the Year 7's yelled.

I pulled up my socks. *No way!* And I bet Mrs Thompson didn't even need the photos laminated. Talk about being sucked in! No wonder Susie kept looking at her watch.

Susie swatted my bum. 'Go on,' she said, and pushed me forward.

What was there to say? It wasn't like I'd planned a speech, let alone expected a party. I flashed a cheesy grin.

'*Speech*! *Speech*! *Speech*!' they yelled. Even the footballers were banging their fists against the tabletop. And John Landy cupped his hands around his mouth and yelled like he'd just kicked a goal.

I gave Susie an 'I'll kill you later' greasy over my shoulder. 'Okay,' I said. 'Ah, thanks. And, ah . . . get lost!'

Thank God they cheered – even though I *was* serious. Some of the nicer girls stepped forward. They hugged me and wished me well. Then the Year 7 captain – Karen Tools, the leader of the cricket-pitch chicks – presented me with a gift. 'This is for Veronica,' she said, dipping her head *oh so sincerely* to one side. 'The *entire* year level *collaborated* to make it in Art.'

Where was my unicorn when I needed him? I took the gift and smiled, and then a strange tingle fluttered inside my chest. I didn't want to cry – not in front of the whole class. So I chewed on my lip, and concentrated on unwrapping the gift rather than stare back at everyone as they stared at me. Immediately, I recognised Susie's handwriting on the gift. She'd written across the base of the large rock:

Each student had painted an individual pebble to have a smiley face and a set of clothes – that looked just like them – and had then glued their pebble onto the larger rock. In the centre of the big rock, some of the pebbles were stacked on top of each other, like they were 'doing it'. Talk about disgusting! And they were obviously meant to be the cricket-pitch chicks.

Susie turned the stereo up. The music thumped out loud enough to be heard from the main road. Within two minutes, Neil Wright had ruined everything – he and the footballers: they'd turned my farewell party into a competition. Who could shove the most chips into their mouth? If you laughed and sprayed chips out of your mouth, you'd earned bonus points. Who could make two Cheezels stick in the socket of their eyes without using their hands? And who could sprinkle coconut from a lamington onto their head and shoulders to look like they had the worst dandruff? And then there was the 'big burp' competition.

'*Righty-right!*' Mr Henski, the Year 7 teacher, yelled. He pushed his way through the crowd, to the troublemakers. '*Pack it up!*' He clapped his hands. '*That's it! Neil Wright! Do as you're told!*'

Even Susie was making heaps of noise and flirting with John Landy, across the other side of the room. They were taking it in turn to cover their heads with the drum kit while the other one whacked the skins.

Mr Henski screwed up his face and covered his ears. '*I said*, "TURN the music OFF!"'

I hated the guys at Yarra Valley High. It'd been my party, and they'd turned it into a mosh pit.

Ding-ding-ding.

The Year 7's cheered and ran out of the room. Suze and me grabbed our bags, pushed and shoved our way through the crowded corridor and ran out the front door of the school.

I never *ever* thought I'd dread the final bell: Yarra Valley High was like a bad dream, but by comparison, the thought of going to Lagilla Convent seemed like a nightmare. Penny had told me about the school: how nuns were the teachers and that they were really strict. She should know, 'cause she'd caught the train to the city every day and gone there for six years. She'd said that if a student didn't sit up straight, or yawned, or chewed her nails, they'd got the strap. And to prove it she'd shown me cuts on the back of her legs where she'd said a nun had whipped her for not doing her homework. Sometimes Penny tells me stuff that's not true, just to tease me or to make me scared, but this time I reckoned she was for real.

At the front gate, Suze and me turned left towards the pedestrian crossing.

I dreaded the six-week summer break between schools. 'Mum finally agreed to let me go to school *here* rather than make me catch the train to Lagilla, that way I'd have time to ride my horses after school, and *now –*' I said, throwing my bag onto the ground as Suze and I waited for Clive, the pedestrian-crossing monitor, to raise his 'Stop' sign and blow his whistle. 'After I've worked this hard to get an Equestrian Federation ranking, Mum goes and says we have to move. I don't get it, *Suze*: why can't my life be about *me* and what *I* want?'

'Bumble.' Susie held my shoulders, forcing me to look her in the face. 'We'll still compete in the Olympics together – won't we?'

'Bumble' is the nickname Dad gave me when I was a baby – not only because my surname's Bee but because I've got a baby blanket that's black and has yellow stripes, like a bee. I still use it as a blanket, even though it's not that big. Mum said Dad used to wrap me up in it and call me his bumble-bee. Penny calls me Dad's favourite: I guess he does let me sit in the front seat of the car and always takes me with him on his fishing trips.

There was no way I would ever be good enough to ride in the Olympics if I didn't get to train. 'Not if I only get to train on weekends,' I replied.

'Yes we *will* – *won't we*?' She dug her nails into my skin.

'Suze, I'll never be good enough: My riding will get worse and I'll look like one of those stupid trail-riding kids.' I flapped my arms as badly as they did: '*Giddy-up, hee-haw; yee-hah!*'

'You promised,' she said. 'You hooked pinkies with me. Remember? In the library?'

I lifted my bag over my shoulder. 'Yeah – well.' I'd been thinking about that promise. 'What if Mum breaks *her* promise?' I asked. 'Then what?'

'Don't say that.' She screwed up her face.

'Suze, but what if –?'

She walked off. Now I'd done it.

'Suze, seriously!' I ran after her. 'Okay,' I said, 'I'll think only good thoughts – so then only good stuff will happen.' She slowed down enough so I could catch up. 'Hey, how about we take the horses for a swim in your dam?'

She tugged on my plaits and smiled back. 'Great idea, race you to the bus stop,' she said, and then ran ahead. As she passed the guys from Year 10 they blew a wolf-whistle. She waved to them, and then indicated with a raised thumb over her shoulder, that she couldn't stop to chat 'cause she'd already made plans with me.

I saw the bus coming and raced to catch up. Even if she *did* have the hots for John Landy and the guys from Year 10, she was still my best-est friend.

The bus chugged along Cherry Tree Road. Suze and me were the only people on the bus, so we sat at the back. We felt like we were top dogs – like we were in Year 12.

Most of the farms we see on our way home are 'working properties'. Neil Wright's dad is an egg producer who keeps 5,000 chooks in super-huge sheds and sells the eggs to city people. When the bus passed his place, we pegged our noses with our fingers. And Craig Berton's dad grows different types of grain – hay and lucerne, for example – and his mum sells it at their general store. Raleigh Berry's parents breed goats, sell the milk at the market and make clothes from the wool. We rolled our eyes when we passed her place. Then we passed some orchards, where Suze and me pick fruit over the summer holidays, to save up for horse gear.

But not all the properties are working properties – some are hobby farms. They consist of small paddocks and a couple of sheep or horses, but the owners don't make money from them: they make money from other things. Michelle's dad's an accountant, who works in an office in a town not far from Yarra Valley, and her mum's a secretary at The Pines, which is a golf course. And Karen Tools's dad's a pilot, who goes away for a couple of days, sometimes even for a week. Their house is on the top of a hill, and we've heard it has an indoor swimming pool.

Suze and me live on hobby farms. We have pets, and grow fruit and vegetables, but our dads travel to an office to make money. Mine's an architect, and Suze's step-dad's an engineer.

Susie started a game in the bus we were in: she made monkey noises as she swung from the overhead handrails. The driver didn't even tell us off: he turned up the radio and tapped his fingers on the steering wheel, to the beat of the music.

I swung like Tarzan over to Susie. Nodding my head in the driver's direction, I asked, 'Can you believe it? It's the first time he's ever been *in* a good mood.' He usually tells everyone to sit down and to shut their gobs.

'Dare me to wink when he looks over next?' Susie asked.

'No way.' I wrapped my legs around her waist, forcing her to fall backwards.

'Hr-hrm.' The PA system crackled through the overhead loudspeaker. The driver was glaring at us in the rear-view mirror. 'Next stop!' he said loudly.

'Thanks . . . See ya!' Susie called out as we jumped off. She blew a kiss as the bus moved away.

'Cheat! Unfair!' I squawked as Susie sprinted off to her front gate. My bag was super-heavy. 'Just 'cause *you're* not carrying a rock!'

'T. U., baby!' she called back. 'Toughen up!'

Susie's property is way cool. There's a ménage, separate summer and winter paddocks, a stable with a loft, a Pegasus horse float parked in their garage – painted blue, with a silver stripe down the side, to match their four-wheel drive – and a wet area to hose down the horses.

Susie reckons my place is better. Sure, my dad's an architect, and he's won awards for his designs. He built our house, and it is different: it's made of glass and shaped like a fishbowl, and we've got a swimming pool that wraps around the outside of the glass wall like a moat around a castle. But besides that, there's only a shed to store my saddle in, and a small holding yard. The rest of the property's taken up with Dad's vineyard. He makes wine, but only enough for him and his friends. It's his hobby, like fishing.

Our families aren't poor, but we're not super-rich. It's not like our dads give us pocket money – that's why Suze and me have to pick fruit at the Hendersons'.

Susie opened the gate to the summer paddock. We clapped, to round the horses up. Susie's horse Sam and her mum's horse Tiger trotted towards the stable. Any other day, I'd have run home to get Ebony, but I didn't want to bump into the Canadians, who were looking at the house, to rent it for the year.

'Skinny-dip?' Susie suggested. She skipped ahead, to grab the halters hanging from the hook of the stable door.

'*Ah.*' I wasn't keen. 'The horses are moulting, and I've got my bathers,' I lied, tapping my bag, pretending my bathers really were in it. *I can wear my sports shirt and bloomers,* I thought. 'You can take all your clothes off,' I said, even though I *was* joking.

'Cool,' she said.

'*No:* could you *not*? I hate it when you do that.'

Susie lifted her top and flashed her bra. 'You're a prude, Veronica; you know that? What are you gonna do when a guy wants to *kiss* you and then –'

'Get lost,' I said, and clapped my hands over my ears to drown out her voice. '*Raaaah-rahrahrahrahraaaaah!*' I waited until her lips had stopped moving, and then dropped my hands back to my waist. I hated when Suze talked about guys and kissing and stuff like that.

She looked at me and shrugged her shoulders, as if *I* were the freak. 'How about double-dinking and riding together on Tige?' she offered.

I shook my head.

She pulled a face. 'Oh, Vee, come on: you know Sam's hopeless at swimming. And I promise I won't skinny-dip – I'll wear *extra* clothes.'

I kept shaking my head.

'I'm flying to Noosa tomorrow,' she begged, and pressed her palms together like she was saying a prayer. 'I won't be back for two weeks. And then, when I come back, you'll have moved. BuUMMmble, I won't even get to see you for Christmas.'

'Do we *have* to dink?' I said. 'Besides, when you get back from Noosa, we'll still ride together, when I come and visit on the weekends.'

'Pretty please,' she insisted.

'Oh, *okay*.'

Tiger trotted around the house, following the circular drive to the winter paddock. Suze had got her way, but had at least let me sit up front. Past the house, we trotted towards the winter paddock, where the dam was.

The grass in the winter paddock had been cut. Bundles of hay were tied with bailer twine, ready to be stored in the loft above the stable. The stubble was dry and brown from the sun – except for a strip of lush, green grass that started at the drainpipe that stuck out of the driveway embankment, and spread on down the hill, to the dam.

In the distance, I could see the terraced grapevines growing across the neighbouring hillside and the glint of glass from my house reflecting from the sun. Soon it'd all be taken away – but not permanently, if I had my way.

'I didn't *ask* for a farewell party,' I thought out loud.

'How cool was it?' Susie declared, and hugged me tighter around my waist.

'Neil Wright ruined it,' I said, 'he was like a clown in a circus. I wouldn't have been surprised if a fire twirler suddenly appeared . . . or a muscle man. And by the way, did we really have to help out in the library?'

She laughed.

'You mean *we laminated those photos for no real reason except –*'

'Yep!' she cut in. 'And you did *such* a good job!'

'Suze! That is *so* not funny. Oh, yeah: hilarious!'

I pulled gently on the reins, bringing Tige back to a walk. We leant back on him as the paddock sloped towards the gully. His whither stopped our backsides from sliding forward over his neck. I turned him right, moved closer to the green grass, and then kicked him on when he jerked his head down to grab a bite.

When we got to the dam, we sat in silence and watched the water. A ripple formed across the surface. It wasn't really a dam – more like a lake filled by a creek that flowed through the gully during the winter. There was a man-made island in the middle of it, and a bridge joining the paddock to the island. We'd ridden the horses over the bridge once, but Morris, Suze's stepfather, had nearly killed us when he saw hoof marks indented in the wood. I pointed to another ripple in the water, underneath the branch of an overhanging gum tree.

'Trout,' Susie whispered. 'Morris put a hundred of 'em in the other day.'

I whispered back. 'Aren't trout *saltwater* fish?' I was sure Dad and I had hired a boat and caught some in Port Phillip Bay – and the Bay *was* saltwater, not freshwater.

'Morris: what a wanker – they probably are.' It wouldn't take anyone long to realise Suze hated her step-dad. She cast a glance at the dam and its doomed saltwater trout, and shouted over her shoulder towards her house, 'They'll all die, *murderer*!'

We laughed. I kicked Tige forward. With the splash of his hooves, the water was churned into clay. Suze and I folded our legs. Tige pawed his front-right leg, then his left. Leaves – covered in slime from the bottom of the dam – rose to the surface.

'*Argh*!' I screamed. I kicked Tige forward, to get away from the sludge. The ground dropped out from beneath. We were floating. 'Feel how cold it is when you drop your legs right down.'

'No shit,' Suze agreed. 'But the top layer of water feels warm, like piss.'

'*Suze*! Do you *have* to be rude about *everything*?'

Tiger's head was raised above the water. He snorted, and his head bobbed up and down as his shoulders powered forward; he was working one front leg, then the other. His back hooves kicked out. Tightening my grip around a chunk of his mane, I held on as the three of us moved forward towards the island. He blinked his eyelashes, and flashed the whites of his eyeballs as his head rocked from side to side.

Suze pulled back on the elastic of my bloomers; I twisted my hip to keep them from slipping, and screamed back for Suze to hold onto *me*, not my clothes: '*Meee*, idiot!'

'I'm trying,' she screamed back.

'*Suze, watch out: shark!*'

'*Loch Ness!*'

We laughed, then coughed and spluttered: Susie thumped my back, to clear my throat.

'Thanks,' I said, and elbowed her hand away. 'That's enough! *Argh: piranha!*' I thrashed my arms below the water as if there really was a school of piranhas down there.

'*Loch Ness!*' Suze yelled again.

'Good one! Original: you've already said that.'

She thought about it. '*A huge Loch Ness floater, then.*'

'*Argh!*' We both shrieked.

We'd had enough of swimming, so we cantered up the hill. I stopped at the fence, where my property meets Susie's. There's a huge blackberry bush growing over the fence; we call it the Igloo, because it's shaped like an igloo and hollow in the centre. We camp out in it some nights. There's a fireplace in the middle, and a hole in the roof so the smoke can get out.

I lowered myself onto the ground. 'I still can't believe Morris hasn't sprayed it yet,' I said. Susie's stepfather was obsessed with making their property look like one of those English gardens they show on *Burke's Backyard*. And he hated the horses.

'*Morris*? Morris *who*?' she asked, and squeezed the water from her hair.

I opened the gate to let Susie and Tige pass, and then slipped the chain around the post. She not only had a creep for a stepfather; her real father had run away when she was six. Suze said she didn't know why her dad had run away – so one day we asked her mum, and she said he'd drunk too much and one night he'd never come home from the pub, so she'd decided to move herself and Suze to Australia, to make a fresh start. And then she said something about gifts being wrapped in the strangest of packaging.

We thought about that, and finally agreed it meant 'a good thing happening in a strange way'; like, Suze and I would never have met if her dad hadn't run away, because her mum would never have moved to Australia.

'Remember,' I began, 'when Morris hit me for dropping saddle soap on your lounge-room floor?'

'Vee, it's no secret we both *hate* Morris.'

'I didn't say I "hated" him – but the thing is, my dad would never hit you, and it's not like I'd meant it.'

Susie slid off Tiger's rump, like how an Indian would slide off. 'I hope Mum divorces him,' she said.

'You can't say that.'

'Yes I can: I hate him; I hope Mum divorces him – and I hate how Mum doesn't believe me when I tell her some of the stuff he does. Like, remember when he threw my saddle blanket in the fire because I'd left it out overnight? And he won't let me look after Eb and Maje while you're away. Seriously, the property's big enough for four horses.'

'Don't worry,' I offered; 'Eb and Maje are *my* problem – besides –'

'That's it! I'll *kill* him!'

'Oh, yeah: right!' I said. 'And I bet you want *me* to help!'

Susie narrowed her eyes. 'You *are* my best-est buddy, aren't you?'

I ignored her, and tied the reins to the post.

She walked off. '*I'd* kill someone if *you* asked me to,' she shouted over her shoulder. 'Just 'cause *your* dad's so nice.' She raised her arms above her head, and spun around and around till she'd got dizzy and fallen to the ground.

I looked over to Suze's house, and then looked back at mine. I stared out across the valley: I loved this time of day, when the shadows got long. The grass looked golden brown, and the setting sun made the sky an orangey-pink colour.

What about Wish Two: for Suze and I to train together and be selected for the Australian Olympic Eventing team? To travel with our horses on a plane to another country: like New Jersey, where the US Equestrian Centre is? To ride a clear round of the cross-country course without any time penalties? And a perfect dressage test? And a clear round of the showjumping? Then we'd gallop our lap of victory, our blue ribbons and the Australian flag flapping against our knees. And then, as I was sponging Ebony down, I'd meet some guy from another team, a guy who was just as horse mad as me . . . and he'd kiss me – a real kiss, with tongues and –

What was I thinking? I *hated* guys: they were all creeps who had nothing but *girls-girls-girls* on their mind; not that they had a *mind* – because if they *did* have a mind, they'd have to have a brain, which was *so* not possible. I *so* wish guys didn't exist . . .

Oh, noooo: I'd just wasted Wish Three. Not to worry: it wasn't wasted – was it? I don't think so. Hang on – choice A: a world *with* guys. '*Urgggh.*' Or choice B: a world *without* guys. '*Yeeaah!*' Phew – certainly not wasted: all guys are creeps, especially Neil Wright, John Landy, Craig Berton, the Year 10's . . .

'Boo!'

'Argh!' I spun around. 'Don't do that – it's *so* not funny.'

'Is too,' she said. 'You're such a space cadet.'

'At least I don't act as if I'm Maria in *The Sound of Music*.'

Susie spun around again: '*The hills are alive* –'

'Spare me,' I demanded, and walked off.

We decided to hang out in the Igloo, even if it would be for just a minute. I wanted to say goodbye to our secret hiding place. Suze crawled in first then I crawled in behind her. We sat on the log beside the fireplace, stabbing toasting forks into the ashes.

'I'll miss you,' she admitted.

I dropped my fork onto the ground. 'I thought you couldn't wait for me to go – so you could start your fabulous, super-cool and amazing "Vee-less" life. You'll get to hang out with the cricket-pitch chicks.'

'Don't be stupid,' she replied.

'I'm not,' I said, then went quiet. 'Okay: I guess I'll miss you, too.'

'You won't,' she said. 'You'll forget all about me. I'll call your place and you'll say, "Suze? Suze who?" You'll meet so many *cool as* people, and I'll just be dull and boring within a week.'

'You – "dull and boring"?' I fell off the log from laughing.

'Vee, sit up.' She waited till I'd stopped. 'We could be blood-sisters: so whenever we were apart, we could still be together.'

I gave her a look. 'That is *the* stupidest idea.'

23

'Crap,' she said; 'it's the *coolest* idea: it'd be like this invisible connection; it'd be like *our* secret.' She broke off two barbs from the blackberry bush. 'Go on.'

'You first,' I dared.

We held our breath and watched as the blood rose from Susie's pierced thumb. A dark-red blob spread across the tip of her finger.

'Hold still,' she said.

'*Argh*!' I drew back my thumb from the pain as I felt the prick in my skin.

We lifted our hands; our fingertips met. This was it: our last day together. I wanted to be brave, brave enough to tell Suze I couldn't imagine getting through the next year without her. And that – no; I couldn't: I knew better; I'd thought about this. If I blurted out how much I loved her, there was a chance I'd ruin our friendship: she'd think I was a *lezzo*, or a freak. I cleared my throat. 'Thanks,' I said, 'for the party, and the rock – even though it *was* stupid. Yarra Valley High *so* does not "rock".'

Susie wiped the tear from my cheek. 'Sshh, Vee; it's okay.'

I folded my knees closer to my chest.

She leant over and kissed my lips.

I got a huge shock. '*Suze*!' I scrambled, lost my balance, and fell. '*Argh! Shit*! You just kissed me. *Ouch*.' I rubbed my funny bone, which I'd landed on and knocked against the log.

Suze leant back and laughed; she wasn't even embarrassed. 'I'll show you,' she said, as if nothing had happened, 'how I'd do *it* with John Landy if we were boyfriend and girlfriend.' She got up and straddled the log.

'Spare me,' I begged. I turned away, knowing she'd show me anyway.

'Oh, John! Oh, John!' She rode the log as if she were riding a rodeo bull. '*Yee-hah*!'

'Suze, I gotta go.' I crawled out of the Igloo super-quick. Even though, I was laughing.

Susie sat on top of Tige, bareback. She waved from her side of the fence. Long shadows had formed around me, but Suze was illuminated in the golden light of the sunset. Her curly hair looked like a halo.

I waved back from my side of the fence. *Can we still be best friends*, I wondered, *even if we only see each other on the weekend?*

I didn't want to go, but walked backwards anyway. My throat tightened. I crossed my fingers and hoped the next year would pass quickly and that Susie knew our kiss hadn't meant a thing.

We waved one last time before she disappeared over her side. As much as I didn't want to, I turned to face the vineyard and headed towards the hill, where my house was. I got a fright when a bird swooped down and flapped its wings right in front of my face; one of them clipped my nose. I could see the bird's nest, up above in a gum tree, and hear her little chicks chirping. Below the nest, on the ground, I could see a dead chick that had fallen out. Beside the chick was a real four-leaf clover growing amongst a patch of grass. The mum swooped a second time. I didn't want to worry her, so I grabbed the clover for good luck and bolted. The rock in my bag banged against my hip with each hurried step.

When I got halfway up the hill, I stopped running and pressed the clover between the pages of my Math book – where I'd also put the scrap of Mum's letter. It was getting late, and now only a quarter of the sun was peeking over Cockatoo Ridge. Surely the Canadians would have left by now. The little chicks weren't the only beings who were hungry: I was starving – especially after vomiting.

'*Hey*!' I yelled. I could see Penny heading away from the house, following the line of the fence that led back down the hill. I recognised her black clothes and bright-blue hair, even though her hair had been bright red the last time I saw her: she called her style 'goth'. '*Penny*!' Two weeks had passed since we'd last talked. She was never home, and spent most of her time at her boyfriend Nick's house. He lived about a 'k' down the valley. She'd just finished her Year 12 exams.

She looked back. She had both her arms raised, holding the barbed-wire fence away from her clothes. She was about to climb through the fence, and was taking a yellow-hessian bag from her shoulders to make the passage easier.

I could see the wooden legs of her easel sticking out of the bag's top flap. 'Penny! Wait up!' I yelled. I really wanted to talk to her about the Canadians: maybe they hadn't signed the contract to rent the house.

She folded one arm on top of the other and gave me an 'up yours!' sign.

I didn't care; I kept running, and climbed over the fence when I got to it. By the time I caught up, I'd started puffing. 'What happened with the Canadians?' I asked. 'Did they –'

'As if I'd know,' she muttered, and walked away.

'Come on.' I chased after her. 'Neither of us *wants* to move.'

Penny had said that Kew was too far from Nick's place, and M said that if Penny ran away, and lived at Nick's house, she'd ᴗ ᴗ ᴗ police.

'Go and find out for yourself,' she said.

'Just tell me,' I insisted; 'at least tell me if they've left or not – I don't wanna go up to the house if they're still there.'

She pointed up the hill, towards the house. 'Look,' she teased: 'there's Black Beauty.' She was always saying stupid stuff like that. It sucked, being the younger sister.

I kept following her as she walked away, but kept a safe enough distance. The last time we'd talked, we'd had a huge fight, and she'd ended up squashing my head between my bedroom door and its frame. We'd been fighting about Mum and Dad, and the bushfire. I'd been mad that she'd said the Waring bushfire wasn't the reason why Mum had decided to move. But it *was* because of the bushfire – that's what Mum had said. 'So, have they rented the house?' I asked again. I could tell, by the look on her face, that they had.

'Yes,' she finally admitted. She went to walk off, but changed her mind. She sat down and pushed off her right boot, and then tapped its heel against a rock.

I leant back against a tree. I heard a click as she undid the buckle of her bag. Then she took out a roll-your-own.

The wind blew her cigarette smoke past my face.

On the night of the bushfire, the locals had crowded into the carpark of the Yarra Valley Pub. We'd watched the flames as they'd crossed Cockatoo Ridge – 60 kilometres away. It'd looked like a volcano had erupted orange lava and huge fireballs of gold and red into the night sky. Craig Berton's mother had said that if the wind shifted south, Yarra Valley would be right in the path of the fire. The wind was blowing at 60 kilometres per hour, and I knew my maths, so if the wind shifted our way, the fire would reach us within an hour. The Chief from the Yarra Valley Fire Brigade told everyone not to panic, to go home and get some rest – and then sent four fire trucks to Waring. That meant that if the wind shifted overnight, Yarra Valley wouldn't have a back-up fire truck.

If it wasn't the Waring bushfire, I wondered, *what was it?* 'Remember the fire?' I asked Penny. 'I woke up, and my bedroom was full of thick, black smoke. The weird part was how quiet it was. I always thought a bushfire would be this huge . . .' I stopped to find the right word. 'Oh, I don't know – like, *loud and crackling*, like in the movies, you know?'

'Making the glass shatter and buckle?' Penny asked. 'Making the house cave in, melt onto your skin and burn you to death?'

'Yes!' I felt goose-pimples prick my skin as I remembered how scared I'd been. 'I ran out of my bedroom, I remember screaming for Dad. I panicked. I ran into the upstairs bathroom rather than Mum and Dad's bedroom.'

'Dickhead!' she spat.

'Oh, and *you* weren't scared?' Dad had gathered the family into his bedroom. He'd checked the phone by his bedside, making sure the electric cable was still connected. Then he'd called the neighbours. The Gibbses had said the fire was 30 kilometres away and that the wind had blown the smoke ahead of the front.

'Mum was crying, remember? Even she was scared; her whole body was shaking.' She'd been saying for years that a bushfire was going to happen and we'd be trapped inside the house. She'd paced up and down, and hugged Amy as she yelled at Dad. 'Mum said it was Dad's fault – that the design of the house was too dangerous for the country! And *that's* why we're moving!'

Penny took another drag.

I kept talking, hoping she'd agree that I was right. 'Even *you* were scared,' I insisted. 'There *was* no other reason!'

She stubbed the ash end of the cigarette onto a rock. 'What would you know?' she said. 'You've never even had a boyfriend.'

'As if I'd want one! And what's that got to do with it?'

She screwed up her face as she forced her boot back on. '"What's that got to do with it?" That'd be right: no one in this family knows a thing about love.' She walked off without tying up the laces.

'You don't know everything!' I yelled back. 'You're hardly ever home. Besides, no one died: the fire didn't come anywhere near the house – or Yarra Valley – so there is no need to move.' I ran off. 'Go on, then!' I yelled over my shoulder. 'Run off to your stupid boyfriend! *See if I care!*'

I stopped running when I got to the top of the hill. I couldn't stop thinking about the bushfire. After speaking to the Gibbses on the telephone, Dad had left the three of us with Mum, in the kitchen. He'd turned on the sprinklers and pushed wet towels into the cracks under the doors. I'd wanted to run outside to see whether Eb and Maje were okay, but Mum held me back against the fridge door.

We'd spent the rest of that night huddled around the kitchen table. Mum had phoned the Gibbses every 30 minutes to see whether they were okay. We never did have to evacuate. The wind had shifted, and blown the fire back into its own path, so the firefighters had been able to control the blaze. The following afternoon, the bushfire had been re-classified, from 'Emergency' to 'Contained'. We'd survived – so what was the big deal? There *was* no need to move!

I could see Dad's dual cabin ute, Mum's four-wheel drive and a green stationwagon parked in front of the carport beside the house. I didn't recognise the wagon. I crossed my arms, wondering what to do. The wagon had to be the Canadians'.

I kicked a rock into a nearby bush. Even though our house *was* pretty amazing, Dad's fishbowl design was the reason why Mum wanted to move. Dad called it a 'fishbowl design' because the outside was made of mirrored glass – rather than brick or wood – and the outside was round-shaped so the house looked like a giant-sized fishbowl. If the bushfire had come through the valley and up our hill, our house *would've* shattered and melted from the extreme heat. About two months earlier, Suze and me were camped out one night at the Igloo, and we'd thrown a bottle into the campfire and *it* shattered and melted. It even exploded and a made a huge popping noise that'd made us scream.

I stood there with my hands on my hips. The golden light of the sunset reflected off the mirrored glass wall and onto the surrounding bush. The glass wall was actually made up of lots of triangular pieces of glass joined together like pieces of a jigsaw puzzle – each triangular piece was about five metres long and three metres wide. I counted the number of triangular pieces of glass: 'Twenty-seven, 28, 29 . . . 52, 53, 54 . . .' Altogether, 76 triangular pieces had been joined together to make the house look like a giant-sized ball of glass bursting from a wall of sandstone: the sandstone was a cliff face that the house backed onto.

My favourite time of day was sunrise and sunset when the sun's light reflected off the pool's surface, bounced up and onto the glass wall, which then reflected shimmers of golden light onto the surrounding bush. Some mornings, I'd set my alarm clock to wake me up at 5.00 a.m. just so I could watch the sunrise and see the mist lift out of the valley.

When the mist lifted as high as Cockatoo Ridge, I could see right on down to the next town. It *was* pretty amazing – most of the teachers and students at school had heard about my house and asked me if it *were* true. They'd ask: *does it really have glass walls and a glass floor, so when you're inside, can you see the creek that runs down the sandstone wall and then flows underneath the floor? Yes,* I'd answer, *but the glass floor is only in the kitchen and the entrance hall so it's not like I can see the creek from every room.* I swear some of the students reckon I'm lying 'cause they'd then go and ask Suze if it were true, and she'd stick up for me and tell them that it *was* true. Then she'd exaggerate and say that there's also a hole in the kitchen floor so my dad can catch fish out of the creek and cook it up for tea.

Sometimes I reckon it'd be so much easier if my house *were* made from brick and wood – with four straight walls, two front windows, and a front and back door. Mum *was* right: I reckon the house would've melted from the heat if a bushfire had come through. If only we lived in a normal house, I bet we wouldn't have to move.

'Veronica!' Mum called and waved. She had shorts on, and her legs were white. For the first time, I noticed she'd lost weight – not that she was ever fat, but I could see she looked different. Even her face was white.

She kept waving, and then smiled as if she had good news.

I stood like a statue.

'Veronica!' Excusing herself from the visitors, she walked around the outer edge of the pool and headed towards me.

I felt trapped; I wanted to run, but knew that if I did, it'd be a super-rude thing to do. I went over. She, Dad and the Canadians were sitting at the table next to the barbecue. I ignored the Canadians and lifted the bottle of wine out of the ice bucket. I posed the question I had to ask: 'What's to celebrate?'

Dad was about to tell me off, but changed his mind. 'Veronica,' he said, 'this is Kieran and Kathy Wilson –'

'So what?' I said, shouting over the top of Dad's introductions. 'You think you're moving in, don't you? I hope you like snakes – especially Red-bellied Black snakes. We get heaps of 'em 'round here.'

Kathy sat up in her chair.

'The nearest hospital takes at least 50 minutes to get to in a car,' I went on. 'Snake venom takes only about 10 minutes to kill you. You start frothing at the mouth . . . your muscles go into spasm.' I threw myself onto the ground, thrashed my arms and legs about and flopped my tongue to the side of my mouth.

Mum screamed: 'Veronica! Get up – *now*! You're in *big* trouble.' She pulled on the ends of her short, blonde hair.

I sat up. 'Oh, yeah,' I said, using my wrist to wipe the drool off my chin. Mum had told me that Kieran was going to look after the vineyard, and that Kathy had offered to look after Eb and Maje. 'Don't go near my horses; they're wild Brumbies, and they'll kick and bite anyone but me.' I stood up and filled their wine glasses, and shoved the empty bottle back into the ice bucket. 'Enjoy!' I dared them, and unfolded the scrap of Mum's letter from between the pages of my Math book. I held up the evidence: 'But don't enjoy yourselves too much – renting this place *is not permanent*!' Then, without looking back, I ran off towards the horse shed.

If only that were true. That's what I'd really liked to have said and done. In reality, I acted as if I hadn't heard Mum. I ran off to the horse shed and didn't go back to the house until the Wilsons had gone.

7

Later that night, I sat on my bed, opened my diary to a blank page, and wrote:

Mum's going to FREAK when she sees my room, but so what. She came in before, and told me to pack my stuff into boxes!!! And divided my room down the middle and said that

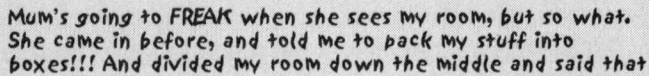

everything on this side is stored in the horse shed

and everything on that side goes to Kew.

She'll FREAK when she sees what I've done. I've dragged everything - bed, desk, wardrobe, trophies, ribbons, transferred all my horse posters and magazine cut-outs - to the 'horse shed' side. So now, there's nothing on the 'Kew' side. If I HAVE to go, then I'm only taking ME (BECAUSE I HAVE TO), Mum's letter because she'd promised we'd move back if the trial year didn't work out, and my new lucky four-leaf clover.

I can hear her and Dad fighting and I'm sick of it. I don't even reckon THEY know what they're yelling about. This is what I have to put up with!!!

Mum: 'Get stuffed. You haven't shaped up, so you can ship out. Or you stay here, and I'll move to Kew with the kids.'

Dad: 'The kids need a father.'

32

Mum: 'Father! Is that what you call yourself? Hah! I can't
        wait to earn my own money and get on with MY life.
        I'm sick and tired of the housewife trap. You've
        destroyed any semblance of trust. Broken MY
        family.'
Dad: 'Fair go, I'm trying here. You don't give us many
        options.'
Mum: 'How dare you. You're the one responsible for our
        lack of choice here, mate. We tried counselling and
        that didn't improve our situation, so face up to the
        fact. The best thing for my children and me is this
        move. I can go back to nursing. And Penny needs
        to get away from Nick. He and his friends are not
        safe. And those children DO NOT need to find out
        about your whereabouts.

Whoa. They never used to fight. Actually, it'd been a long
time since I'd seen my parents hug or kiss. Dad used to always
kiss Mum - on the forehead, the lips, the neck. A kiss to say
hello, good bye, good morning, good night. Instead of a kiss,
now all they did was fight.

It's ok for Penny, she'll be 18 in a month, and she runs away
whenever she wants. And Amy's 5, so she just plays with her
toys.

Yikes! There's no way I'm going to love Veronica Bee. Not for
the next year, ANYWAY!!!!!!!!!!!!!!!!!!X#*+@Y???!!!

PS Still don't know what to think about the k___s that
happened between Suze and me...??

33

I walked into the kitchen. I had to shout to be heard above Mum and Dad.

'Stop it!' I yelled. 'Stop it!'

Mum came over and gave me a hug – to make out that Dad was the bad one of the two of them. Her hands were covered in soapsuds, which were also on Dad's shirt.

I pushed her away. 'I'm sick of it: you two are always fighting! That's all you ever do. You're mad at each other, and all it does is make me mad. It's not fair – so stop it.'

'See?' Mum asked Dad. 'See what you've done?'

'No, Mum,' I put in. '*You're* just as *bad*; you're even worse! You're making the whole family move. It's all about *you*, and what you want. And I don't even reckon you two know what you're fighting about. You don't even make sense.' I pointed at Mum. '*You* sound like you're telling Dad that *he* has to go: that he has to leave the house or the family – or something like that. That's not fair. Dad hasn't done anything wrong.'

I ran out of the kitchen. As loud as I could, I gave my bedroom door a slam, and then wedged the back of my desk chair under the doorknob. My heart pounded inside my chest. I felt terrible for pushing Mum away; I took the chair away from the doorknob in case she wanted to come in. I waited for ages, but she didn't knock . . . At least they'd stopped fighting. I grabbed my diary and a handful of pencils, and jumped back into bed. I didn't feel like drawing, but made myself draw a picture of a unicorn with a rainbow in the background and 10 four-leaf clovers around the edge; then I added blue and red and orange and yellow and purple and pink. I wanted to smudge thick charcoal over the colours – but I didn't want to let myself feel mad.

I must have fallen asleep. The next thing I knew, there was a knock on the door. I lay still, opened my eyes a bit, and watched as Mum crept in. She stared at the furniture. She stood there a long time, her hands on her hips, then came over to the bed. She took the diary from under my arm and gathered the pencils. When she saw the drawing, she smiled.

'Don't bother reading it,' I said.

'I thought you were asleep,' she replied. She passed the diary to me.

'There's nothing about you in there,' I announced; 'it's only for writing about good stuff.'

She looked hurt.

I felt bad, not just because I'd hurt Mum, but also because I'd lied. I had written good stuff about her. But ever since Mum'd said we were moving, I'd written only bad stuff. I missed writing about the good stuff, like what Suze and I got up to after school and on the weekend, and what we did at pony club.

'I want you to know I love you,' Mum said, gently. 'I'm sorry that your dad and I fight.'

I tucked the diary under the doona, and turned away.

She bent down and kissed the back of my head. 'Don't forget I love you,' she said, and then left the door open as she left.

I jumped up and closed the door, and jumped back into bed. I tried to sleep. But couldn't. I watched the moon as it shifted over the ridge.

The next two weeks weren't much fun. Susie was away, and even though I didn't want to move, I had to help Dad.

'Wake up, sleepyhead!' My little sister, Amy, was with me, bouncing up and down on my bed.

I was exhausted from packing. 'Get off!' I ordered.

She wouldn't stop bouncing, out of excitement. 'Penny's here; Penny's here.'

'Big deal,' I said.

'She hasn't got any hair left – it's all fallened out.'

'Are you serious?' I asked. 'Is she *bald*?' I sat up. I hadn't seen Penny since I'd chased after her; the day the Canadians signed the rent contract. 'I bet she did shave it – she'd do something crazy like that.'

Amy ran ahead as I got out of bed. I barged into Penny's room: she was crouched over, throwing books into a box. She turned around. Her hair was the same colour: bright blue, but with orange bits at the ends.

'*Aaaamy*! *Liar*!' I pushed Amy from her hiding spot, behind the curtain, and turned to Penny. 'She'd said you'd shaved your head.'

'Would both of you *get lost*?!' Penny yelled. She threw a book at us, and just missed. 'I know I'm exciting, and everything – but bugger off!'

I pushed Amy out of the room and shut the door. Amy banged and hollered from the other side. 'Liar, liar: pants on fire!' I yelled, loud enough for Amy to hear.

Penny punched me to make me stop. 'Cut it out,' she said.

I laughed, to show she hadn't hurt me. 'Are you leaving with the family in Dad's car?' I asked. 'Mum's driving Dad's car tomorrow, because the Wilsons bought her four-wheel drive. Mum says she wants a smaller car, which is *so* dumb, because she's gonna have to buy another one when we move back. I'm going with Dad in the van.'

'Mum can get stuffed,' Penny offered. For three years, ever since Mum had banned Nick from setting foot on the property, Penny hadn't been doing what she was told.

'But Mum said you have to.'

She punched me again – really hard. I fell backwards; my head banged against the wall; a sharp pain shot up my shoulder.

Amy ran into the room. She thought I was pretending to cry. I was curled up in a ball on the floor. She dumped a box over my head. I pushed the box away and shoved her back. It was a mean thing to do, but it served her right: she'd been acting like the move was a game – jumping out of boxes and hiding in cupboards as Dad and me packed. 'I'm telling Mum!' she cried.

'Amy, come back!' I called out after her – but she'd gone.

Penny shoved me out of her room.

Mum threw her hands in the air when she saw I was lying in bed. 'We're never gonna move at this rate!' she huffed. 'It's 10.30!' She yanked at my doona.

'Mum, don't: I'm hurt bad; I can't get up.' With my good arm, I grabbed hold of the doona and yanked back.

'You're gonna *have* to get up,' she demanded: 'your father needs help – and don't pick on Amy!' She walked off in a huff.

'I'm not!' I yelled back. 'Tell *Penny* not to pick on *me* – I'm not her punching bag!'

I thought Dad would come and tell me to get up, but no one else knocked, so I stayed in bed the whole day. Now and then, I could hear Amy skipping down the hall . . . and the diesel engine of the removal van, which Dad had hired, turning on and off . . . and the electric ramp being raised and lowered as Dad loaded the furniture . . . then Mum and Dad fighting . . . and Mum and Penny fighting.

Later that afternoon, Amy came running in. She jumped onto my bed like I was her best friend all over again. 'Dad wants to know where the tape measure is,' she said.

'On top of the gas meter,' I answered. 'Get off: it hurts.'

She bounced up and down about 10 more times, and then finally ran out neighing like a horse.

Having stared up at the ceiling all day, I was bored stiff, so I shifted onto my side and looked out the window. I could see Eb and Maje eating grass at the far end of the holding yard. They raised their heads and pricked their ears as Penny climbed the gate. She cut across the yard, towards Nick's house. Mum ran after her, then stopped at the fence and cupped her hands around her mouth. She was yelling at Penny to come back. Mum gave up and started walking back towards the house.

Later on, the room got dark. Just after 8.00, Dad knocked. He switched the light on as he came in. 'What's up?' he asked.

'Nothing.'

'You're not claiming sick pay, are you?'

'Very funny, Dad.'

'Are you hungry?'

'No.' I'd thought about sneaking up some leftovers after they'd all gone to bed.

'It's fish and chips,' he said; 'Mum thought that'd be easier . . . If you change your mind –' He tapped the wall.

I rolled onto my elbow and leant my weight on the shoulder that didn't hurt. 'Hey, Dad, what did Mum mean? You know: about what you two were fighting about the other week, when she said you'd done something wrong?'

Dad smoothed his palm against the plaster. 'Mum's uptight,' he answered; 'that's all. She'll settle down. Do you want the light on, or off?'

'On,' I decided. ''Night, Dad.'

''Night, Bumble.'

I thought I'd draw another picture in my diary – but in the end, I didn't feel much like drawing.

That night, I couldn't sleep. I crept outside. It was dark, but I knew the property well enough. The paved sandstone around the swimming pool was warm against my bare feet. I passed the barbecue area and headed towards the holding yard.

The moon was full, so the sky wasn't super-dark. I pressed my palms into my eyelids: my eyes felt red raw and scratchy because I'd been crying so much. I could think of nothing worse than knowing this was my last night.

I sat down on the top step of the herb garden and opened my diary to a blank page. I took the pen from the spine of the diary. *This* was going to be my last entry. If I left my diary in the horse shed, I could write again when we moved back, when I had good stuff to say.

> Who's going to look after Eb and Maje if something terrible happens during the week?
>
> And what about Suze? Will she miss me? Or was she just saying that because that's what I wanted to hear? Who's going to be her new best friend when school starts back? And as for Morris!!!!@#!!!! Will I have to put up with his creepiness if Susie asks me to stay over on the weekend? I don't think I can!!!
>
> What if the Waring bushfire never happened?
>
> If only I were Penny's age!

I chewed on the pen . . . I didn't have an answer to even *one* of my questions.

I snapped the diary shut, and took the shortcut through the herb garden, to the shed.

'*E-e-e-e-e-b*!' I kept my voice low so I wouldn't wake anyone in the house. I climbed the wooden rail. I called again: '*E-e-e-e-b*! *M-a-a-a-ajor*!'

A possum hissed . . . I thought I heard a car coming up the drive, but it was a truck heading over the ridge, towards the abattoir. I knew Dad hadn't returned yet from delivering the last load. Was I the only one who cared? None of the lights in the house were on.

The horses trotted over to me.

'There's my boy!' I patted Eb on his forehead, on his diamond star. He used to be a racehorse, but wasn't very good at racing, so I got him when he was four. Audrey, my instructor, said he might be good enough to be a national 'three-day event' champion – that's if I kept training with him. He's a great jumper.

'I'm gonna miss you,' I whispered to him. '*Yeeees* . . . There's my boy.' I pressed my cheek against his black coat. 'And no eating apples from that Wilson woman!' I told him. I tapped his forehead to make sure the message sank in.

My other horse, Major, was old now – 19 last August, but that didn't mean he'd stopped being cheeky. I had to push his head away to keep him from nipping at my hip. He was a scruffy pony, and I couldn't have asked for a better first horse. At pony club, we'd won every games competition. And he'd never refused a jump. As a jumper, he'd tried everything: twisting his hip to the side; grunting; even farting, once - which Suze always reminds me about – so we'd jump a clear round.

I wrapped my arms around his neck. I wondered whether the horses even cared about what was happening in the family: did they know their lives were about to change? and that I was saying goodbye? Maybe they did, and couldn't wait for me to go, so they could slack off.

Closing my eyes, I pictured my feet lifting off the ground, and my body rising like a helicopter. Instantly I felt better, like I'd left all the crap in my life behind. I rose higher, and then somersaulted – once, twice, three times. Then I stretched my arms, and tucked into a swan dive . . .

My lips curled into a smile as I swooped into the valley . . .

I skimmed over a creek, circled a clump of blackberries, sped down a dirt path, dipped my left shoulder, and circled left towards the pine plantation at the far end of town.

I knew every bit of Yarra Valley off by heart. In winter, I collected mushrooms. In spring, I cut wattle that Mum put in vases. And in summer, I picked blackberries that Mum boiled up to make jam.

I swooped back towards the house. Before the vineyard had been planted, Suze and I had built our own cross-country course: it went down the gully; up over the hill; along the fence where our properties joined; back down the paddock; across the dam wall; and in and out of the fallen logs.

I wondered how Suze was going. I'd been thinking about that kiss, wondering what she'd been thinking since. She'd seemed so cool at the time, but maybe now she was freaking out just as much as me. Maybe she was grossed out, and had decided she didn't like me as a friend. I liked Suze as a friend and nothing more. And now, I felt panicked and confused that something weird had crept into our friendship . . . If only we hadn't . . . If only *I* hadn't . . .

I drummed my fists against my forehead. I couldn't quite wrap my mind around the experience, or find the words to explain how I felt; so many other thoughts about my family were going through my mind. Maybe Suze hadn't even given our kiss a second thought. She got over things quickly. Maybe other girls who were best friends, like Suze and me, kissed just like how we had. And it's not like we kissed like how Mum and Dad kiss, or rather, how Mum and Dad *used* to kiss. At least that kiss was our secret.

Major jerked his head and twitched his ears. Ebony turned. The headlights of the approaching removal van shone across the gully.

I stepped backwards and hid myself between the horses. The van chugged up the hill and took the last bend of the drive. I held my breath and shielded my eyes from the light.

The engine cut out. I could hear the radio, and then heard it being switched off, and the click of a door handle. Then I heard a door creaking as it was being opened. I could hear Dad's work boots crunching across the gravel. Another door was opened. A second set of footsteps stomped across the drive.

'Good one – as if *you* respect rules!'

'Penny!' Dad yelled. He sounded super-angry. 'Do *not* walk *off*!'

'*You're a hypocrite*!' she yelled back. 'The damage is done – you've ruined the family!' She slammed the front door. A high-pitched crack was followed by shattering glass.

'*Penny*, unlock this door – *do you hear*?' Dad knocked on the door. 'Don't make me have to go back to the van to get my keys . . . Penny!'

Well, one of my questions had been answered: Penny was home so that meant she would be leaving with Mum – in Dad's car. At least I'd be driving with Dad, in the van.

I heard the stomping of Dad's work boots – faster, louder, and slightly uneven – towards the yard. I peered over Eb's shoulder. Dad was carrying a box; his tanned skin and sun bleached hair glowed in the moonlight. Every time he inhaled on his cigar, his face was illuminated by the red glow at the tip of his cigar, making his green eyes sparkle. Dad and me had the same green coloured eyes, although the skin around his eyes was wrinkled from all the sun he got from working on his vineyard. Unlike Mum, Dad looked healthy.

I heard the gate's latch click. Ebony turned and backed away, so Dad could see it was just me, standing on my own.

'Struth, *Vee*!' I'd caught Dad by surprise, and he dropped the box. Stuff from inside it spilt out everywhere. He bent over and picked up the hand drill that had fallen out.

I stepped back, and bumped into Major. I couldn't decide whether to help pick up the stuff, or run and hide. The only reason I'd helped Dad pack was because I reckoned Mum had picked on Dad.

'Do you have any idea of the time?' he asked me.

'Just making sure you're not starting any bushfires,' I joked.

Dad wasn't much of a smoker: sometimes he'd lean against the veranda, holding a cigar and a cup of tea, and watch the sunset. I'd run out and bounce on the trampoline, and he'd hang the cigar from his lips and clap when I did a flip. Tonight, he took the cigar from his mouth and stood on the spot for ages, like he was having a private chat with himself, inside his head.

'Dad?' I said, to interrupt his line of thinking.

'*Hh*,' he managed.

'I don't get it: I thought you didn't want to move. You might've kicked Penny and me out of your bedroom that night the bushfire broke out so that you and Mum could have a fight, but I heard what you'd said to Mum. I was listening from the hallway. I heard you say you were happy to keep driving to your office in the city for business if you needed to, and that you couldn't see why anything had to change. And now you're wanting to move as much as Mum – even more so.'

He sighed and wiped his hands across the front of his shirt. 'Maybe the change will do some good all round: your mother can go back to nursing; she can work permanent shifts with one of the larger hospitals – that's what she wants. Her five-year gap's nearly up – and she's aiming to do a refresher course now, so she doesn't have to re-register. And Amy and you will be at Lagilla next year: you'll appreciate being so close – not like Penny: she had to catch the train back and forth.' He began to collect the scattered drill bits. 'Look, sometimes people say things out of anger, and it's not what they intend. Mum'll calm down, once the boxes are unpacked.'

'And then what?' I added. 'Do *you* want to move back?' I threw my diary into the box so Dad could put it in the shed with all the other stuff we wouldn't be taking with us, and ran off.

'*Veronica*, come here!' he called after me.

But I didn't want to hear what he had to say.

'Veronica, would you let me finish?'

I spun around and waited to hear what he had to say.

'Yes,' he went on; 'I do want to move back - when the time's right.'

'"Yes"?' Now I was really confused. 'What do you mean by "yes"?' You bought the house in Kew: why would you buy a house in the city if we're moving back here?'

He considered his response. 'It was one of my developments: the company owns the land, and the final arrangements were only a matter of paperwork – it made sense.'

But his words didn't ring true. 'I still don't get it: are you and Mum getting a divorce? Is that why we're moving? Will it be that you and Mum live in separate houses now that we've got two?'

He stubbed his cigar into the frame of the shed door. 'No; we're just making a bit of noise as Kew gets organised. Mum will settle in.'

43

'"A bit of noise"!' I wondered whether the day would come when I had to choose whom I wanted to live with: Dad or Mum. 'Susie's dad doesn't even write to her; he ran off when she was a kid, and doesn't even call.'

'Well, that's Susie's father, not yours. Believe me, it won't come to that.' He looked up at the moon.

I wondered if he was thinking about his own dad, and how he'd died very young. Dad had often told me how lucky I was to have a dad around.

After a while, he looked back and lifted his arms. 'Listen, Bumble –'

'No, Dad,' I interjected; 'I don't want your hug, I *don't* want to move, and I *don't* want anything to change. I just want to ride every day of my life, and compete for Australia in the Olympics. Audrey said Eb and I have made it to a point.' I closed my eyes and squeezed back the tears. 'She said if we keep training –'. I sucked in a deep breath.

'Bumble, don't be so hard on yourself.'

'What would *you* know?' I shot back.

He dropped his arms. 'I *know* that not accepting change only makes life harder. You'll look back on all this and see it for what it really is. There's a greater purpose to life than fighting for a ten-acre property – that's why I'm okay about moving. You gotta let some things go - even if it *is* just for a while.'

'*No!*' I yelled; 'not if there's a chance that Mum doesn't want to move back.' Now I had a million-trillion-zillion questions bouncing around inside my head. Nothing made sense. And I had a bad feeling, like a knot tightening in my guts. I felt like I was gonna throw up.

'Veronica –' he grabbed my wrists – 'I think you should get some sleep: it's late; we've got a big day ahead.'

'No!' I jerked my hands away. 'You can't keep telling me what to do *all* the time!' I ran into the shed and slammed the door behind me.

Pitch black – the globe had blown the other night. Now what? What the hell was I doing? I slid the bolt across. I wasn't an idiot – I was proving a point, expecting Dad to knock . . . any minute . . . any moment . . . any second . . .

But he didn't; I didn't even hear him walk off – though he must have. I'd been standing in the shed for more than an hour, maybe an hour and a half. I'd calmed down. And I swear the temperature was rising – hotter and hotter. I was feeling pretty stupid. And as much as I'd tried, *and tried*, *AND TRIED*, the lock simply *would not* budge. *Maybe Dad's right*, I thought; *maybe I'm not the only one going through a hard time . . . Maybe . . .* 'Daaad! Muuum! HELP!' This was an emergency: I was busting to take a pee. I searched through a box to find a hammer, but found only a couple of tennis racquets. *Now, which one's Penny's?* I recognised the soft fuzz of my sister's terry-towelling handgrip. I raised the racquet above my head, and:

The lock shifted. I burst out of the shed and gulped huge hits of air.

That night was a sleepless one. I lay on the horse shed's tin roof and watched the sun rise over the ridge. *What was the 'greater purpose of life' Dad had mentioned, and what had he meant by it?* Without horses, my life had no other 'purpose' . . . And what if Mum and Dad got a divorce? No matter what Dad had said, I knew something was up between him and Mum.

I sat up. My shoulders were stiff from lying on the hard tin. I felt a bit silly, wearing pyjamas outside. I glanced at my watch: 7.30 a.m.

What about wish number four: could I make time stop? If I could, we wouldn't have to move – but then again, if time stopped, I wouldn't be able to do all the cool stuff, like compete for Australia in the Olympics.

Okay. Wish Four: rather than get mad, I wish I could always see the funny side of everything – there had to be *something* funny about all the crap in my life, something that'd make me roll around and laugh out loud.

I thought long and hard, but couldn't think of anything that was funny. Instead, I wondered, *what if my world were only as big as our property, and the rule was that I were never allowed to leave it: would people visit me?* Suze would, of course. And I had my family: my Dad, and my Mum, and Amy . . . forget about Penny – I tried to roll both my shoulders back, but the left one that she'd hit still hurt a lot . . .

Then again, though, maybe everyone would leave this place, to get away from me, because I'm such a pip and such a worry-wart. That's certainly not funny, 'cause then I'd be lonely . . .

I snuck back to my room, unpacked the four-leaf clover – from between the folded scrap of Mum's letter – and gently pressed it to my lips as I made my wish again . . .

I placed the four-leaf clover flat on the carpet of my bedroom floor. I rocked back and forth and hugged my knees to my chest, and cried for ages. I didn't like what was happening, not one bit. I gave the four-leaf clover another kiss, and tried desperately to think of something funny, then refolded it into the scrap of paper, and cried again . . .

It was 9.56 a.m. Mum had called me a couple of times, and in the end, Amy came looking for me. 'Mum wants you,' she said, matter-of-factly. She barged into my room. 'We're leaving. You'll get left behind.'

I threw my pillow at her. Amy thought I was playing a game, and tried to start a pillow fight.

I could hear Dad yelling, '*Penny, can you come here a minute*?' He'd been loading furniture by himself for the past two hours, and now, the ramp of the van was making a weird noise, and wouldn't go up or down. I could see him from my bedroom window. '*Penny*!' he yelled again.

Penny was by the pool, stretched out on a reclining deck chair. For the past hour, she'd been laughing at Dad, driving both him and me crazy. Amy and I watched from my window.

The ramp jolted – as if it were stuck. The side table, that Dad was in the middle of loading on to it, almost tipped onto the ground. It was a French antique that he'd inherited from his mother, Flo, after she'd died. '*JACQUIE*!' Dad yelled: if Penny wouldn't help, maybe Mum might. The table's top drawer hit the edge of the ramp and fell to the ground. Dad used his left boot to stop the other drawers from falling. He lost his balance, though, and the side table came crashing down.

'*Dad! Hang on: I'm coming*!' I yelled to him. I ran out of my bedroom, hopped down the stairs, pounced out the front door and sprinted down the drive. Not even the crushed gravel cutting into the soles of my bare feet slowed me down. When I got to Dad, I knelt down and pushed the drawer off his chest. He must have got a deep cut above his left eye, because he was pressing his hands against his forehead and blood was trickling down his wrists. 'Are you okay, Dad?' I asked. 'I'm sorry: it's all my fault – I said I'd help, and I didn't. And if I had've helped, none of this would've happened.'

Mum came running out, holding a bundle of newspaper; a glass vase was sticking out of the top of it.

'Mum!' I waved her over. 'Quick: Dad's head! It's cut!'

Dad pushed my hand away. 'Here – let me stand,' he gruffed.

Mum knelt down.

I stepped back.

'It's bad,' Mum declared, and tried to pull Dad's hands away from the wound. 'What were you thinking, loading the side table on your own? Something like that weighs a tonne. Honestly, Richard, I told you not to lift it on your own.'

Dad looked at her. 'I don't need a speech at the moment. If you'd step back and give me some space, I'd get up.'

'You need stitches,' Mum announced. 'Richard, are you listening? If you'd let me have a look, and settle down enough to come inside, I'll dress the wound: we need to stop the bleeding.'

Dad shoved her hand away. 'Blazes, I needed help *then*, not *now*!' He leant back against the van, found a garbage bag and took a white cloth from it.

'*Richard*! Do *not* use *that* to wipe the blood!'

Dad spun the tablecloth in front of Mum's face, windmill style. '"Not *that*?"' he mimicked.

'*Richard*, stop it!' She pushed Amy out of the way. 'Veronica, take Amy inside,' she ordered. 'I'll be with you two in a minute – go!'

Typical: Mum and Dad were having another screaming match. Rather than take Amy inside, I decided to gather the pieces of splintered furniture into a pile. I wanted to fix everything, and right now: that meant stopping Mum and Dad from having yet another fight. 'Stop it!' I yelled back.

'Certainly not "*that*"!' Dad yelled, yanking a towel from the bag. 'Or *these*!' He screwed a napkin into a ball and pitched it, as if it were a baseball, towards the carport. 'How about *these*, Jacquie: is *this* precious?' He held up another napkin. 'Is this more *precious* than my *table*: *my blazing* –' kicking the van, 'good-for-nothing *table*?'

'*Richard, stop it!*' Mum yelled. 'Have *some* self-control, for God's sake!'

'"*Self-control*?!"' he yelled back and kicked the pile of wood I had just gathered.

I grabbed Amy by her T-shirt and ran towards the house, to get out of the way.

Amy held onto my pyjama pants and cried, '*No, Mummy; no!*'

'*Whoo-hoo!*' Penny cheered, bouncing up and down on top of the reclining deck chair as if Mum and Dad's fight were something to celebrate.

Dad tossed the towel aside and charged like a wounded bull towards Penny. 'There's a rude awakening in store for you!' he roared.

Penny leapt off the chair and dodged him.

'Richard, leave her alone,' Mum demanded, and ran over to stand between them, holding her arms out as if she were a police officer directing a traffic jam.

Each time Dad shifted, Penny shifted away. 'Penny, I've had it!' he yelled. 'Honestly, I don't know what to do! You've got a serious attitude problem!'

Penny took a drag on her cigarette, totally enjoying his bad mood.

Dad pointed to the ground at his feet. He glared at Penny: 'Come here: it's *pot*, isn't it?!'

'"It's *pot*, isn't it?!"' Penny mimicked. 'Why – you want a toke?' She lifted her skirt to her knees and waded into the shallow end of the pool, keeping out of Dad's reach. 'Come on, then!' she dared. 'Come and get it, if you think you're such a Sherlock Holmes!' She flipped the butt inside her mouth, chewed, swallowed and then grinned like she was proud of her effort. 'I guess you'll never know now, *Daddy*! There goes your evidence – oh, and by the way, you look like crap! And I thought you were the master of bleaching the crap out of our family strife: all your smooth white lies, your neat little boxes of betrayal and deceit filed away so Mum couldn't see – *whoops!*' She clapped both hands over her mouth, as if she'd accidentally spilt the beans.

The vase Mum was holding slipped out of her hand. The glass smashed across the tiles. Mum wobbled, as if she were about to faint.

'Penny, I've had it!' Dad roared. 'I've tried; I've had it with your attitude, your meddling in matters that don't concern you, your disregard –' He stopped and turned towards Amy and me – '*Veronica, go inside! You've been told!*'

Amy tried to run towards Mum, but I wouldn't let go of her. 'No, Mummy; no!' she cried. I pulled her back.

'Don't talk to me about *"had it"*!' Penny shouted. 'I told you *I'd* had enough of your "Pauline-thing" *three years ago*! And *you*: you didn't stop that, did you? I've had to stand by and watch you hurt Mum – and follow your orders to keep my mouth shut, so Mum'd think I didn't know.'

'Penny, *no*!' Mum cried. 'Both of you, *stop it*! *Veronica*, take Amy inside. Both of you, *inside – NOW*!'

I fumbled with the door handle, pretending to go inside.

'*Richard*,' Mum began, '*did you know this*? *Did you know Penny knew and never told me*? *Do you know the difference this makes*?'

'*Mum*!' Penny rolled her eyes. 'Do you think I'm an *idiot*? I can't *believe* you think I didn't know.'

'How long have you known?' Mum asked.

'You want to know what I *think*?' Penny said, now that she had her moment. 'I hate *both* of you – for everything you've done, and haven't done, to stuff up my life! When I first found out about Dad, I didn't say anything: I thought I could convince him to stop it – so then *you* wouldn't have to know. But you know what? You're just as sick – because you *do* know! He told me it was none of my business. But it is, because he *is*, or *was*, my dad. Why do you think I spend so much time at Nick's place? Why? Because this family is fucked up in a major way! I hate *both* of you! I don't even want to look at either of you, let alone talk about this! How can you accept *him*?' she asked Mum, as if Dad didn't even have a name. 'How can you even sit at the same *table*, let alone sleep in the same *bed*? I don't get you, either of you, accepting this! Mum, I didn't want to tell you I knew . . . ' Penny's eyes glazed over and her lips quivered. 'Ah, forget it: I don't care. Mum, you were a good mum until Dad ruined you – and now you're just as much to blame!'

Dad squatted onto his heels. 'I think we all need to cool off,' he suggested, sensibly. 'We can talk about this later.'

The loud revving of a car's engine made us all look towards the drive. Two vehicles were making their way up the drive: a removal van, like the one Dad had hired, and a green stationwagon following behind.

'"*Ze Canadians*"! "*Ze Canadians*"!' Penny cheered in a mock-French accent, spreading her arms wide. 'Everyone, *zmile*!'

Mum waved as if she were really pleased to see the Wilsons. She smoothed back her hair, and used the heel of her shoe to sweep the broken glass aside. Dad cupped his hands, scooped water from the pool into them and used it to wash the blood from his arms and face.

I pushed Amy towards Mum, and ran towards the herb garden. I felt that no matter how fast and hard I made my legs pump, there was no way I was ever gonna make it to the shed. I felt like a cartoon character stuck in the air, like my legs cycled madly below my hips and I'd got nowhere.

Wish number five: to have superpowers so I could fly. As a superwoman, I'd have sprinted towards the shed, flapped my arms and:

I'd have been airborne, like a plane, way before I'd made it to the holding yard.

Fffweeeeehhh!!! Fffrrooommm!!! First stopover Disneyland – riding in the 'cup and saucer'. *Yippee!* Hurtling through 'Space Mountain'. *Wheeee!* Waving from the porthole window of the 'Yellow Submarine'. *G'daaaay!!!* Galloping on a horse, through the township of 'Frontier Land'. *Yeee-haaaaaah!* Second stopover, flying back through time to the '1920s' – watching Phar Lap being born, blinking his big round eyes for the first time, then standing up on wobbly legs and taking his first steps.

"'Cause it's a small, small wo-ooorld!"'

Fffrrwooosssh!!!

Where was my four-leaf clover when I needed it?!

Later on, Mum came up to the holding yard gate and waved to me.

I pretended I couldn't see her.

'We're leaving!' she called. 'Come on: the five of us are leaving in the ute. The Wilsons have offered to drive the van later this afternoon. Your dad's not feeling so well.' She didn't care that I was giving Eb and Maje their last hug.

I turned the bucket upside down and tapped the last bit of grain out of it. I joined Mum at the gate and asked her, 'What was Penny going on about?'

She watched a peewee circling above us. 'I think Penny's upset about leaving Nick. She's taking it out on your father. Come on.' She opened the gate to let me out.

I chose to climb over the fence instead. 'I don't believe you,' I said. 'Something's up. Why won't anyone tell me what's going on? Are you and Dad getting a divorce?'

'No,' she replied, matter-of-factly. She massaged the back of her neck and rested her arms across the top rail of the gate. 'Everything's going to be fine.'

'What was Dad going on about, then?'

'You're making something out of nothing,' she reasoned. 'Your father was concussed – that's all; he was talking gibberish.'

I walked off, back towards the house, with Mum following me. I put the bucket down by the back door where there were small splinters of shattered glass from when Penny slammed the door the night before. 'You're lying,' I said to her. 'There's something going on.'

She went to touch my cheek. 'What happened to my cute little Bumble-bee, and her beautiful smile?'

I turned my face away. 'Your cute little Bumble-bee buzzed off when she stopped believing in the tooth fairy.'

'Veronica, it's gonna be okay.'

'"Okay"?' I repeated. 'Okay for who?'

She tightened her lips into a straight line and pinched up the skin between her eyebrows. She turned away, but I could tell she was about to cry. I didn't know what to say. Without thinking, I gave her a hug. She held on to me for a long time. Her melon-scented perfume reminded me of when I was a kid. Her body shook as she cried.

'What's gonna happen?' I asked. 'Why can't you and Dad just get along?'

'It's not that simple, Veronica,' she replied. 'We're trying. We've got a couple of problems to sort out, but we'll be okay.'

'You and Dad never used to fight.'

'Sometimes marriages go through a hard patch. Your dad and I need to sort a few things out. We're seeing a counsellor.'

'Why? Can't you, just like, wave a magic wand?'

She smiled and wiped a tear from her face. 'That'd be good, wouldn't it? If only it *were* that simple. We might need a bit more time, though.' With that, she stepped back and stared out across the valley. 'I'll be glad to leave here: there's no way your father and I can both work, travel back and forth from the city, *and* look after you kids.'

'We don't need looking after,' I said; 'we're old enough – and it's not like we're poor: you don't *have* to work.'

'Veronica, we've been over this before.'

'I know: bushfires; blah-blah-blah.' I didn't want to push the point – not when she was feeling this upset.

The phone rang, and she went off to answer it. I hung out in my bedroom, staring up at the ceiling and the emptiness of the bare room, until it was time for us to get in the car.

Mum steered the ute down the drive.

'I look ridiculous,' Dad suddenly said. He was sitting in the front passenger seat, a bandage wrapped around his head.

'Don't take it off, Richard,' Mum ordered, and pushed his hand away from the bandage; 'not till we get you to the hospital. You'll have to put up with it. You need stitches, and the pressure from the bandage stops the bleeding.'

Dad sat back in a huff. 'I could've stitched it myself: I don't need to go to the stupid hospital. People come out of those places sicker than when they went in. I've stitched up rips in tents, and they've never bloody-well leaked.'

Penny, Amy and me were sitting in the back seat. Amy was in the middle and had her head resting on my lap. She giggled at what Dad had said. I unfolded my baby blanket and tucked the edges of it around her waist. She smiled back, and snuggled closer to my hip. Penny's music was blaring from her headphones; she hadn't heard a word of what Dad had said.

The vineyard's terraces flashed past.

I closed my eyes and focused on the swirling colours rather than on the blackness. I thumbed the piece of paper I'd torn from Mum's letter and pushed it deeper into my pocket, but careful not to crush the clover inside. I still wasn't sure what the 'hard patch' she'd mentioned was. What *was* wrong? And what if they couldn't sort it out: then what?

Mum turned on to Cherry Tree Road and accelerated towards Melbourne.

1

We arrived at the new house. It was easy to recognise because it was the only house on the street made entirely from glass. Rather than fishbowl-shaped, the new house was wave-shaped: curving inwards to the second storey and then curving up and over at the top – like a massive wave rolling towards the beach. And the front garden even looked like a beach: instead of lawn, flowers and trees, there were beach shells, sand, driftwood, rocks and sea-grass. The pathway, leading from the front gate to the front door, was paved with smooth, black rocks that were neatly placed. Anyone could recognise that my dad designed both the old house and the new house, 'cause of the mirrored glass wall made up of smaller triangular pieces of glass. The new house's wall – from the second storey to the top where it curved up and over – reflected the beach-styled garden. And from the second storey to the ground – where it curved in and down – the sky was reflected.

Unpacking was a lot of hard work. My body was aching. We'd been shifting furniture the whole day, and we still had heaps of stuff to move. Paintings were leant up against walls. The couch was blocking the hallway. The lounge-room chandelier was lying on the floor. Boxes were stacked up at the top of the staircase.

The new house was a mess.

I had to squeeze past a bookcase to get to my room. Once through, I closed the door, wedged the desk chair under the knob, sat down and slumped my back against the wall. *If it wasn't the bushfire,* I wondered, *why did we move? What did Penny mean by 'Dad is or was my dad'? Were Penny, Amy and I adopted? No: that was crazy – we looked like Mum and Dad. Had I done something wrong? Was that why I was told to go inside the house?*

The wind pushed the curtain back from the window. I noticed that the back garden hadn't been landscaped yet: bags of sand and cement were lying all around, and a blue tarpaulin was flapping against the fence. And the pool was empty. I guessed Dad planned to finish the garden at some stage and it'd probably look similar to the front garden's beach-styled theme.

The evening sky was being darkened by a summer storm, making it seem later than it was. The new carpet and paint smelled, like cleaning products; and then there was also that unmistakable smell of the fat plonks of rain falling onto the hot, bitumen streets.

I looked around my bedroom. The sheets that Mum had given me were folded at the end of the bed. Cardboard boxes were stacked on top of each other. Between the bed and the boxes, the floor was covered with clothes and junk. I switched the light off, jumped into bed and wriggled into my sleeping bag. The room was lit up by lightning: 1-2-3-4-5-6-*boom!* More lightning: *BOOM! Why have we moved so suddenly? I* wondered. *What's Dad done wrong?*

I hated not knowing the answers: my mind was ticking over and over and over, and no matter how hard I was trying, nothing would make it stop.

Still in my sleeping bag, I sat up, shuffled across the room, pulled the chair away from under the knob and opened the door. The hall light was on. I squeezed past the bookcase again, shuffled across the hall and knocked on Penny's bedroom door. *'Penny,* open up! It's me!' I whispered. 'I want to come in for a sec.' I turned the knob and stuck my head through the doorway.

Lightning struck. The room turned an eerie blue-grey. *BOOM!* I switched the light on, and once inside, gently closed the door. Knowing Penny, I figured she'd run off to Nick's – she'd probably caught a train or hitched a ride there. Her bed wasn't assembled: its wooden pieces were lying scattered in a pile on top of the mattress. However, she'd stuck six poster-size photos of her goth friends up on the wall. There they were: climbing on top of cars that'd been dumped in a gully. They were naked – but not so you could see anything that mattered – and their bodies were covered in tattoos. Seeing the mist in the gully, I felt a chill go up my spine. *BOOM!* They were the same photos from her bedroom at Yarra Valley. But they now had graffiti on them: thick, black words scribbled in Texta, in another language. She must have stuck the pictures up and then written on them; I could tell, because some of the graffiti had gone onto the wall.

I sat down on the mattress and read the labels stuck on the boxes:

Human Remains
Illegal
Poison XXX
digital/audio
Tracks to trip and rip
Boring School Shit
Veronica's brain

'Veronica's brain'? *What?* I shifted that box closer to me. It hardly weighed anything. I ripped the tape off and pushed the flaps open. Nothing – except writing at the bottom:

Empty! What did you expect?
Now piss off and stop looking through my stuff you little shit!

Penny wasn't always this mean. We used to hang out and do heaps of cool stuff together: we made cubbyhouses, skipped with one end of the rope tied to the veranda and played Marco Polo in the pool.

I opened some of the other boxes: candles; incense; art stuff; tiny bowls and tobacco pipes. Another one had jewels and crystals; another, sketchbooks filled with magazine clippings and tattoo designs. And then I found heaps of books on how to make films, and hundreds of discs containing digitally recorded sound effects. And her 'black only' clothes, decorated with beads and leather strips.

A photo of Nick fell out from between the pages of a book. His dreadlocked hair was hanging down past his shoulders, and his skin was covered in tattoos. He was holding a video camera above his head. I could make out a forest in the background; it was probably Thailand – they snuck off there once to make a documentary. When Mum found out, she chucked an absolute barney.

I threw the photo back into the box. *Gross!* I thought. *And to think she's actually kissed him!* He looked like he'd never showered – and he'd left school midway through Year 11, after his parents were lucky enough to win Tattslotto and they'd left Nick to look after the house when they'd moved overseas. Penny says Nick earns money as a filmmaker, but Mum reckons he's living off money his parents set up in a trust fund for him. Penny refuses to show us his documentaries – she says there for 'goths' only. Anyways, he's *feral*, and the kids at school called him the Yarra Valley Freak. And he'd changed his family's house to make it spooky. Suze and I had ridden past it and seen the wind chimes hanging from the trees: animal bones and feathers were tied to the strings. Even Eb had got the spooks: thrown his head in the air and bolted off.

BOOM!

I grabbed the disc that had 'Yarra Valley' written on its packet, shuffled out of the room and closed the door behind me. *Dad hasn't done anything wrong,* I thought; *Penny was just being Penny – but then, I didn't totally believe what Mum said: that Dad was 'talking gibberish'.*

Someone had switched the hall light off, and the light in the study was on. I figured Mum was probably unpacking. I went to my room, closed the door behind me and wedged the desk chair under the knob again. I lay down on the bed and curled up in a ball. The house was dead quiet now that the lightning had stopped. *What exactly's going on out there?* I wondered. *Amy seems okay – but everyone else's acting like it's World War 3.*

I turned my computer on. The screen saver – a picture of Eb and Maje leaning over the holding-yard gate – popped up. I kissed the screen, slid the 'Yarra Valley' disc into the CD-ROM and turned the volume up. I could hear the 'ping' of bellbirds echoing from the gully to the ridge . . . the buzz of Dad's chainsaw . . . a magpie calling . . . a flap of wings . . .

. . . and finally, exhausted from crying, I fell asleep.

When I woke up, the first thing I did was check my email Inbox.

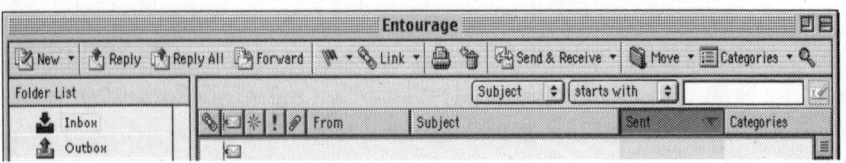

>From: susie@bumble.com.au

>To: veronica@bumble.com.au

>Subject: Cyber hugs from Noosa!!!

>Sent: 14 December, 10.20 a.m.

Hi there, my Miss-Vee-Bumble-bee. How cool is this? I've found an Internet cafe on the main street! Wish u were here. Noosa is THE biggest Perv Fest!!! There's a couple of spunks sitting at the computer beside mine, & I'm talking THOROUGHBRED. I met a guy last night (called Guy!!!!) at the hotel swimming pool. He's from Sydney & holidaying here with his parents. He's 16! Spiky brown hair with a bit of blond at the front (surfie), tanned & a total SPUNK!!! I'm meeting up with this other hotbod called Aaron in (checking watch) 2 minutes, & he's going 2 show me how 2 boogie-board. Watch out! Hawaii Five-O!!! 'Da-nah-nah-nah-naaaah-naah!!!' Guess what? I've got a tan - & I can prove it, because I've got photos. Surf's up. I'll let u know how I get on with Aaron & Guy & Thommo & Arty & Jezza & Luke & Steve . . . Remind me NOT 2 4get 2 tell u about STEVE!!! He gave me a bracelet, but I lost it last night at the beach. (Doi! Typical me!!!) Hugs & big, wet, sloppy kisses on the lips. Your best-est buddy & blood sis.

XXOO Susie-Suze

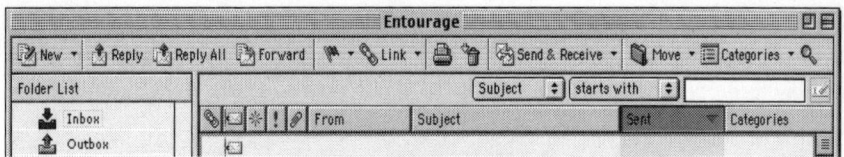

>From: susie@bumble.com.au
>To: veronica@bumble.com.au
>Subject: Where's my Vee?
>Sent: 16 December, 4.40 p.m.

HELLO! Have u moved & forgotten all about me? Let me at least pretend that you're still my best-est buddy & write me an email! Not like u not 2 write back ASAP. Last night - FYA! Aaron asked me 2 do it. We were sitting in the dark on the beach. Then after he'd asked me 2 do it he turned around & (ready 4 it?) SPEWED. How disgusting! I've spent the whole day (bored out of my mind!!!) watching movies in the hotel room so I don't bump into him - which is ridiculous. HE should b the 1 who's 2 embarrassed 2 show HIS face. I'm wearing Mum's beach hat & a pair of daggy sunglasses as a disguise so I can at least sneak out & send u an email. Wish u were here to ROFL with me. XXOO (Still the virgin!!!) Susie-Suze

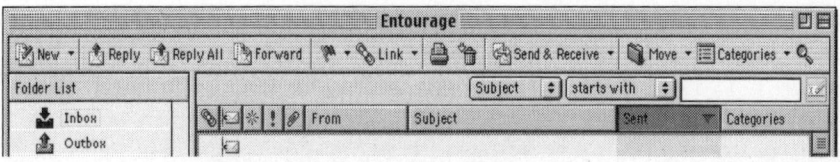

>From: veronica@bumble.com.au
>To: susie@bumble.com.au
>Subject: RE: Where's my Vee?
>Sent: 18 December, 7.04 a.m.

SUZE, u have soooooo made my day!!!!

I've just got up & I'm kicking myself for not thinking B4 now 2 check my emails. We moved yesterday. It's been full on & NIGHTMARISH. I'm sorry I didn't write back ASAP, but my computer was packed away. Missing u2 X 1000. Make that X 1 million. Everything sucks right now. Hang on, BRB . . . Dad just knocked on my door. Mum wants 2 c me. Pluttthh! She can go jump. She's booked me in2 this stupid holiday program. As if. She starts back at nursing today.

Gotta go. If I don't catch Dad right now, I WILL have 2 go 2 the holiday program. His work's boring, but not as bad as. Mum's even talking about sending me 2 the holiday program between Christmas & when school starts back. Hah! She's dreaming!

TTYL, till then, miss ya. Your best-est buddy & blood sis. (NO kiss) XO - Vee

I chucked on a pair of shorts and a T-shirt, and grabbed my runners. The bookcase was gone, so I sat on the top step of the staircase and tied my laces. My tummy was rumbling. I was about to step off the landing, but stopped when I heard Mum shout, '*Penny!*'

The study door was open a bit. There wasn't much time – but one peek and I'd be off.

Mum was sitting on a bed, her back to me. She had the phone pressed to her right ear, and was using her other hand to go through her handbag. 'I'm sorry you had to find out this way,' she was saying. 'At least come home so we *can* talk. I don't like you being at Nick's – you know what I think about him, and my opinion *has not* and *will not* change.' She ran her fingers through her wet hair and waited for Penny to stop arguing down the line. 'I'm more than well informed about what goes on up there, she went on; 'the whole town knows. And the Gibbses have had to send Clare to her grandparents' in Ireland to get her to a safer place. No, Penny; *no*! By being tough, I'm letting you know how much I *do* care. That environment isn't safe; it's detrimental. Am I making myself clear?'

I noticed she'd put her clothes in a pile at the bottom of the bed. Her make-up – lipstick, mainly – was scattered across the bedside table. And the sheets were crumpled as if someone – she? – had slept in them the night before.

'Penny,' she continued, 'I want you to come home *now*. I don't get my new car till Wednesday, but I'll ride out in a taxi. I don't condone your friendship with anyone from that place – not till you listen . . . and I'll make it as impossible for you . . .' She raised one of her hands, and sighed to herself. 'Would you consider staying at Lisa's, then? She's as concerned about you as I am – she's even offered to have you live at her house until things settle down here.' She turned and looked around her – she must've sensed I was there. 'Hang on,' she said to Penny. Then, holding the phone away from her head, she asked, 'Veronica?'

I pushed the door open. 'I'm going with Dad,' I announced.

She placed her hand over the mouthpiece. 'Veronica, it's organised: you're booked into the holiday program.'

'No – I've already told you: I don't want to go; there's no way I'm gonna be the oldest person there.'

'But you –'

'No! Amy can go by herself.'

She gave up. 'Okay – as long as it's okay with your dad.'

Dad drove the ute down the centre lane, where the tram tracks ran. Everywhere I looked I could see concrete: on the footpaths, on the driveways – on the left, I could even see a *concrete park*. And the traffic crawled as slow as a snail. On both sides of the road, I could see that the writing on the shopfront windows was painted in red and gold, and that none of it was in English. An Asian woman shuffled across the street, fanning her face with a newspaper to cool herself from the summer heat. 'Look at the rubbish,' I announced, pointing at the Yarra River: 'gross.'

As we crossed a bridge, Dad moved over to the outside lane. He looked at me. 'Grumpy *speaks!*' he joked.

'I'm not "grumpy",' I explained; 'I'm tired – that's all. I hardly slept: I kept waking up from all the weird noises I was hearing.'

'You'll get used to it,' he said. 'Lagilla's down there.' He pointed down a side street. 'It's close enough for you and Amy to walk when school starts back.'

'Yeah, great,' I said, totally lacking in enthusiasm: 'I can't wait. Where's the eject switch? I'll pass on the guided tour, thanks.' I crossed my arms and chewed on a fingernail. So much stuff was going on inside my head, and I had *the* worst-est headache. 'Why's our family so weird?' I asked.

He laughed.

'*Dad*, I'm *serious!*'

He took his time, and switched the radio station to his favourite news programme. 'It all depends,' he began, glancing over his shoulder at the tram coming up behind us, 'on how you look at things.'

'Well, I'm looking,' I reassured him. 'And Mum's sleeping in the study. Are you gonna tell me *that's* not weird?'

'Oh that. That's short term,' he replied. 'She'll be working odd hours while she's doing the nursing refresher course, coming and going late at night; then, once a permanent position in a bigger hospital comes up, we'll look at reorganising the set-up – it's only a coupla weeks – months – at the most.'

I felt like Tarzan falling to the ground after he'd failed to grab onto a swinging vine.

Swissh swisssshhh waaaa iiie!!

It *was* true: Mum *was* sleeping in the study. 'See?' I said to Dad. 'Weird! And what about Mum's family? I've never even met her parents – and she hasn't spoken to her twin sister for years!'

THUD

Ouch! I thought. 'You can't tell me *that's* not weird!'

He ruffled my hair and remarked, 'You're certainly a fountain of conversation – for someone who shut herself up in her room last night and told everyone she wanted to be left alone. Speaking of Lisa, she dropped by last night to welcome us into our new house.'

'Yeah, right – as *if*,' I blurted out. I thought he was lying
But he didn't give me a knowing wink.

'You're serious, aren't you?' I said. 'That's just *too* weird! Mum hasn't spoken to her for, like, years – and Lisa wouldn't even recognise me if I did come downstairs. And no one told me, anyway.'

'Your mother tried,' he explained, 'but you were sleeping.' He stopped to let a group of kids, kicking a soccer ball, cross the street. After they'd crossed, he turned the car into a side street. 'You're right, they hadn't spoken for a while,' he said, 'so it was a big deal, her dropping by.'

'How come I've never met Mum's and Lisa's parents?' I asked.

He had to think about that one. After a while, he replied, 'When your mother was your age, Lisa was the one person she felt connected to. They were adopted, so they never knew who their real parents were. Lots of kids are adopted and have a happy childhood. But your mother and Lisa were sent to Lagilla's boarding school when they were very young. Ideally, they should have lived at home and spent more time with their adoptive parents. But it was probably best that they didn't spend much time with them: they were always comparing the two girls, and favouring Lisa over your mum. In the end, the favouritism came between them all.'

His explanation wasn't making much sense to me. 'If Lagilla's so bad,' I asked him, 'why am I being forced to go to school there?'

'Veronica,' he began, switching off the radio, 'you're a day student, not a boarder; Mum and I would never allow that.'

'Well, it must be a crap school,' I insisted, 'otherwise Penny wouldn't have wagged so much.'

He shifted gear. 'You're not Penny. She has a bad habit of running away from challenges and complexity. You're different.'

'Well,' I spat back, 'maybe she's *on* to something.'

Neither of us said anything for a while, so I sat staring out the window. Years ago, Mum had said that if Lisa moved into the house their parents had bought as an investment property, she'd never speak to her again. Obviously Lisa wasn't worried about what Mum'd said, because she did move in. I'd seen the house: I was with Mum when she drove over there about two years before, parked out the front but changed her mind about going inside. 'Lisa's weird,' I decided: 'she painted her house purple and orange.'

'I've seen worse,' Dad said, with a hint of a smile.

'Yeah, like in cartoons – but not in real life.'

He chuckled.

I thought about Mum and Dad. 'How old were you,' I asked him, 'when you and Mum first met?'

He shrugged his shoulders. 'Thirteen, I think.' He counted aloud, on his fingers.

'Thirteen?! That's how old I am! Were you two kissing when you were that age?'

'No,' he assured me, and shook his head.

'That's disgusting.' I knew he was lying: he just didn't want to admit they'd sucked face when they were 13.

He explained, 'We were friends for a long time before we started going out together as boyfriend and girlfriend. Your mum stayed over at my place during her holidays because she didn't like going home. Even Lisa stayed over if she didn't stay with a friend. We didn't start *seriously* dating till we were much older.'

'Yeah, *right*.' I played air violin and hummed a romantic tune.

'Cute,' was all he said.

Then, suddenly, it occurred to me: 'Why,' I asked him, 'are you all of a sudden sticking up for Mum when you two fight so much? And why is it that everyone in our family's so unhappy? Except Amy – are we jinxed or something?'

'We're not "jinxed",' he replied. 'But maybe your mum's parents should never have adopted the girls. If you're gonna have kids, you should be there for them. The girls suffered a marked absence because of their parents' selfishness. It's sad, growing up without your parents: you miss out on a lot of love – you're lucky you've got both.'

'Dad, all I'd said was that our family was weird - and now you're *blah-ing on* like you're Oprah and saying big-word stuff like "marked absence". Like, what does that have to do with it? The fact is our family *is* weird, and you won't admit it. If I had a twin sister, she'd be my best friend, and I'd hang out with her every day.' I switched the radio to a music station. 'Can we talk about something else? Or how about we don't talk at all.'

He stopped at the lights and looked at me. 'Your mother and Lisa are working at getting close again – and that's *great*. No one's "jinxed". And our family's not "weird". Life isn't always a fairytale, as much as you'd like it to be. We've invited Lisa over for Christmas lunch, and she's said yes, so just go easy, Bumble . . . See if you can be nicer to your mother, too.'

'I have been,' I said, matter-of-factly. 'I unpacked the boxes in the kitchen, even when she didn't ask me – and I helped Amy set up her room.' Ever since Mum had told me about her and Dad's 'hard patch', I'd been making an effort. I wound down the car window. 'Maybe, I'll run away like Penny.'

'You wouldn't do that,' he said, playfully tweaking my nose, 'you're my Bumble.'

'Dad, that is *so* corny.' I pretended to gag.

'Guess stopping off at the Pancake Parlour for breakfast's ruled out, then.'

I could see the sign up ahead. '*Oh*, Dad, *please!*'

'Do you promise to be nicer to your Mum?'

'Dad, that's blackmail!'

He drove super-slow past the entrance to the restaurant.

'Okay: I'll make her a cuppa when she gets home from work . . . and I'll finish unpacking the boxes in my room – but *only* if *you* promise to be nicer to her too.'

'Deal,' he said, and held out his hand for me to shake.

We shook on it. Then he reversed, and turned into the entrance.

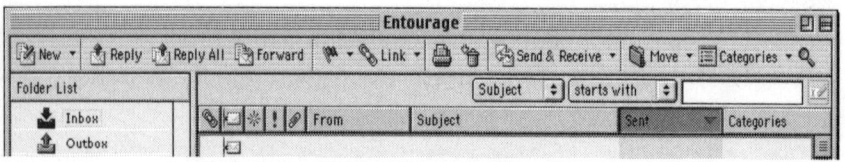

>From: veronica@bumble.com.au
>To: susie@bumble.com.au
>Subject: HELP!!!
>Sent: 19 December, 9.21 p.m.

Suze, HELP!!!

Nothing's changed. Mum & Dad just had another huge fight. It all started when Mum screamed at me 4 asking Y Penny was living at Lisa's place. (Remember Mum's twin sister Lisa? The 1 who showed us how 2 fold pirate hats out of newspaper when we were kids?) I didn't realise the subject was so touchy. And Mum & Dad aren't sleeping in the same room.

Don't u think that's weird???

I do.

TTYL, your best-est buddy & blood sis. XO - Vee

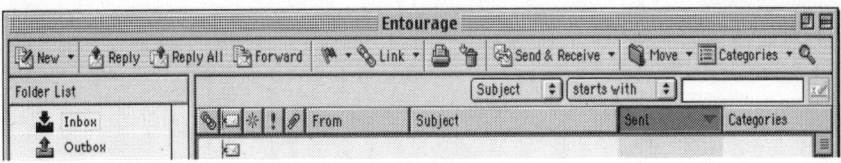

>From: veronica@bumble.com.au
>To: susie@bumble.com.au
>Subject: SOS!!!!
>Sent: 20 December, 8.01 p.m.

Hi, Suze. Weekdays I'm helping out at Dad's work & Mum's finally agreed I can keep going there until school starts back. If only they'd let me stay at home. I hate that they treat me like I'm Amy's age. Everyone in the office is super-duper nice & slurping up 2 me bcoz of being Dad's daughter & everything. Even when I stuff up big time. Like yesterday, I filed the contracts by Project Name rather than Company Name & had 2 do it all over again. But I couldn't remember which 1's I'd filed. So then, Pauline (Dad's business partner) thought I was so hopeless that Dad said I could clean out the fish tank instead. I was cleaning the glass when the bottom plate cracked & water spilt everywhere. I'm talking all over Dad's development models, & Pauline cracked it, making this huge fuss about the fish & saying they were this crazy exotic breed that costs $1000 each. As if. The fish were flapping around on the carpet, & Pauline threw her coffee in2 the nearest pot plant & scooped the fish in2 her mug. She had an absolute barney.

Now Dad's given me (what he calls) a 'Low Risk Project' where I have 2 take photos of the CBD. They can be of anything - whatever I think captures 'the essence of Melbourne'. Talk about DUMB!!! I think it's just an excuse 2 get me out of the office so I don't trash the place. There's this really geeky guy who's working in the office over his uni summer break, & he's disgusting. He's always making up reasons 2 come in2 the room I'm in. He's worse than Neil Wright. His name's Vincent Gee. More like Vincent VOMIT!!!!!!

Have u checked out any trail rides that go along the beach? Or r u full-on despo & chasing guys all the time? EVERYTHING SUCKS, IN CASE U HAVEN'T CLUED ON!!! SOS. HELP!!! (I'm serious.) – Your best-est buddy & blood sis. XO – Vee

PS Still waiting 4 u 2 write back about Mum & Dad & the separate-room thing...

It was about 9:30 a.m. when I got off the tram at the corner of Bourke and Swanston Street, and the city was super-busy.

Earlier that morning, Dad'd said the camera didn't have a fantastic zoom and that "you'd need to keep a wide perspective when taking the photos, unless you got up close and personal with your subject". I had no idea what he was talking about, so straight away I took a tram – from Dad's office – into the heart of the city, to avoid hearing any more of his photography lecture.

The first thing I did was look up: there was a massive poster of a soccer player that covered the wall of an entire office-building; actually there were tonnes of pictures, billboards, advertisements and giant TV screens everywhere. Only when I looked directly upwards could I see the sky. Even though the sun had risen hours ago, I was shaded by the buildings and had to walk into the middle of the city square before I could stand in its warmth. A bike courier hopped up, onto the sidewalk, then rode the steps upwards and into the square and did a wheelie right in front of me. I jumped backwards to get out of his way, only to have something wet and sharp jab my ankles.

I screamed – imagining a snake had bitten me – and turned around to face a giant green vacuum cleaner that had sharp black bristles at ankle-height. The city cleaner driving the vacuum – dressed in blue overalls, a bright orange vest and ear muffs over his head – kept on vacuuming the sidewalk even though every other person walking through the square paused to stare at the girl who'd just screamed at the top of her lungs.

I wanted to run, jump on a tram and go back home. But, I was also curious about the camera and the photos it'd take. So I went over to the far side of the square, away from the early morning rush, sat down on a metal bench and looked for things to photograph.

Everything I saw, I hated: the city was ugly! All around me was cement, smoke, noise and garbage. Even the air stunk of diesel fumes from the delivery trucks. And everyone was in a hurry to get somewhere. Or if they were sitting down, they were drinking coffee, writing notes or talking on their mobile phone.

I heard the *kl-kl-klop* of horse hooves and looked right to see a big grey horse coming down Swanston Street, pulling a shiny black wooden carriage. The horse wore a beautiful silver studded ornamental bridle – even the blinkers had matching silver decorations – and a plume of scarlet feathers sprouted from the top of the horse's head that perfectly matched the carriage's velvet upholstery. I scrambled to grab the camera out of my backpack. *Piiii* – the sound that told me the camera was ready to take a picture took forever – *iiing*! By now, the horse was directly in front of me and centred within my viewing screen so I quickly pressed the shutter button halfway down to focus, just like Dad'd shown me. The camera whirred into focus. I pushed the button all the way down – *click*! How cool! My first picture of the city was going to be of a horse and . . . What?! A poo bag?!

I hated poo bags – it was cruel to strap a bag to the bum of a horse so that it didn't poo on the road – and horses shouldn't really be in the city. When I looked back the horse didn't appear as majestic, and it's back right leg looked lame. *Poor thing*, I thought, *probably from trotting all day on the bitumen*.

Heaps more people rushed to and fro, car horns tooted, whistles blew. The city was very different from Yarra Valley.

Bourke Street Mall seemed like a good place to take more photos. The street was closed to cars, although there were still bikers and trams, and buskers played drums and guitar to the passing crowds. At the far end of the mall there was an old man sitting on a bench surrounded by a flock of pigeons: there must've been hundreds of 'em; thousands. The pigeons fluttered about, and lots perched on the man – his shoulders, arms and legs – and two of them even fighting to get the highest perch on top of his head.

The man's hair was long and dreadlocked like Nick's. I bet Nick'd end up like this guy, when he got older. I moved closer to take a picture, so that I could email Suze a photo of 'Nick the Pigeon Man', but when I lifted my camera the guy jumped up.

'*Don't* you take a picture of *me*,' he hollered above the flutter of wings as the pigeons flapped and flew upwards to the rooftop ledges of the post office. 'I will *not* be the subject of your interrogation. *They* told me about *you*. *They* told me that spies were coming –'

I ran. I didn't stop until I'd sprinted the length of the mall and turned the corner into a side street. I decided not to take any more photos of city people; instead I wandered down the side streets and alleys and found myself looking through the lens at graffiti and garbage . . .

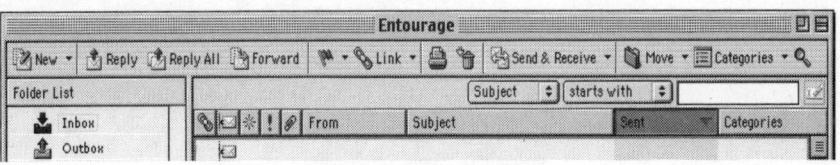

>From: susie@bumble.com.au
>To: veronica@bumble.com.au
>Subject: I'M FAMOUS!!!
>Sent: 21 December, 7.23 p.m.

La-la-la. I saw Thomas Kirkland from Ace20 on the beach 2day. I AM NOT KIDDING!!! He looks a bit like how he does in the video clip, but is heaps SHORTER (bummer) in real life. All the girls were asking 4 his autograph, & he was really sweet & said I could be in his next video clip. I spotted 2 new girls at the hotel (in the lobby), but haven't spoken 2 them yet. They look pretty cool. The taller 1 looks older than me, about 16... maybe 17. Morris is giving me the shits. He is SUCH a WANKER!!! He keeps perving on me in my bikinis!!! I squirted Tabasco sauce in2 his porridge this morning, when he wasn't looking. I had 2 run out the room. It was 2 funny. Look out 4 my video clip on Channel V!!! Your best-est buddy & blood sis. XXOO - SuzieAce20

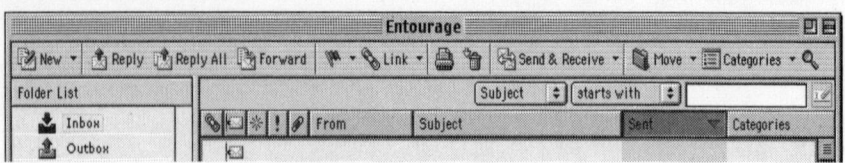

>From: susie@bumble.com.au
>To: veronica@bumble.com.au
>Subject: DAN!!! HOT! HOT!! HOT!!!
>Sent: 22 December, 2.06 p.m.

DAN AND I WENT TO 3rd BASE LAST NIGHT!!!!!! Mum & Morris didn't even say anything about me getting home at midnight. They weren't even home 2 c what time I got home. Dan's last name is Princeton. What do u think? Susie Princeton? Or Susie Kirkland? Let me know. XXOO – Susie _ _ _ _ _ _ _ _ (Fill in the blank.) PS I'm going out with the 2 girls I saw yesterday in the hotel lobby. I met them at the beach 2day. We bought fake IDs from a backpacker at the Internet café & we're gonna see if we can get in2 the Pub. Can't wait!!!

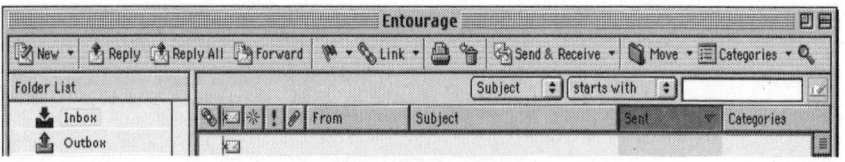

>From: susie@bumble.com.au
>To: veronica@bumble.com.au
>Subject: MAJOR HANGOVER!
>Sent: 23 December, 4.28 p.m.

Hi, Vee. Susie's told me all about u. U sound really cool. If u ever come 2 Perth, come & stay over at my place. Not during exam time though. I'm doing Year 11 next year, which'll be a bit stressful. Cool. Bye from Bells :-)

Hi! Heard ya cool. Bye! :-) Briggs

Vee, last night was THE BESTEST night!!! We tried to get in2 Steamers (this really cool club on the top of the hill) but the bouncers didn't let us in. So we went 2 this beach party & it was packed. I kept bumping in2 all these spunks I'd seen on the beach during the day. We had a competition 2 c who could kiss the most guys. Bells won (SLUT!!!). Only saying that coz she's reading over my shoulder as I write. Really, she's cool - hot-to-trot!!!! Anyways, we're going 2 a beach party again 2nite. There'd better be heaps & heaps of spunks. XXOO - Susie-Suze.

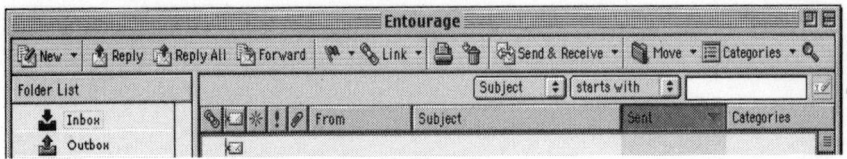

>From: susie@bumble.com.au
>To: veronica@bumble.com.au
>Subject: SHARK ATTACK!!!
>Sent: 24 December, 10.12 a.m.

Hi, Vee. The Surf Club's banned everyone from swimming at the main beach. & now there's a helicopter flying above the water, checking 4 sharks. JAWS!!! YIKES!!! Everyone's standing around in Hastings Street watching, & the helicopter's really LOUD!!! The lifeguards r saying there's a school of 5 & they're trying 2 round them off 2 stop them from going in2 the Sound. Once they get in2 the Sound, they say it's really hard 2 get them out, & people windsurf in there. (Hopefully vomit-head Aaron - he said he does. Suffer!!!). It's stinking hot right now!!! CONES is this gelati place next door, and there are like 1000 flavours & I'm thinking of getting another 1. YUMMMM AS SCRUM AS!!!!! Last night, I had a tongue-fest with Steve again. (Did I tell u he's a Melbournite?! & that he turns 17 in 4 months!) Big hugs & kisses from your best-est buddy & blood sis. XXOO - Susie-inlovewithSteve-Suze!!!

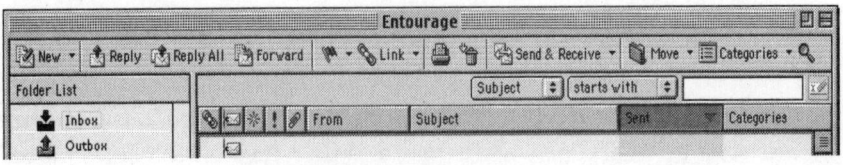

>From: susie@bumble.com.au
>To: veronica@bumble.com.au
>Subject: PS!!!
>Sent: 24 December, 10:14 a.m.

PS We're checking out of the hotel & going 2 Fraser Island later this afternoon (staying 3 nights, sleeping in Eco Cabins, whatever they r???). U can't phone in or out bcoz there's no electricity, phone etc. So 'HAPPY XMAS!' now 4 then!!!! Stuff your face & eat xtra 4 me in case there's no real food on the island & I have 2 run around naked (which wouldn't be so bad), living off nuts & berries!!! Doi - there'd better be a toilet, or else!!! XXOO. Your best-est buddy & blood sis, Susie-Suze

6

Ah, Christmas: '*Tra-la-la la-laah-La-La-la-La! Deck the halls with –*'

As I grabbed some candles from Mum's bedside table, I heard a loud bang coming from a room that seemed to be Penny's. I sprinted across the hall and ran into the room. '*Penny*! Oh, my God!' My mouth dropped open: she'd knocked out a hole in the wall where one of her giant-sized photos had been. 'Dad's *so* gonna kill you! What do you think you're doing?'

'Nothing – nick off,' she replied, in her usual charming way. She went back to thumping the wall with a hockey stick. Plaster flew out everywhere. 'You heard me,' she said: 'nick off.'

'No: you're crazy – you know that?'

'Four-eyes, *piss off*!' She swung at the wall again.

I jumped back. Some candles broke as I fell backwards against the wardrobe. 'Now look what you've done! You think you can just come home, stuff up everyone's Christmas and then nick off to Nick's place!'

'You are *so* naive,' was all she could be bothered saying.

'I am *not*!' I lashed back. 'At least I'm not a nutcase!'

She changed her mind, and decided to rip into me: 'Hoh! And what about *you*? Walking round with your head stuck up a horse's arse! You're life is *so* cushy. The only thing you're trying to deal with is this family's move. And here's an update for you! Get your facts straight before you open your stinky mouth: I'm living at *Lisa's*, which is a huge, *major* improvement on this dump.' She stuck the photo back over the hole.

'Don't think you can hide it,' I told her. 'Dad's *so* gonna find out.'

'Good – I hope he does.' She punched her fist through the centre of the photo so the hole could still be seen. 'I hope he keels over when he sees it and has a heart attack, for all I care.' She stared at me with an 'I know everything and you know nothing' kind of look. 'Poor, little, precious Bumble: thinks she's an only child.'

'I wish I *were*,' I said. 'And anyway, what were you crapping on about that day by the pool? Don't give me that dumb look – what were you saying about Mum and Dad?'

I knew by the smirk on her face that she knew exactly what I was talking about. 'Do your own research, Sherlock. Apparently I'm not allowed to breathe a word, because poor, precious Bumble's got a soft head and she couldn't cope.'

'*Tell me!*' I yelled at the top of my voice.

She eyed me off, savouring the moment of knowing something I didn't know.

'Veronica! Penny!' Mum was calling from the bottom of the stairs. 'I need your help!'

Both of us ignored Mum.

'*Tell me!*' I begged, 'or I'll tell Dad about the wall.'

Penny pushed me back against the door then backed off towards the hall.

I rose to my feet and chased her out of the room. There was no way I was gonna let her get away with that – not any more. Drawing my arm back, I aimed a candle at her head.

She didn't duck in time. '*Ow, bitch!*' she yelled, rubbing the back of her head, where the candle had hit.

I ducked as she threw the candle back. 'Stop it!

She gave me an 'up yours!' sign and ran down the stairwell, two steps at a time.

I reckon I had *the* worst-est older sister in the whole, wide world. I gathered the candles – even the broken ones. There was no way Penny and me were related, I decided: surely someone in the hospital had jumbled the files. Surely I *was* an only child.

Wish number six: to *be* an only child so that Christmas Day would be as cool bananas as this: '. . . *boughs of holly; Tra-la-la la-laah –*'

'You're such a *darling*!' It's Mum, interrupting me as I waltz into the dining room. She takes the candles and slots them into the candelabra at the centre of the dining table. 'Now,' she begins, 'Dad and I have been discussing –' she strikes a match – 'Do you want to open your presents first, before we eat, or after?'

I gaze at the huge pile of presents under the tree. There are so many of them – all neatly wrapped and ribboned – that they spill out across the carpet. Some are square-shaped, others round-shaped and squashy. I've already checked them out: each night I've crept down the stairs to suss out the shapes and bulges. For some, I've peeled back the tape and then carefully sealed them back up again; for others, I've guessed what they are straight away.

Because I'm an adorable child, I say to Mum, 'Oh, Mum; oh, Dad, don't you want to open your presents from me first?'

Dad gives Mum a sloppy kiss on the cheek as he refills her wine glass. 'We've done such a great job, haven't we, Jacquie?' he asks her. He wraps his arms around her waist, and looks over at me: 'Our little Bumble's so thoughtful, isn't she?'

'She's perfect,' Mum agrees. 'Go on: you first, love.' She takes an envelope from the mantelpiece, which I know is my Christmas card.

'Okay,' I say, 'but *only* if you insist.'

I take the card and hug it to my chest. The presents under the tree are always the little 'itsy-bitsy piecy' things: turnout bridles, new brushes for my grooming kit, rugs, saddle blankets; the real gift is always written in the card. Last year, Dad sticky-taped a piece of straw to the inside of the card, and the message was that he promised to build me a new stable. The year before that, the card contained a key to a Pegasus horse float.

'Did you?' I jump up and down. 'Did you *really*? Is he? IS HE?' For the past year, my loving parents have been writing everything I've asked for on a whiteboard in the kitchen. 'Is Safari really *mine*?' I ask. He has to be: I stuck his photo on the whiteboard. Anyone who rode Safari would definitely be chosen to ride for Australia in the Olympics. '*Yippeeee*!' I shout.

'Open the card,' Dad says, just as excitedly.

'Go on!' Mum adds.

I tear open the envelope:

Hah sucked in, loser!

Firstly, you wished for a unicorn.
Then you wished for you and Susie training together
to qualify for the Australian Olympic Eventing team.
Thirdly, you wished for a world without guys -
get a life. Fourthly, to see the funny side of
everything - are you laughing YET?????
Then fifthly, to fly. Get real.

So. We're sorry. We're really horribly, terribly,
awfully sorry, but you're NOT an only child.

Happy Happy Christmas All our love,
Mum and Dad

'. . . La-la-la-la-laaah; 'tis the season to be –'

This is how Christmas *really* happened.

My job was to set the table. First, I'd laid the tartan cloth, then the embroidered tablecloth, six china plates, the best silver cutlery and the crystal glasses. 'What's wrong with having a barbecue?' I asked, loud enough for Mum to hear. She was in the kitchen, panicking that the turkey was too dry. I was in a bad mood because Penny kept coming in and pulling my plaits. I ate another lolly, probably my sixtieth. I stuffed some of the empty wrappers towards the bottom of the bowl, rolled some of the others into tight balls about the size of a chocolate, wrapped them up again and twisted the ends to make them look brand new.

Finally, we all sat down to eat. Dad insisted Lisa sat at the head of the table so she'd be sitting next to Mum. Amy and I burst out laughing when Lisa started talking about the 'Third World' and how she'd been adopting a goat as Christmas presents for poor villagers. 'It's true,' she confirmed: 'my shop raised enough money to buy two goats and build a toilet for an African village – it flushes and everything.'

Amy fell off her chair when Auntie Lisa started making flushing noises.

Lisa didn't really look like Mum: her hair was short, like Mum's, but spiked up, like a punk's. She wore crazy clothes, like what dancers wore in video clips. Her shirt was shiny and purple, and had red buttons. She didn't say a word when she opened one of my 'chocolates' and saw that there was a wrapper inside.

I thought Mum was going to kill Amy when she spilt her Coke.

'Good one,' Penny said to Amy. 'Just don't spill the bloody wine, dickhead.'

Amy burst out crying.

'Penny, be nice!' Lisa warned, pointing a finger at her rude niece.

Penny went to say something, but changed her mind. She came back from the kitchen carrying a roll of paper towel and a wet sponge. We had to re-set the table so Mum could soak out the stain.

When we sat down again, Lisa told us about the latest shop she'd bought; she now had eight florist shops altogether. 'We make arrangements out of cork, bamboo and chicken wire. Once, we did a rowboat filled with lilies and water and silver birch.'

'It doesn't sound like a typical flower shop,' I said.

'You're right,' she agreed. 'Floristry's not like it used to be: it's installations now – not boring old bunches of flowers. It's clients and contracts and storyboards.' She sat up, slipped off her shoes and tucked her feet under her bum. 'We're talking 'themes', 'events', 'weddings',' she enthused; 'booked by celebrities, corporate companies – six months or up to a year in advance. If it wasn't so busy at the moment, I'd ask Veronica if she'd like to hang out at the warehouse –' she looked at me – 'but I'm flat out. I'm thinking of employing an assistant manager. I've employed six juniors, about your age, over the summer break. They're good sorts: you should drop by one afternoon, even if I'm not there. It's not far from Richard's work. Sometimes I have to kick them out at the end of the day. I can't complain – I guess I'm lucky: some bosses have to take the whip to their workers. God, I remember when I worked my first few jobs and I'd have a half-hour snooze in the loo with my head propped against the toilet roll dispenser – no wonder I kept getting the sack.'

We laughed. Lisa made life sound interesting. She crossed her arms, pretending to be hurt. 'You think *that's* funny,' she went on; 'I'll tell you what's funny: I hear you two are enrolled at Lagilla next year. That school is horrible: at the boarding school they forced us to eat rotten cabbage soup –' She jumped in her chair as if someone, obviously Mum, had pinched her on the leg. '*Did* I tell you how *good* that school *is*?' she yelped, and winked at Penny.

'Let's eat,' Mum announced, and passed the bowl of roasted potatoes.

'This is lovely, Jac,' Lisa remarked. 'Thanks for the invite. You were always the killer cook. Me? I've burnt water in a wok!'

'It's good to have you,' Mum replied, and squeezed her sister's hand.

Penny rolled her eyes, typically.

We passed the food around the table: steamed peas, leg ham, cranberry sauce, roast turkey, gravy. When Mum wasn't looking, Amy and I mashed up our potato.

'Veronica,' Mum snapped, her eyes narrowing, 'you know about mashing!'

'*Mum, look!*' Amy yelled, pointing at Lisa's plate.

'Oops!' Lisa put on a face as if she'd been sprung, and stopped in the midst of mashing a spud. 'Must be the Irish blood.'

'How do you know?' I asked her. 'You're adopted; I thought you didn't know who your real parents were –'

But Dad cut me off. 'Could you heat this up in the microwave?' he asked curtly, and passed me the jug of gravy.

'It's okay, Richard,' Lisa assured him.

I went to get up, but Mum told me to sit down. 'How about grace?' she suggested. She did the sign of the cross: pointing her right hand from her forehead to her chest. 'In the name of the Father,' she began, 'and of the Son, and of the Holy Ghost.' She was really serious.

Lisa unfolded her legs and bowed her head.

'Bless this food we are about to receive . . .' Mum went on and on. It was the longest prayer she'd ever said.

I looked up: Penny had given herself permission to drink her *and* Dad's glass of wine. She gave me a dirty look when she saw I'd seen her. I ran a finger across my throat to let her know she was in big trouble about the hole in the wall – not that I was really gonna tell Dad: she'd kill me if I did.

'Amen,' Mum finally said.

'Amen!' Amy and I shouted. We did a quick crucifix, like it was a competition to see who could finish first. Then we piled more food onto our plates. Amy and I were the first to help ourselves to seconds.

Dad and Lisa did most of the talking. '. . . Of course Veronica would,' Dad said to Lisa.

'No, *Daaaad!*' I poked my tongue out at him. 'You *can't* make me.'

'Go on,' Lisa said. 'Richard says your photos of Melbourne are brilliant. You *must* show us – I insist.'

'N.O.' I deliberately opened my mouth wider on the 'o' of 'no', to gross everyone out with my mouthful of mushed potato. 'Besides,' I added, 'Melbourne stinks: the air pongs; I might as well throw my alarm clock in the bin: the tram's so loud, *it* wakes me up.'

Lisa laughed.

'Maybe later,' she whispered to me.

After we ate the Christmas pudding, we cleared the table and swapped presents:

To Mum & Dad
Happy Xmas

- double movie pass.
Why don't you go out
and stop fightting.

xo vee.

Nothing from Penny
-surprise surprise!
Didn't get her
anything,
anyway.

To our Deerest Bumble-bee
wishing you a
Happy Happy
Christmas

boring, predictable:
digital camera.
(I had asked for a lift
to Yarra Valley.)

All our love Mum and Dad

And a drawing
from Amy:
Ebony and Major
Jumping.

'Advanced – real talent!' Lisa announced, admiring Amy's artwork. She gave her youngest niece a hug. 'And *how old* are you?'

'Five,' Amy replied, holding up three fingers on one hand and two on the other.

'Wow: five! or five and a *half*?'

'Five and a *half*!' Amy answered. 'And Mum's taking me on a tram ride tomorrow.'

'*Ohh*, lucky you!' Lisa tickled her.

And a locket -
Happy Chrissy,
love Lisa.
Looking forward to hanging out.

'Thanks,' I said to her. I ran up to my room, slipped my four-leaf clover and the scrap of Mum's letter into the locket and clipped the chain around my neck. *On second thoughts,* I paused on the way out, *why don't I grab that folio of photos? So what – see if I care: she's given me this necklace, and it's not so bad.* I ran down the stairs.

Penny was standing by the dining-room window. She'd wrapped tinsel around her head and was drinking wine from the bottle.

'Have you seen Lisa?' I asked her.

'You've got glasses,' she answered: 'put them on.'

'You're feral,' I said back: 'you don't even brush your hair – and I'm *so* gonna tell Dad . . .' I ran out before she could say another word about the threat.

Lisa was in the kitchen, scraping food from the plates into the bin. Her voice was cutting in and out of the conversation she was having with Dad, but it sounded pretty much like she was lecturing him.

'Richard, I'm not gonna pretend I don't know,' she said. By the sound of the clatter, I could tell she was scraping the plates way too hard – much more than she had to. 'Jac's told me,' she went on; 'she's pretty traumatised and broken up by it all . . . Jesus, Richard.'

I pressed my body against the pantry door and kept out of sight. It was kind of hard to hear what they were saying. I leant forward and cupped a hand around my ear.

Dad took the plate from Lisa and loaded it, with the other dishes, inside the dishwasher. 'We married so young,' he said. 'I need time apart.'

I stepped back as I heard a plate clattering against the knives and forks.

'Richard, she's devastated,' Lisa continued. 'She's never known anything else.'

'It's a break, Lisa – not a break-up.'

'I don't think that message is coming across – not from what Jac's said. She thinks you're leaving her – and you need to let that other thing go if there's any chance of a future between you two. I can't believe you're doing this. It's hurtful for everyone involved. Jac and I have our differences, but we're *still* – and always *will* be – sisters . . . What about the kids?'

'I know; *I know* –' Dad said, 'I don't need *you* to remind me. I think about those kids all the time. I, for one, know what it's like growing up without a father – I was eight when mine died.'

'Richard, it's obvious you're *not* thinking about the kids – because it's pretty clear why Penny's living with me: she's affected. If you're prepared to meet Jac halfway, she'll give you another chance . . . it seems she's willing to give both you and *me* a second chance.'

I stepped back further into the pantry when I saw Penny walk past.

She saw me, doubled back, and looked wrapped that she'd uncovered my hiding spot. 'What's that?' she asked me, noticing the folio of photos in my hand. 'Give it,' she demanded, tugging it from me.

'No,' I shrieked, and tugged back. Then, locked in our struggle, we tumbled out of the pantry, and in the process almost knocked the turkey on the silver platter off the marble bench top. '*Penny*!' I yelled. '*Stop it! Dad, stop her!*'

'*Penny!*' Dad yelled, and pushed us apart.

'I just wanna have a gawk,' she said.

'Oh *yeah*,' I shouted. 'Show me one of your stupid *documentaries*, then!'

'*Girls, stop it!*' Mum screamed from the hallway, like a kettle going off.

Penny pushed the folio of photos hard into my chest. 'Here: have your photos,' she said. 'No one *wants* to see your ridiculous photos anyway.'

'They're not "ridiculous"!' I yelled.

'Prove it,' she teased.

'I will,' I said defiantly, and flicked the elastic band off the folio. I held up a picture: an A4-size photo of a rubbish bin on Little Bourke Street, noodles dripping onto the pavement from it.

Mum walked in. I held up another pic: a collage of graffiti, traffic lights, a 'Stop' sign in the middle, a 'Hazard' dazzle-board bordering the A4 sheet. Then another creation: a close-up of a thick, black cloud of smoke spewing out of the exhaust pipe of a delivery truck on Spencer Street.

Lisa was waving a tea towel in front of her face and covering her mouth with her other hand – it was obvious she was trying not to laugh.

Penny didn't hold back, though: '*Hah! Too good! Too good!*' She slapped her right hand against her right leg.

I held up another photo: a close-up of a hessian poo bag strapped to the bum of a horse pulling a carriage down Swanston Street. That certainly wasn't funny!

'Veronica, what about the Shrine?' Mum asked, and burst into laughter harder than Penny's. It made everyone else bend over and have to wipe the tears from their eyes. 'Or the Botanic Gardens; ducks on the lake; Flinders Street Station; boats on the Bay?'

'What is it?' Amy asked, running into the kitchen – she hated missing out on anything.

I decided to run for cover – up the stairs, across the hall. I slammed my bedroom door shut, dived under my sleeping bag and hugged the folio of photos to my chest.

I hated my life. I hated Mum for laughing at me. I hated Dad for hiding their 'break', or whatever *it* was, from me. I hated Lisa and Penny for knowing more than I knew . . . Why did my life have to change?

'Knock-knock!' I heard Lisa calling from the other side of the door.

'Your photos are excellent,' she called out; 'you've captured some ugly truths about living in a city – the rubbish and pollution – and you've shown it in a way that makes the ugliness look beautiful. That's a really mature insight for someone your age.'

'So what?' I said, pretending like I didn't care.

'Veronica, I'm sorry – we weren't laughing *at* you.' I could hear the buttons of her shirt clicking against the door. 'The world's not against you, even if that's how you feel. I know you're hurting, what with everything going on, but it won't feel like that forever. And I didn't mean to say that Lagilla was a bad school; they've raised truckloads of money to make it a fantastic school – there's a new Science wing and a recording studio in the music hall. You must be excited about going somewhere new.'

As if she knew how I felt. 'Go away,' I pleaded; 'leave me alone.' The last thing I wanted was for Mum's sister to be waltzing back into our lives and thinking she knew everything – like an instant Einstein . . . But then again, maybe she did know more than I knew. 'Is Dad dying?' I asked her. I wasn't sure whether she was still standing by the door.

'No – whatever gave you that idea?'

'Nothing – forget it,' I answered; 'I'm just being an idiot.'

'Veronica, let me in.'

'No; leave me alone.' I was in no mood to talk to her. 'Isn't it time you left?' I wrapped my pillow around my head. Five minutes later, I checked that the hall was clear, and jumped back into bed.

First I heard Dad yelling. Then it was Penny yelling at Mum. Then the front door slammed. Then Lisa's car drove off. I rolled onto my stomach. *Pu-thump; pu-thump*. I could feel my heart beating. *Tick; tick; tick*, and the clock beside my bed shrieking: one hour . . . one hour and 15 . . . one hour and forty-five – every second felt like an eternity . . .

Finally, the white walls turned pink as the sun set. The room then darkened to black. I rolled over in my sleeping bag and tossed my wet pillow onto the carpet. A funny feeling came over me. My knees jerked up to my chest; my feet kicked the air once, twice; I stuffed a corner of the sleeping bag into my mouth – what the hell was so funny? Certainly not my life! Why the hell, then, was I laughing and rolling around from side to side? *Ah*, bum. I *was* trying to make Melbourne look bad, and then Aunty Lisa reckoned I'd turned the 'ugly' into 'beautiful'. I laughed harder. If I'd managed to do that to a photograph, couldn't I also turn the ugliness of my life back to beautiful? Couldn't life be that simple?!

Maybe, they *were* just having a 'break' – that's what Dad had said – and everything would fall back into place once Mum's nursing hours became 'permanent'. Silly me – a total worry-wart. Everything was gonna be A-okay. If it *was* only a break, there was still a chance everything would go back to how it had been . . .

Walking back to my room from the bathroom, I noticed a gift by my door, on the floor. I nearly died when I read the card and saw it was from Penny. Inside the wrapping was an oil burner, some tea-light candles and a bottle of Sweet Dream oil . . .

Noticing that the light in the study was on, I went downstairs and made a cup of tea. Then I came back and knocked on the study door.

'Who is it?' Mum called from within.

'Me.' I walked in with the cup of tea and the oil burner. 'I made your favourite,' I said: 'chamomile.'

'Thanks, love,' she said; 'that's really sweet.' There were already two half-empty teacups on her bedside table. 'They're old,' she said; 'I was about to go downstairs and make myself another one.'

'Perfect timing, then,' I said, and passed the tea to her. I put the oil burner down on the table. 'Can I show you something?' I asked her. 'I have to turn the light off.'

She was about to say no, but didn't. 'Yeah: sure,' she said.

The flickering shadow of the tea-light candle bounced happily off the walls. The room looked like a fairyland. I lay on Mum's bed, and together we watched the dancing shapes . . .

After a while, I got up. ''Night, Mum,' I said. 'Do you want the light on or off?'

'I might read for a bit . . . But Vee, we weren't laughing *at* you.'

'I know, Mum. When I took the photos I was trying to make Melbourne look bad – I could take *nice* photos if I wanted.'

'I'm sure you will,' she said, 'especially now you've got your own camera.'

'Yeah: thanks for the camera. Maybe if we went to Yarra Valley I could take nice photos of the horses – I promise they'd be good.'

'I'm working Saturday *and* Sunday – but I'm sure your dad could take you.'

I backed out of the room and switched on the light. 'Okay: I'll ask Dad. 'Night. Love you.'

As a way of thanking Penny for the gift, I decided to do something extra-special for her. It wasn't as easy as I thought it would be, but after about half an hour, I managed to put her bed together. There were no black sheets in the linen press, but I thought the blue sheets with the sunflowers on them would be okay: they were a bit more interesting than white. Then I unpacked the boxes and set her room up exactly how I thought she would: her clothes folded inside the dresser, the bottles of oil and incense lined up around the mirror, the photo of Nick by her bed, her CDs stacked along her bookcase shelves – I even stuck a couple of her drawings on the wall. Our Electrolux makes a lot of noise, so rather than vacuum up the plaster beneath the hole in the wall; I got the dustpan and broom from the laundry and swept it up. When I stood back, I couldn't help thinking the room looked good – kind of like her room at Yarra Valley . . .

I had one more thing I wanted to do, though: I lit a stick of incense, to make the room smell like her. Then, taking one last look, I turned off the light and closed the door behind me. I was so tired I fell asleep the moment my head hit the pillow.

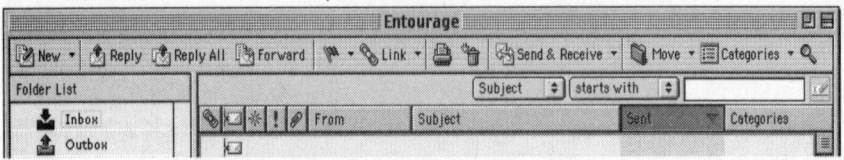

>From: susie@bumble.com.au
>To: veronica@bumble.com.au
>Subject: I'm back!!!
>Sent: 30 December, 8.53 p.m.

Vee, just tried calling your place but your dad said u were out. Call & let me know if u can sleep over 2moro. Remember we promised we'd spend New Years 2gether? I have so got 2 tell u about Steve. We're ON!!! I've got a boyfriend!!! I've got a boyfriend!!! He gets back from Noosa in 6 days. He is so hot-scrum-HOT & THOROUGHBRED.

Your best-est buddy & blood sis. XXOO Suzie-INLOVEWITHSTEVE-Suze.

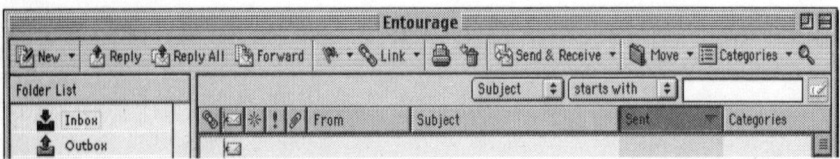

>From: susie@bumble.com.au
>To: veronica@bumble.com.au
>Subject: What's with???
>Sent: 4 January, 8.53 p.m.

Vee, what's with??? I've tried calling your house heaps of times & you're never home. I spent New Years on my own! Raleigh rode past yesterday, wanting 2 go 4 a ride, & I nearly died. I said I was sick, & pretended 2 spew in the water trough. She got a new horse for Xmas & was going on about how much her parents paid 4 him, & how he'd qualified 4 the Nationals last year. WHAT A WANK!!! It was so obvious she was lying. Call me, or else! Your best-est buddy & blood sis.XXOO Suzie-Suze

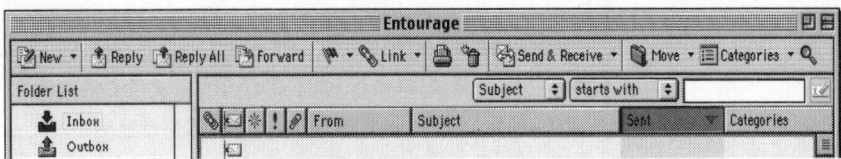

>From: susie@bumble.com.au
>To: veronica@bumble.com.au
>Subject:)-: Not happy!!!
>Sent: 8 January, 2.06 p.m.

U r so rude. What's with???

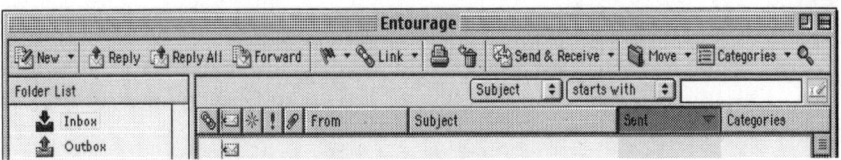

>From: veronica@bumble.com.au
>To: susie@bumble.com.au
>Subject: RE:)-: Not happy!!!
>Sent: 9 January, 9.37 p.m.

Hi & goodbye.

I'm really hurt that u never replied about Mum & Dad not sleeping in the same room. If you'd sent me an email like that I'd have called you back ASAP.

NOT your best-est buddy & had a full blood transfusion. Vee

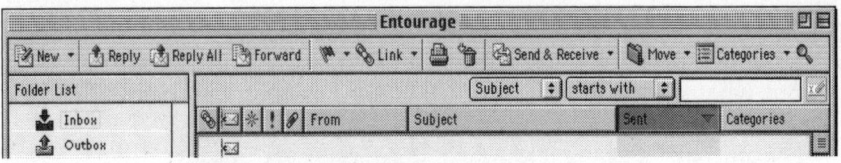

>From: susie@bumble.com.au
>To: veronica@bumble.com.au
>Subject: I'M SORRY!
>Sent: 10 January, 1.06 p.m.

Vee, I'm sorry!!! I just tried calling your place again but you're out. My head's been stuck in the clouds since Steve asked me 2 go out with him. Forgive??? PLEASE!!! I took Sam 4 a ride yesterday & he so wanted 2 cut across the paddock 2 your place. I miss u!!! Call me, please!!! XXOO Susie - I know I'm hopelesshopelesshopeless & don't deserve a best-est friend as good as u - Suze

Friday night: Mum was working late, so Dad, Amy and I ordered pizzas. We ate them in front of the TV – we did that a lot now because Mum was working late shifts. Sometimes it was just Amy and me. If I was cooking dinner, I made scrambled eggs, toasted cheese sandwiches, two-minute noodles or baked beans on toast.

Dad stood up when the closing song from *Burke's Backyard* came on.

'Where are you going?' Amy cried out to him, and hugged his leg to stop him from walking away.

'I won't be late,' he said.

'*No!*' Amy wailed. 'You went out last night – you always go out. *No, Dad*!' She flopped like a rag doll when Dad picked her up and sat her on the couch.

Her crying got louder as I followed Dad to the door. 'Where are you going?' I asked him.

'Out,' he replied. 'I've got a work thing on.'

I walked with him to the garage. 'Can we go to Yarra Valley, maybe tomorrow?'

'I'm busy,' he said in his 'no frills' voice. He was definitely in a bad mood.

'What about Sunday?' I suggested, as the central locking beeped.

'I can't,' he said. 'Ask your mother.'

'That's what you said last week – and Mum works weekends. You said you and Mum would take it in turns to drive me out every second weekend, and I haven't been once – not since we moved.'

'We'll talk about it later.' He was fobbing me off. 'I'm running late.'

'But what if something's wrong?' I asked as he got in the car. 'What if the horses are sick?'

'I'm sure the Wilsons would call if anything happened.'

The car-engine revs drowned out my voice. He closed the door, but I made him wind the window down. 'You and Mum are having a break, aren't you?'

The engine quietened down. He used his shirtsleeve to give the dashboard a wipe. 'True,' he said. 'But it *is only* a break.'

'How long is a break?'

He buckled his seatbelt. 'Not long.'

'But why?'

'Because, your mother and I decided it was a good idea. Both of us have a lot of stuff on. It's only for a short time.'

'So you're not getting a divorce?'

'No,' he said.

'I thought you'd promised you were gonna be nicer to Mum.'

'Maybe we should've asked your mother to promise to be nicer to me.'

I had to think about that one. 'Mum's not that bad, Dad – and you guys have been married for a long time, so you must have a lot of good stuff you can remember.'

He squeezed my hand. 'You're right,' he said. 'Especially memories of you three.'

'Maybe we could go fishing,' I suggested.

'That'd be great,' he said. 'We'll talk more about it tomorrow. Mitchell River might be the place to go. We caught a lot of good-sized fish when we went there last time.'

'And if it's warm enough,' I added, 'we could sleep in our swags.'

'Sounds perfect . . . Watch your feet.'

I stepped back and watched as he reversed the ute out of the drive.

When I went back into the house, I let Amy choose a DVD. She fell asleep within five minutes. I snuck up to Mum's room and dialled Susie's.

'Hi – is that you, Suze?' I asked.

'*Aboooout tiiiime*!' came the reply.

'"About *tiiiime*", yourself!' I snapped back, and waited a couple of seconds while saying nothing. I picked up the oil burner from the side table. It smelled like the lavender bushes in Mum's herb garden at Yarra Valley.

'*Buuuumble*, be nice: I'm your blood sis,' she said. 'And *I* should be the one mad at *you*. Remember – New Years – you and me? You said we were gonna hang out together . . . What's with?'

I couldn't be bothered making it easy for Susie or pretending I still wasn't mad. I twisted the cord around my wrist.

'Vee, it's your Susie-Suze: talk to me. I tried to call and tell you I was sorry. I can hear you breathing – I know you're there.' She panted like a dog into the phone. 'I rode over to your place this arvo and checked on Eb.'

I flopped onto Mum's bed. 'Eb! How is he?' I asked, suddenly interested in what she'd said.

'I knew that'd get you talking. He was covered in dust. He looked like he'd been rolling around in a mud bath.'

'That'd be right,' I replied.

'But I washed him for you,' she said. 'And Maje.'

'Thanks,' I said. 'You didn't have to, but thanks anyway. It's probably a camouflage – so the Wilsons can't see him. Were they there?'

'Only the guy – what's his name?'

'*Craphead* Kieran.'

'Yeah – that's it. *Craphead* didn't mind me mucking around the holding yard.'

'He'd better not,' I said. 'Dad told them I'm allowed to go there whenever I want.'

'He said he hadn't seen you – not since you'd moved.'

'Tell me about it.'

I was about to go on and on about how much the whole thing sucked, but for the next five minutes, Susie blabbed on about Steve. 'You have *so* got to meet him: his smile is *sooooo* hot-scrum-hot – and his teeth are as-white-as-white. He's a total spunk! If he wanted to, he could be a model.' She yakked on and on. 'He'd look really hot in one of those surf mags. And he'd earn heaps of money, and we could run away, so then – how brilliant! – I'd never have to see Morris's ug-*as* ugly face again.'

'Does he ride?'

'*Doi*! Fat chance,' she replied. 'We were piss farting around in the stable the other day, and the only thing he said I could get him riding was his surfboard. Then he pushed me onto the ground and said, "And your tight arse". Not that we've done *it* yet. But he's so *hot-to-trot* and *laaah* . . . *Doi*! Know what I mean?'

'No – not really.' I decided to change the subject. 'So, what about my Mum and Dad? Don't you think it's weird they're not sleeping in the same room?'

'Vee, big deal,' she said; 'when Morris and Mum fight, *they* don't sleep in the same room.'

'You don't think it means they're getting a divorce?' I asked her.

'So what if they are? It doesn't change anything.'

'Are you kidding?' I couldn't believe she'd said that. 'It changes *everything* – and then there's this secret they're not letting me in on, and I know it's got something to do with why we moved so suddenly; it wasn't because of the bushfire – I swear, Suze.'

'Secret-*schmecret*!' she jeered. 'There probably isn't even one. *Your* mum told *my* mum that your family were moving because she'd freaked out about the bushfire – I was there when she said it.'

'But Dad told me he and Mum were having a "break".'

'Vee, half the kids at school have parents who've divorced – so even if it's a "break", a "break-up" or a "divorce", I don't see why it's such a big deal! My Mum divorced, and now she's married again.'

'And look how much you hate Morris!' I said. 'I knew you wouldn't see it my way – you never do.'

'*Buuuumble!*' I heard her say.

'"Bumble" yourself – and I thought you were my friend!'

'I *am!*' she assured me. 'You're the one not being a friend.'

'*Me?*' I knew then that I shouldn't have phoned her; now I felt even worse than before. Suze was raving on about divorce and how normal it was, but what I really wanted to hear was – God, I don't know, so I asked, 'What do you mean *me?*'

'I didn't mean it: I just said that – I wasn't for real.'

Then Mum walked into the bedroom; she'd finished her nursing shift.

'Suze, hang on,' I said; 'just a tick.'

'Veronica,' Mum hissed, flicking my runners off her bed, 'it's past your bedtime.'

I waved her away. '*Mum, but I've only been on for, like, two minutes. Oh.* Suze, I'm gonna have to go: Mum's hanging around like a bad smell . . . Yeah, I'll call tomorrow: I'll let you know.' There was no way I was gonna ask Mum whether I could sleep over at Suze's place – not with Morris creeping around. 'See ya,' I said. And with that, I slammed the phone down. '*Muuuum!*'

She grabbed my elbow. Her nails dug into my arm. 'I told you to put Amy to bed,' she yelled.

'I hate you!' I yelled back. 'And Dad hates you too. You're sleeping in here because Dad can't stand you. Who'd want to sleep in the same room with someone as horrible as you?'

She let go. 'I asked you to put Amy to bed.'

'I'm not her *mother*,' I shot back; 'you are!' I slammed the door as I ran out . . .

Two minutes later, I knocked on the door.

'Hang on – just a tick,' she said; 'I'm getting changed.'

I called through the door: 'Do you want a glass of wine – or a chamomile?'

'You can put Amy to bed – that'd be a help,' came the response.

'Okay.' After I'd put Amy to bed, I found an opened bottle of white wine in the fridge. I knocked on the study door.

'It's open,' Mum said.

She was sitting in the chair by her bed reading a piece of paper.

'I'm sorry,' I said, and passed the glass of wine.

She looked up from the letter she was holding in her hand. 'You're a life saver,' she said. She sipped the wine, and glanced back at the letter.

'What's that you're reading?' I asked.

She turned around and looked out the window. I noticed her eyes were watery and red. 'We'll talk about it in the morning,' was all she managed to say.

'Okay,' I said. ''Night, Mum.' I gave her a quick hug and a kiss. On the way out, I closed the door . . . That night, I hardly slept.

Next morning, Amy came running into my room. She was dressed in a Lagilla uniform and black lace-up shoes.

'What a loser,' I said, 'it's Saturday!'

'Mum said I could wear my new dress.'

'Good one: school's not till Monday – talk about a dag!'

She twirled around and waved her arms above her head. 'I'm beau-ti-ful,' she sang; 'I'm a princ-ess.'

'"Princess"? No you're not,' I said; 'you're my slave: go and make me breakfast . . .'

By the time I'd put on my slippers and sat down at the kitchen table, she'd put a daisy in a milk glass, the toast had gone cold and the Sultana Bran had turned soggy. '*Mmm*,' I said, though: 'looks super-yummy – thanks, my slave.'

She squirmed in her chair. 'Do the tongue thing,' she begged.

I showed her how I could make my tongue touch my nose, and then made my eyes go all bulgy.

'Urgh! You're a Martian,' she said; 'Martians have green eyes like yours.'

'And my snot's green, too,' I warned. 'Look out!'

She squealed, jumped down from her chair and held up a shopping bag as a shield: 'There's three uniforms for you!'

I pushed the family-size packet of Sultana Bran in front of my face so I didn't have to look at the bag. 'You can have my uniforms if you want,' I offered.

Mum walked in, dressed in a cream shirt and navy pants. She'd put make-up on, and looked really nice. I peered over the top of the Sultana Bran and watched as she waited for the kettle to boil and her toast to pop. The last thing I wanted to do was try the uniform on to see whether it was the right size. I hoped I was invisible.

'Damn it!' she said, annoyed that her two pieces of rye toast were burnt. She threw them in the bin, while they were still smoking, opened the window and waved a letter – the same one she was reading last night – around the smoke detector. Luckily the alarm didn't go off. Then she made herself a coffee and sat down in the chair beside mine. She put her hand on my forehead to check to see whether I had a temperature.

I pushed her elbow away.

'You look pale,' she said: 'do you feel okay?'

'I'm fine,' I said, and picked out some sultanas from the bran.

I hadn't asked her about her new car – a new-model Volkswagen; it'd been really late being delivered at the caryard, and she'd only just picked it up last night. She'd been driving a hired car ever since she'd sold the Landie . . . She crossed her arms and rested her coffee mug against the cradle of her arm. 'I know you were mad last night,' she began, 'and I shouldn't have yelled – but you have to understand I'm trying to do the best I can.' She took a deep breath and unfolded the letter in her hand. The paper had creases in it. She smoothed them out against the table's flat surface. 'I was hoping we could talk about this. There *is* no easy way to tell you what's in it. It's a letter from your father's lawyer. We've decided to get a divorce.'

I stared at the letter, and looked up at her. I didn't know what to say. Maybe I'd heard wrong. 'What about counselling?' I said, ever positive. 'I thought you said you and Dad were working everything out, and that it'd be okay.'

'We tried,' she started to explain, 'but sometimes married couples fall out of love. Your father and I can't keep living together in the same house. It's not healthy to keep living like this. We need to move on and live our own lives. We love you children very much, and we want the best for everyone. Your father's gonna move out, and you girls will live here with me.'

I couldn't believe what she'd said. 'Where's Dad going?' I asked. 'Do we have to stay here? Can't we move to Yarra Valley?'

'We need to live near the city,' she said. 'Yarra Valley's too far from the hospital – I have to work and earn enough money to pay the bills, and be back in time to look after you girls.'

'We don't need looking after,' I yelled. As I stood up, my chair fell backwards and banged against the floor. 'We're old enough to look after ourselves. And I know Lagilla costs a lot of money, so I won't go, and then you won't have to work so hard.'

She waited till I'd calmed down. 'Your father'll continue to pay the school fees. I *have* to work to pay for everyday things, like food and gas and electricity. And you need an education. Imagine if I didn't have a nursing qualification: we'd be stuffed. I need your support right now. I'm doing everything I can. Please – I don't have the energy to argue: I can't afford to get run down.'

Amy climbed onto the table and took out her new set of coloured pencils. Mum helped her open the packet. My sweet little sister had no idea our mum and dad were about to get a divorce. I burst out crying. Mum put her arms around my shoulders, and rocked me back and forth, like she'd done when I was a kid. I couldn't believe Dad was gonna live somewhere else – it didn't seem right. Did that mean Amy and I would never see him again? Did it mean he'd come home one last time, pack his bags and drive away?

Amy took one of my uniforms out of the bag. 'Put it on,' she said, and waved it above her head. 'Mum said you could wear yours today too – I asked her, didn't I, Mum? And she said you could. Put it on; put it on.'

'Go away!' I snapped at her. 'You're a loser – no wonder you don't have any friends.'

She jumped down from the table. 'You're a meany!' she cried. She climbed onto Mum's lap and snuggled up against her chest.

Mum's tears welled up again.

'Where's Dad?' I asked. I had a bad feeling he'd already gone.

'He left early this morning,' she replied. 'But he asked for you to call him on his mobile.'

'You mean he's gone forever, and didn't say goodbye?'

'No,' she said. 'He's not moving out for a couple of weeks.'

I didn't want to call him from the kitchen phone, not with everyone around to listen in, so I asked, 'Can I use your phone upstairs?'

'Of course,' she said.

I ran up to the study. I dialled Dad's mobile number. The phone rang out and then went to message bank. I didn't want to leave a message; I wanted to talk to him. I went off to my bedroom.

Mum came up and knocked on the door.

'It's open,' I said.

She came in. 'Did you speak to your father?'

'No. He's not answering.'

'I'm sorry,' she said. 'Maybe he's out of range. Try again in about 20 minutes. He said he wanted to speak to you after this –' She looked away. 'I know it's bad timing, but I have to go to work for a second interview for the promotion in the new psych ward. I'd like you and Amy to come – they make nice milkshakes at the cafe.'

'No thanks, I want to try calling Dad again.'

'But you can still come, and call him on my mobile.'

'No. I'd rather stay here.'

'Are you sure?'

'*Mum!*'

She looked at me. 'Are you *sure*?'

'Yes!'

'Well, I'll be back in an hour; I won't be long, and I'll have my mobile on.'

'Leave Amy. We'll be fine,' I said.

She kept standing by the door, staring at me with a worried look on her face.

'Go: you'll be late. And good luck – you look nice.'

'Okay,' she replied. 'Keep an ear out for Amy – she's out in the yard. And let me know if the uniform and shoes don't fit; I'll leave the bag by the front door.'

I watched from the stairwell as she reversed the VW out of the driveway. It was a tiny car, compared to the Landie.

I went downstairs and noticed the bag by the front door. I put the school shoes on and slipped the uniform over my head. *Bugger*, I thought, *they were a perfect fit.* Amy wasn't in the yard when I went out there looking for her. I was about to call out to her, but then saw a movement behind a reclining chair. Even though the pool was empty, I stepped into it and pretended to swim. A puddle of water had formed at the deep end. I pretend-freestyled over to it and pushed the toe of my right shoe into the edge of the water. I nudged it an inch further . . . then another . . .

Amy jumped out from behind the chair. 'Don't! You'll ruin them!' she yelled.

'Big deal,' I said, and dunked the shoe deeper into the water. I stepped back and flicked the water off the leather. The sock was wet up to the ankle but I wasn't in the mood to care.

Amy climbed down the ladder and joined me in the deep end. We pretended to swim laps. She copied everything I did. It didn't take long for her to start annoying me again. I went back up to my room and hung the uniform on the back of my chair. Then I sat down at the computer and connected to the 'Net:

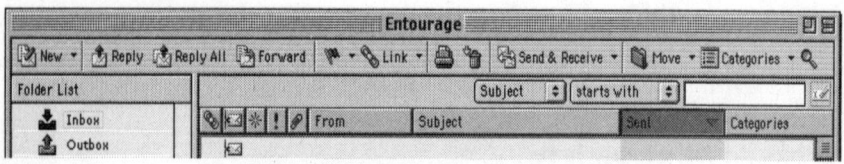

>From: veronica@bumble.com.au
>To: susie@bumble.com.au
>Subject: Missing u, love Vee
>Sent: 13 January, 9.21 a.m.

Suze, sorry I had 2 go last night. Mum was chucking a spaz attack. I guess things aren't going 2 well. She's just told me she & Dad R getting a divorce. She says I have 2 live with her at Kew. I know I'd rather live with her, coz she's my mum, but what if Dad moves back 2 YV? Suze, I love them both, but I'd rather live at YV than Kew.

I'm not looking 4ward 2 school on Monday. I'd rather be going 2 YVHigh with u. I wonder what the girls will be like? I can't tell them about Mum & Dad, they wouldn't understand.

I miss u, Eb and Maje. SOS. Your best-est buddy & blood sis. XO - Vee.

I tried calling Dad's mobile again.

This time he answered.

'Dad, it's me,' I said. 'Mum's just told me you're getting a divorce – you told me last night you weren't and that it was a break.'

'Hang on,' he said; 'I'm parking the car.'

I could hear the indicator blinking, then the engine cutting out, then the jingling of keys, and then him shifting some stuff around. 'Dad, are you there?'

'Yeah: hang on,' he replied. I heard the car door opening and closing, and then some more shuffling. 'Vee?' he asked.

'Yeah, Dad; I'm here. Mum's just told me you're getting a divorce – how come you didn't tell me last night?'

I could hear the tapping of his shoes across concrete; it was an echoing sound, like he was in a tunnel – maybe an underground carpark. 'Your mother and I talked about it,' he began, 'and we decided it was best if *she* told you.'

'Why couldn't *you* tell me – or were you lying?' I put him on the spot.

The tapping of the shoes stopped. 'No, that's what we both decided. We wanted the three of you to be told at the same time. I've just been over to see Penny. We had this idea of holding a family meeting, but Penny wouldn't come to the house.'

'"Family meeting"?' I couldn't believe he'd suggested it. 'How can we have a family meeting if we're not even a family? What's gonna happen now? Mum says you're moving out.'

'Yes: I am moving out,' he said. 'But I'll be living in an apartment around the corner from my office, so I won't be far away. You can come and stay. I know it's not an ideal situation, and I'm sorry this is happening.'

'It won't be the same,' I said. 'Dad, how come you're not moving back to Yarra Valley?'

'We've rented the house for the year,' he replied. 'I can't kick the Wilsons out.'

'Yes you can: it's *your* house.'

'It doesn't work that way.'

'Dad, this sucks.' I started crying again: I still couldn't believe what was happening. 'Mum says you're moving out in a couple of weeks.'

'Yes, but not until I get back from my conference.'

'What conference?'

'Didn't your mother tell you?'

'No.'

'It was only decided late last night,' he explained. 'The development in Hawaii's going ahead. I'm away till the end of the month. I wanted to wake you this morning and tell you, but you were sound asleep. I left a box of chocolates on the floor, by your bed.'

'I don't want chocolates, Dad; I want you and Mum to stay together. You said parents should be there for their kids.'

'I can still be there for you, even if your mother and I aren't together.'

'That's not true – where are you *now*?'

'I'm at the airport.'

'See!' He'd flown overseas for business before, when he was building a development in Italy and another one in Spain.

'Bumble, I'll see you when I get back,' he said. 'And you can call my mobile, any time – I'd love to hear from you.'

'Dad, I miss you – and you haven't even gone yet!'

'I'll be back before you know it.'

'Three weeks is ages,' I said. 'What about the fishing trip?'

'I promise to take you as soon as I get back: we can go camping along the Mitchell River – we've been there before, and you liked it.'

At least that meant he still loved me. 'I'll save the chocolates,' I promised. 'We can cut up some bananas and stick the chocolate inside and wrap them up in tin foil and cook them in the campfire.'

I could hear a man announcing a flight over the airport loudspeaker.

'Sounds good,' Dad said. 'We'll talk soon – and don't forget: I love you.'

'I love you too, Dad.'

I waited till he'd hung up. Then I went back to my room and put the chocolates in the top drawer of my desk. I didn't know what to do next. I looked around my room. I decided to arrange my pencils from the dark colours to the light ones. I looked up Hawaii in the Atlas. Then I lay down on my bed, and got to thinking about Penny . . .

I ran down to the kitchen and looked up Lisa's number in the address book. When I dialled it, Penny answered.

'Hi – it's me,' I said.

'Hey,' she said back. 'I guess you've been told – are you okay?' She actually sounded like she really cared, talking to me nicely, like how she used to.

'No,' I said; 'I can't stop crying. Mum's at an interview, and Amy and me are on our own.'

'Do you want me to come over?' she asked. 'Maybe we could watch a DVD.'

'Mmm,' I replied; 'that'd be great.'

She did come over, it didn't take her long, and later that night, she, Mum, Amy and me watched a DVD. When the movie was over, Mum asked her whether she'd like to stay the night.

'I'll stay tonight,' she said. 'And then, when Dad moves out, I'll move back.'

Mum gave her a hug.

We went upstairs together. 'Thanks for the oil burner,' I said. 'I never did get to thank you.' I knew she hadn't been into her room yet, so she wouldn't have seen how I'd set it up. 'I'm glad you're moving back,' I told her.

She rolled her eyes to the back of her head. 'I'll still pull your plaits,' she teased.

'Yeah, well, I'll snoop around your room – I know you hate that.'

'Do and I'll kill you,' she warned.

Maybe I shouldn't have unpacked her stuff. ''Night,' I said, and ran into my room before she'd opened her bedroom door.

Next morning, I woke up early.

Penny came into the bathroom as I was brushing my teeth. 'Thanks for unpacking my room,' she said; 'don't know about the "sunflower" sheets, though.'

I spat the toothpaste into the sink. 'It was either sunflowers,' I said 'or Amy's spare set with the "Roadrunner" print.'

'I think I'd rather the sunflowers,' she agreed, and gently flicked a towel against my leg. 'Are you done? I wanna have a shower.'

'Yeah.' I tapped the water off my toothbrush. 'Do you reckon we could make pancakes?' I asked, because that's what we used to do, on Sunday mornings when we were kids.

'Sure,' she answered. 'I'll be down in a minute.'

By the time she arrived, I'd made the mixture. Dad wasn't there, so she did his job and cooked. We laughed and joked around a lot, but underneath it all, I still felt sad.

Mum and Amy joined us, and we sat at the table. Dad's chair was empty. I couldn't believe he'd never sit with us, as a complete family, again.

1

On Monday, Mum drove Amy and me to the same school grounds. First we dropped Amy off at the prep-school gate; then we drove around the block, to the senior-school gate. The driveway was in the shape of a huge horseshoe, and both sides of it were lined with a hedge.

Mum chatted on and on about her new car. 'It's so easy to park – and it hardly uses any petrol.'

'Mmm. Green's a good colour,' I said – but what I really wanted to say was, 'It's dumb: it can't pull a horse float.'

But Mum had asked me not to argue with her, no matter how much I hated the idea of going to a new school. She pulled over, to the left-hand side of the driveway, as a police officer signalled for her to slow down. It looked like something was going on up ahead. Part of the hedge was burnt, and smoke was rising out of the top of it. Orange tape had been used to section off the damaged area.

'Hah: look!' I yelled. 'It's gotta be the hedge burners!' I wound the window down and leant out. I'd seen the hedge burners on the news – well, not the actual hedge burners, because no one knew who they were, but I'd seen what they did: they set fire to hedges all around Melbourne. And part of the hedge lining the main entrance of Lagilla Convent was now burnt to stumps.

I coughed, and banged my right hand against my chest; I wasn't trying to be super-rude, but it *was* funny. 'Looks like we'll have to move back to Yarra Valley,' I said.

Mum was satisfyingly unimpressed. 'Veronica,' she screamed. 'Cut it out! I mean it, just cut it out, I've had enough! I can't take this! Not another word!' The police officer looked over to see if everything was okay. I guessed he'd heard Mum having a screaming fit. She gave the officer a friendly wave, and then took a deep breath. 'Right, better now,' she said. I didn't dare say one peep. She really had lost it there for a sec.

Mum drove forward after the police officer signalled that it was okay for us to move on. She parked in front of the sporting complex. Even though it was a modern building, a lot of the other school buildings were old. The convent's brick wall towered over us, three storeys high. It looked creepy: there were cracks in the brickwork and peering down from the corners of the roof were statues of birds with wings spread wide. And the windows were odd shaped: tall and narrow.

I knew I'd promised, and everything, but I couldn't help myself. 'Talk about a prison.' No way was I getting out of Mum's car – I was buggered if I even knew why she was bothering to drive me there, let alone park. If she was so excited, *she* could put the uniform on.

'Veronica, we talked about this,' she said, grabbing her handbag as she got out.

I pushed the button down, to lock the car from the inside.

'Veronica, you can't do this.' She rapped her knuckles against the window. 'We're late enough as it is.'

'No: there's metal bars on the windows.'

'Veronica, *now*!'

As slow as a turtle, I got out of the car. I followed Mum across the garden and up the steps to the administration entrance.

The floorboards creaked as Mum and I walked down the ancient corridor. My new shoes tapped on the polished wood. I glanced from left to right, and now and then glimpsed a classroom full of students through a side door.

'And *please*,' Mum said, ticking off her mental list of possible stuff-ups: 'I want you to speak in a clear voice and *stop* that walk – you're bopping up and down –'

A nun appeared from a side door and moved from one side of the corridor to the other. She was hunched over and her back looked like it was about to snap. I spun around, and walked backwards as we overtook her. Her outfit was navy rather than black – and from her neck swung a huge set of rosary beads. *Maybe* that's *what gave her the hunchback,* I thought, and then bumped into a wall. '*Ow!*'

Mum hadn't seen: she was a couple of metres in front, talking to another nun.

I snuck over and pretended I'd been standing beside her all along.

'I'm very well, sister, and Veronica's so looking forward to settling in.' Mum did drone on.

'And is this –?' the nun asked.

'Yes, sister,' Mum began. 'I'd like you to meet Veronica. She's so excited about studying here.'

The nun peered over her spectacles. Dried, white crusty bits were stuck to the creased corners of her lips . . . And her eyes were freakish: the pupils should've been blue but they were so pale they looked almost white. She held out her hand and, with a very firm grip, shook mine . . . She wouldn't let go, and looked me straight in the eyes. I had to look away.

Mum raised her eyebrows, a gesture of warning to me to be on my best behaviour. 'Veronica, this is Sister Therese Cecilia, Lagilla Convent's principal.'

The nun's hand felt soft and slippery, as if it were covered in talcum powder. Instantly, I thought of hospitals and illness and death. 'Hello, *ah*, sister,' I mumbled.

Even though Mum had 'walked' me through the conversation at least four times that morning, I now forgot what to say.

Sister Cecilia frowned.

I pulled my hand back.

She held on.

A shrill bell rang.

She closed her eyes; her eyeballs flickered. 'Heaven help!' she said, and crossed herself.

The bell rang a second time, this time longer and louder than the first.

The principal knitted her eyebrows and pursed her lips.

Face like a cat's bum, I thought to myself.

Students crowded into the corridor. Not everyone realised that Sister Therese Cecilia was there. The ones who did realise she was, stopped shrieking and backed off towards the wall.

'If you don't mind excusing me for one moment –' Sister Cecilia began. She turned around but didn't let go of my hand. *'Certainly*, it would *not* –' shouting, and squeezing my hand tighter – 'be *too* much to ask that we conduct ourselves *more* in the manner of ladies!'

The students froze. Their conversations ceased mid-sentence, mid-shriek.

'Well, go on!' she said. 'Assured you do have classes to attend.' Then she directed Mum and me through a doorway and into a large room.

Everyone watched as we walked away.

The room was dark until sister turned the light on. It was decked out in lounges and side tables and lampshades – and there was a piano, which had a stuffed owl standing on top of it. When I saw its 'eyes' glaring at me, I nearly jumped out of my skin. They were just like Sister Cecilia's

'Sit,' sister commanded, like an army major. 'Please.'

I wanted to bolt, and wash my hands – I couldn't see any white, powdery stuff on my skin, but you never knew. I wondered whether my arms were about to shrivel up – or worse still, fall off. The skin on my palms had started to feel itchy. I copied Mum by folding my dress under my bum as I sat down. I forced myself to smile. I pushed the cushion aside, shifted an inch to the left, and then shifted two inches to the right. No matter where I sat, I could feel the red-tapestry upholstery through my dress, itching and pricking me.

Mum glanced over at me, unimpressed by my fidgeting.

I smiled back at her, and placed my bag next to my feet.

Mum and the sis were waiting for me to say something.

'Ah –' I began, not quite sure what to say. I must have missed the question, if one had been asked.

'. . . much like your sister Penny,' Sister Cecilia noted. But she didn't look very pleased about the resemblance.

'Mmm,' I said – but what I really wanted to say was, 'Get lost – as *if*: I'm nothing like Penny.'

Rather than sit, the sister stood behind a chair. She made her fingers claw into the leather cushioning. 'Lovely to have another girl from the Bee family attend,' she said. She twitched her lips. 'Such a shame it's not at the *beginning* of your education: it's best to begin where one can impart values from the start. But needless to say, it's never too late to impress guidance on a young girl. We have excellent success with the scholarship recipients who join us midway through their secondary education.' She tut-tutted . . . 'How is our young Penny?'

111

'Oh, she's doing well.' Mum had decided to lie. 'She's accepted a place at the VCA, studying Fine Arts.' She went on to talk with the sister for a while, while I looked around: a fireplace; a grandfather clock that ticked loudly; lots of portraits on the walls – faces with beady eyes that made my skin crawl. Bugger! Now my *whole* body was itchy, and my forehead felt hot. What if I died? What if I carked it, right then and there?

'Penny did have . . .' Sister Cecilia was pausing to find the right word '. . . what would one say? A keen *interest* in her *sketches*.' She took off her glasses. Then the twitch started up again. 'Now, our young Veronica Bee: *she* –' (unlike Penny) – 'will do fine under the hand of the Lagilla Sisters.' Her kneecaps clicked as she sat down in the chair . . . The leather wheezed, crackled, farted.

'*Oh*,' I managed. I wanted to hug my knees to my chest, roll around on the uncomfortable lounge and laugh out loud. As Sister-Therese-*Holy*-Cecilia sat back, I felt my stomach tighten into a cramp. Whatever was gonna happen at that moment, I was definitely *not* allowed to laugh. '*Hr-hrm*,' I said, to clear my throat. 'Sorry.'

'Bless you,' Sister Cecilia offered, and passed me a neatly ironed hanky from the cuff of her cardigan. 'There does seem to be a lot of pollen in the air - especially for this time of year.'

Mum gave me one of her deadly out-of-the-corner-of-the-eye looks.

If only I'd had tongs . . . I took the hanky. 'Thank you,' I said.

'Veronica, your mother has brought to my attention your sadness with regard to your family's move to Kew.'

My stomach tightened. I was still thinking about sister's 'farting chair' and didn't dare open my mouth in case laughter burst out. I nodded my head and then shook it from side to side.

Sister Cecilia placed a student diary and a bible on the table. 'In sufficient time, you'll settle in, no doubt. These are matters for your concern. And I suggest you learn, by heart, the Code of Conduct at the front of the diary.' The leather chair gave a gasp as she stood up. 'Let us adjourn to the chapel. Father Curry would be most interested to meet you before we settle you into class – oh, and Veronica, it is a delight, none the least extraordinary, to see one of our girls do so well at maths and science. What degree do you plan to study, to further your education, from here?'

'Veterinary Science,' Mum proudly replied on my behalf.

'Your marks from Yarra Valley High are impressive,' the sister remarked. 'But, as always, there are weaknesses, no doubt – are you up to the challenge?'

'*Ah*, . . . yes, sister.'

'Excellent. Now, come along: no dawdling; back straight.'

Sister Cecilia introduced me at the senior-school assembly. I couldn't believe how many students there were: more than a thousand, I'm sure. I couldn't hide, because I was raised up above everyone, on a stage . . . and I didn't want to flash a huge smile . . . and if I stared, they'd think I was weird.

So I looked down at my shoes. I could feel the girls' looks crawling all over my skin. Was I cool? I deliberately wasn't wearing my glasses. Was I good enough to be in their group?

I had a bad feeling: if a group called the Starched with Pressed Folds existed, I was daggy enough to be their leader. Even my backpack had a crease across the front, from the way it'd been crammed into its packaging. I looked brand, spanking new. I wanted to hide, for a trapdoor to magically open:

'Don't bother trying to be my friend: I'm leaving at the end of the year!' That's what I wanted to yell.

Sister Cecilia told me to sit down. My shoes squeaked as I walked across the stage. Everyone stared at me as I walked up the aisle. The Year 7 and Year 8 girls were seated at the front, the 9's and 10's were behind them, and the 11's and 12's were up the back. Each row of girls was raised higher than the one in front of it.

I couldn't find a spare seat.

Sister Cecilia spoke into a microphone. 'Miss Bee,' she began, 'to your left: just there will be sufficient. Year 8, House Group Thoroughgrove, shuffle up and make space – we don't have all day.'

Students shuffled about. I quickly sat down.

Sister Cecilia talked on and on, standing behind a lectern. Her voice rose when she got to words such as 'expectation', 'performance', 'example' and 'excellence'. She paused and looked over her glasses a lot. Four rows of teachers were seated behind the lectern. Lagilla had more teachers than Yarra Valley High had students. Some of the teachers were nuns; some were dressed in casual clothes – but most had a black gown on and wore a funny, flat hat that had a tassel hanging to one side.

I sat still and let my eyes roam the room . . . One thing I realised was that I'd never seen so much black hair. My aunt, Lisa, had told me that most of the girls were Italian. I counted the girls that had blonde hair . . . 13, 14. They were easy to spot because their hair stood out so much. I didn't dare turn around.

The walls were covered with heavy, dark-red curtains, and the carpet had the school emblem stitched into it. At Yarra Valley, we'd sat on the concrete quadrangle when the weather wasn't good – or crowded into the music room when the weather was crappy. And the principal, Mr Woolsley, had spent most of his time shouting to be heard above our gossiping – unless he'd totally cracked it and told us to shut up, which we did, but only for a little while.

Sister Cecilia took a deep breath and sat herself down – finally.

Clank-clank-de-de-daa-daah: a roly-poly, red-faced nun seated at the piano to the right-hand side of the stage started belting out the school song. Everyone jumped up and sang. Some of the lyrics were in Latin. The girl beside me sang *extra* loudly. Her mouth opened up to form a big 'O' when she hit a high note. Sister Cecilia was the only one who didn't sing; instead, she sat in her chair and watched the proceedings.

When we sat down, Sister Cecilia ordered a girl to stand up. Then she addressed the rest of us: 'Does anyone else wish to conduct a conversation behind her hand?'

By the end of the assembly, six girls had been ordered to stand up. Sister Cecilia was first to leave, and was followed by the nuns and then the six standing-up girls, who, I figured, were about to get into huge trouble.

We filed out, keeping to our year-level house groups. All I had to do was follow, like a sheep: out of the hall; down a corridor; up three flights of stairs; down another corridor; down another two flights of stairs; left at a side door opening into a locker room. Every girl was talking – that is, every girl except me.

Another nun brought us to attention with the statement 'I do hope you all had an enjoyable summer break. You look radiant and refreshed. Now, there are some familiar faces.'

Everyone cheered.

'Welcome; welcome – a bit of shush, please! I'm Sister Frances, and I have the lovely privilege of being your Year 8 Thoroughgrove house-room teacher.'

The cheering started up again.

She did look younger than the other nuns – and actually smiled.

Someone shouted from the back, '*Thoroughgrove! Thoroughgrove! Oi! Oi! Oi!*'

'Samantha Porcello!' Sister Frances glared at the girl. 'I believe that type of behaviour is more suitable for a rowing carnival.'

The sounds of shuffling feet and laughter filled the room.

'*Sshh,*' Sister Frances insisted. 'I'll be taking you for morning and afternoon roll call, Compulsory Religious Education, and English.'

Everyone groaned.

Sister Frances handed out a combination lock to each girl and instructed her to remember her code.

Eventually, I found a spare locker – right beside the locker-room door, on the lower row. I chucked my bag in and took out my pencil case, my school diary and an A4-size notebook . . . Oops: maybe not, though – every other girl was grabbing everything and leaving only her bag behind. I quickly pulled my blazer back on. It was obviously compulsory to wear it: every girl still had hers on. I emptied my bag and proceeded to carry everything in one ginormous armload. Then I hitched my laptop carry bag over my shoulder. At Yarra Valley, hardly anyone could afford a laptop, but here, I thought, every girl must have been really, *really* rich.

We followed Sister Frances down the corridor to the house-room. 'Quiet, girls,' she warned; 'a bit of shush, please.'

It's not like I'd never worn a uniform. I'd worn a uniform to pony club, and a navy-velvet jacket for shows, and a compulsory sports uniform at Yarra Valley – but here: even the slightest thing – socks up or down? T-bar or lace-up? belt tightened or loosened? top button pinned or opened? back of collar pushed up like Elvis's or folded over? jumper baggy or folded at the hip? We were all wearing the uniform, but somehow each girl wore hers differently – or just like her friends'.

'Hi. I'm Cas,' I heard someone say to me.

I gave the girl a wave, and walked off ahead.

'A bit of shush,' Sister Frances insisted. She opened the door and everyone barged in. 'Ladies! Ladies! That will do. I'll thank you to line up in the corridor, once more, and try that again.'

This time, everyone walked into the room *quickly*. No one pushed, but the girls were in just as much of a hurry to 'bags' a seat next to their best friend.

Once we were seated, Sister Frances marked the roll. Thirty girls were present: six in the front row, including me, and six more in each of the four rows behind. We voted for a house-room captain, and some girls got really excited when the show of hands was asked for. One girl cried when she didn't win. Then our books and study guides were handed out to us. I put my glasses on and flicked through the school diary: the other houses were Chastleton, Manuka and Sargood, and each was named after a principal who'd died.

'Would someone like to read from the Bible?' Sister Frances asked.

Every girl but I raised her hand. One girl stood up and waved her arms wildly above her head. She was drop-dead gorgeous, and had tanned skin and big, blue eyes. Every single one of her blonde hairs was perfectly brushed into place.

'Yes,' Sister Frances remarked: 'Miss Debbie Forshaw – most enthusiastic, as always. And most fitting for our house-room captain to grace us with the first reading of the year. Please, Debbie, go ahead.'

School was definitely different without guys: a lot quieter. And no one 'piffed' spit balls at anyone or anything. And when Sister Frances asked a question, every girl raised her hand.

Ding-ding-ding. Recess: thank God; at least I knew where the locker room was. I copied the other girls and carried my laptop. The corridor was packed. When I bent down to open my locker door, I felt something sharp and hard hit me on the head. 'Ouch!' I turned around: some girls had formed a starfish and were playing 'stacks on'. 'Thanks!' I said to them – but what I wanted to yell was 'And by the way, don't think you're special: the girls at Yarra Valley play "stacks on" as well!'

'Hey, like your bag.' It was the girl who'd said hello to me earlier. I guessed she was Chinese: her skin was a browny-yellow colour and her eyes were shaped like teardrops. She was super-tall and super-thin – good looking, but in an exotic kind of way. I felt plain, next to her.

'My bag?' I asked. 'Oh!' And that's when I realised I was the only one carrying a dark-red backpack: everyone else had a navy shoulder bag. I backed away and ran out for recess: I had to get rid of that bag ASAP; I had to steal Penny's old one.

I sat down on a bench at the far end of the lunch yard, nibbling on two Ryvitas smeared with Vegemite. I was the only girl wearing a blazer, so I quickly took it off, bundled it into a cushion shape and sat down on top of it.

Four nuns were patrolling the yard. They made some girls untie their jumpers from their waist, handed each one a cotton ball soaked in nail-polish remover, made her tie her hair back if it was past her collar, and confiscated any jewellery.

I recognised Sam Porcello. She almost got a detention for wearing runners to school rather than the regulation footwear. 'But sister,' she reasoned, 'Mum's ordered new shoes; she's paying off the lay-by.'

The biggest of the four nuns stepped forward to meet Sam. 'As much as I'd like to believe that's *not* a fib,' she began, 'I *will* call your mother. And if it is a fib, you'll find yourself in Sister Therese Cecilia's office. I know very well your family's financial circumstances, and that your mother is paying off a loan for your laptop – but so, too, are many other scholarship recipients, and *they* manage to purchase regulation footwear by the first day of term.'

'But sister –'

'Do not "but" me!'

'I wasn't going to,' Sam managed to get out; 'I was just going to ask if you could not say such personal stuff in front of everyone – it's embarrassing.'

'Very well,' the nun replied, and straightened her cardigan. 'But I would like to see you collect 10 pieces of rubbish before you return to class.'

Sam walked off, dragging her runners along the concrete.

Ding-ding-ding. And back to prison it was, for period three. I threw open the door to my locker and grabbed my laptop. Then I ran back to the house-room; grabbed my textbooks, pencil case and A4 notebook; and opened my diary to the back page, where the timetable was: eight periods each day, eight days rotating, so every week each term wasn't the same. Talk about complicated! Let's see: day one – yes, I knew that much. Periods three and four: just as I'd thought - double 'Biol' in the 'Science Lab' . . . Oh, God: period five was a free period – I thought only Year 12's had frees. What was I gonna do? Where was I gonna hide? *Quick*: think about – or rather *dread* – the free later . . . But where was the science lab? Bugger: I checked the timetable again. Languages were taught in the Languages wing, Maths in the Maths wing, Science in the Science wing . . . Oh, God: better check the map . . . new girl; new girl; looks a bit flustered . . .

Ding-ding-ding.

Ding-ding-ding.

Ding-ding-ding.

Period eight – at last! – and I hadn't spoken to anyone all day, except to ask my way around the maze of buildings and corridors. As I walked out of the building, I felt like someone was gonna yell, 'Next! . . . Get lost! . . . Go on: pick up your sister from the prep school . . . Loser! . . . Only junior-school kids have a backpack . . . Hah – and don't bother coming back!'

Mum's 'Vee-Dub' was parked at the front gate of the prep school: she'd organised to have another nurse cover her for the afternoon shift. Amy and I jumped in.

'How was school?' Mum asked us both.

I wound the window down. 'It totally sucked,' I replied: 'I didn't talk to anyone.'

Amy blabbed on and on about how cool bananas her day had been:

'I've got a chair bag, and a library bag with "Amy the Ant" on it!' She held up a bunch of picture books.

'Want to talk about it?' Mum asked me.

'No – not really,' I answered.

She waited for the car behind us to pull out, and then headed off down the street. I nearly died when we pulled up at the pedestrian crossing and I saw Cas, who was waiting at the tram stop, waving. She smiled as if I were her best friend.

'She seems friendly,' Mum commented. 'Is that one of the girls you didn't talk to?'

I slouched down in my seat. 'Go – Mum – the lights are green! Everyone's staring.' I looked down as we drove off. 'I don't even know her,' I said. 'She must've got me mixed up with someone else.'

After we'd worked out the best route for walking home, and where the nearest tram stop was, we went to the supermarket. We were allowed to choose two snack-packs each for our school lunches. 'Only two,' Mum confirmed when Amy wanted boxed sultanas, Fruit Wraps, Smarties *and* Yoghurt tubs. She made her put two items back. I chose Twisties and Cherry Ripes. 'At least choose *one* thing that's healthy,' Mum said, sensibly.

'But cherries *are* fruit,' I replied.

But Mum wouldn't have a bar of it.

I rode the trolley down the aisle and swapped the Twisties for Muesli bars.

Mum made us put other stuff back as well. 'We're on a tight budget,' she explained; 'nurses aren't millionaires.'

'But what about the promotion?' I asked: 'you went for that second interview the other day – didn't you get it?'

'I'm at the top of the list,' she replied. 'But they don't decide for a couple of months. They're waiting for the funding to be approved.'

I picked up the broccoli. 'I know what I'd put back,' I said. I put the broccoli back in the trolley – but later, when Mum wasn't looking, placed it in the supermarket freezer section, well hidden behind the dim sims.

When we got home, Amy and I put the shopping away. Later, while Amy was watching cartoons, I helped Mum plant a herb garden in the backyard. It wasn't anywhere near as good as the herb garden at Yarra Valley – that one was about half the size of a tennis court, and had all kinds of herbs and vegetables, little stone paths winding around the various sections, hedges, agapanthus and lavender bushes, and a fish pond with a fountain in the middle . . .

We spent about two hours planting seeds and shoots. The garden didn't even have enough room for herbs *and* vegetables – only herbs.

'That's it,' Mum finally announced, and stood up and wiped the dirt off her hands.

I brushed the dirt off my knees. 'Mum, it sucks: it looks like a square box of dirt with some green stuff growing in it.' I knew that Mum loved cooking and had spent heaps of time in the garden at Yarra Valley: weeding, pruning, tying vines to poles, clipping the hedges. 'You can't even walk around in it – or sit down on a bench and read a magazine.' She'd enjoyed reading on a bench in the other garden.

'Well, we haven't finished yet,' she declared enthusiastically: 'I've got big plans to make a colourful mosaic of broken tiles along the wall, there.' She held out her arms to visualise what it'd look like.

'Yeah: like, when?' I asked. 'You're always working – you don't even have time to drive me out to the horses.' I turned the tap on and adjusted the hose nozzle. 'You and Dad aren't exactly earning brownie points,' I said: 'you said you were going to drive me out, and we haven't been once. I know it's not that you don't care, but Eb and Maje probably think *I* don't care – which is so unfair, because I do. And the last thing I want to do is hurt them. And I don't know horse language – and they don't know English – so there's no way I can tell them what's going on. And one day, they'll stop waiting by the gate. And then one day, I'll call out and they won't come.'

'At least you know the Wilsons are keeping an eye on them,' Mum said. 'Would you like Kathy to exercise Ebony for you?'

'Are you kidding?!' I was amazed she'd even suggested it.

'It was just a suggestion,' she said. 'Look, I'll talk to your father when he comes back from Hawaii – maybe we can come to some kind of arrangement. You're right: my weekends are full for the next couple of months, what with extra training shifts for the new job – I don't even have time for myself . . . Look at my hair: I keep meaning to go to the hairdressers'.'

'I like it long,' I said. 'It's not *long* long – but it's the longest I've seen it, and it makes you look younger: you should grow it *more*.'

Mum looked at her reflection in the window and fluffed out the ends of her hair. 'Yeah – maybe,' she replied, 'but I need to bleach the grey out.'

'Your hair's not grey.'

'I'm a lot greyer than what I was,' she insisted.

When she bent over, I took a closer look: there *were* grey bits near the roots, but I didn't say anything.

Later that night, I snuck into Penny's room. I grabbed the chair and climbed up to the top shelf of her wardrobe: I meant to sneak the blue shoulder bag back to my room – but I heard Mum coming up the stairs. The door was open and the light was on, so she was probably checking to see who was in there. I hid inside the wardrobe and clutched the bag to my chest. The wardrobe door was open – just a crack, so I could spy.

Mum walked in. 'Penny?' she asked. She looked around the room as if it were the first time she'd seen it unpacked and set up – maybe she thought Penny had set it up, on Saturday night, after we'd watched the movie. She ran one of her hands along the oil bottles I'd lined up along the dresser. The top drawer creaked as she slid it out. She unfolded a jumper and then rubbed the wool against her face. Her throat made a strange noise, and then she took a couple of deep breaths, folded the top and put it back in the drawer. Noticing a certain way in which she shifted her head, from side to side, I could tell she was trying to make sense of the graffiti marked on the wall. Luckily, I'd covered the hole with one of Penny's drawings. I watched Mum massage her neck and heard her yawn. On her way out, she turned off the light and closed the door. I snuck back to my room. It took a while, but eventually I slept.

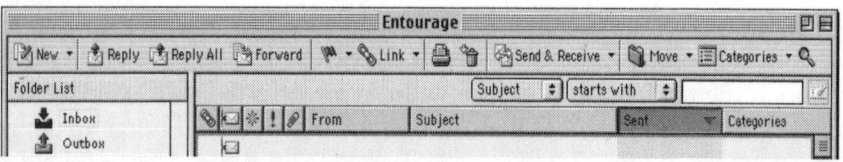

>From: veronica@bumble.com.au
>To: susie@bumble.com.au
>Subject: Dad's moving out!!!
>Sent: 10 February, 7.26 p.m.

Hi, Suze. Get this: when a student does something really bad, instead of being suspended, they have 2 spend a week studying with the students in the Year below. I just read the rule in the Code of Conduct section of my diary. Talk about embarrassing! Penny said students get the strap, but surprise surprise! she'd lied. No one gets the strap, but Lagilla IS really strict compared 2 YVHigh.

But the real reason I'm flicking through my school diary on a Friday night (coz I never would any other time - don't think I've turned in2 a total dag!) is bcoz Mum's just sent Amy & me up 2 my room. She & Dad r downstairs fighting right now. Like, full-on!!! I can hear them, & my door is CLOSED! Dad's been moving his stuff out all day, & when I came home from school, there was hardly any furniture left. About an hour ago, Mum came home from work early, & she chucked a total spaz attack. Just b4 we were told 2 go upstairs, they were fighting about who's getting what. Mum was crying & shouting, & they were doing a tug-of-war with the photo albums. The photos went everywhere.

Dad's leaving 2nite 4 good, & he's not moving back 2 YV. Instead, he's rented an apartment around the corner from his office. It's not far from here. He said I can come & stay weekends or whenever I want. It's gonna be super-weird packing a bag 2 go & stay with him. I don't know if u can remember when your dad left. U never really talk about him, & I know your Mum doesn't say much. But I tell ya, it sucks! You're pretty amazing how things never bug u.

If u get a chance, give me a call. Haven't heard from u 4 ages. How's Steve? R u missing me? I'm missing u more than anything! Your best-est buddy & blood sis. XO - Vee.

Amy and I heard a knock at the door; she'd stopped crying, at last, but now she saw Dad coming into my room, she burst out crying all over again. She knocked the pencils off the desk as she ran over to him. He picked her up. She had no idea what was really going on.

I looked at Dad: even his eyes were red, and I felt really bad for him. The furniture *was* his, so no matter what Mum said, he was allowed to take it.

'I'm going,' he announced. 'I'm really sorry about this; I just wanted to say goodbye, and that I'll pick you up at six o'clock tomorrow morning.' He and I were to camp out on Saturday night, at Mitchell River.

'We don't *have* to go,' I said to him; 'we could go any other weekend – I mean, you didn't promise what weekend we'd go; you just promised we'd go – so we could go the weekend after, or something.'

'I'd really like to go fishing with you *this* weekend,' he said, firmly. 'I'm sorry about all of this – I know it's not pleasant; I didn't expect your mother to come home early; I was trying to avoid a confrontation, and thought I'd be gone by the time she'd finished work. I didn't take *everything* – not like how your mother says.'

'I know, Dad,' I replied. 'All the stuff in the kitchen's still there – and the TV room. And you didn't take anything from anyone else's room. And the antiques were your dad's, so you should get them.' I took the box of chocolates out of the top drawer and pointed to the bag on the floor. 'I kept the chocolates, like I said I would. And I'm packed – so, if you really want to go, and –' Then I burst out crying.

He came over and hugged Amy and me at the same time. Then he kissed the tops of our heads. At least I was getting to spend weekends with him, even if we never lived in the same house again. 'You can come and stay, any time,' he said. 'And we can set up your rooms exactly how you want them – there's a room each.' He looked at me. 'Did you pack the head lamp?'

'Mmm – *oops!*' I replied. 'But I remembered my sleeping bag – and my swag, in case it's hot enough to sleep outside.'

He checked that I'd packed waterproof clothes. Then he hugged Amy and me one last time. We went downstairs and out to the front yard, where the removal van was parked. We kept waving from the driveway even after the van had turned right into the main road.

Mum was watching us from the lounge-room window. I didn't want her to think I cared more for Dad than I cared for her, so I stopped waving, grabbed Amy by the hand and went back inside.

Because the carpet in the house was brand new, the imprints in the wool were standing out. Mum and I walked around the house together . . . not much stuff was left.

I put the kettle on to make her a cup of tea, and made Amy and I a mug each of hot chocolate. When I went to get the milk from the fridge, I found a bunch of photo albums hidden on the shelves inside. It was kind of funny but kind of not funny too. I put the photos on the bench.

Mum gathered the snaps that'd fallen out: 'The bastard thought he could take *all* of them.' She looked dead set and furious.

'Don't call Dad a "bastard",' I said to her. 'And who cares about the stupid photos? It doesn't matter who gets them – all I have to do is scan them and print copies.'

'Well, there's no bloody furniture in the house,' she spat; 'it's a wonder he didn't take the oxygen! Do you know how much furniture costs? It's gonna take me years to replace all this.' She flared her nostrils, dragon style.

'Mum, don't worry,' I said. 'I can eat, sleep, drink, do my homework, watch TV and everything in a beanbag – and I know beanbags don't cost much.'

She looked horrified: 'I can't believe it – no wonder I love you girls so much. Come here: I wouldn't mind a hug myself.' Amy joined in the group hug. 'I'm sorry,' she said; 'I know you don't need to hear me speak about your father like that – it's not healthy for you.'

'I'm hungry,' Amy said excitedly.

Mum glanced at the microwave clock. 'Oh, God!' She jumped up. 'It's nine o'clock!' She got all flustered, and closed rather than opened the pantry door.

'Here, Mum; sit down,' I said. 'You're shaking. I'll get us something to eat.' I turned the oven on to heat up some frozen chips, and then opened a can of baked beans.

Later on, when Amy and I had gone to bed, I snuck out of my room and sat down on the top step. Lisa had come over, and I could hear her and Mum calling Dad all sorts of names. They walked around the house, each carrying a bottle of champagne. When I went back to my room, I heard a cork pop, and both of them cheering . . . I couldn't believe what I was hearing: first, Mum angrily saying mean things, and then carrying on like she was at a party. I clumped the doona around my head. I thought their laughing was disgusting – but then again, I hadn't heard Mum being this happy for years. No matter what, no way was I gonna tell Dad . . . I set my alarm clock for 5.30 a.m. Then I shut my eyes and counted horses jumping over a fence.

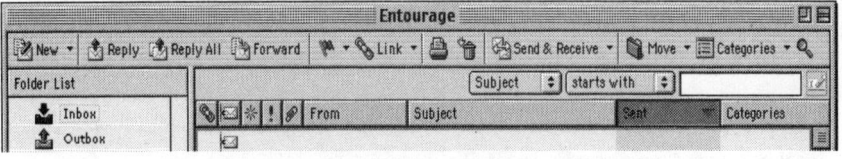

>From: susie@bumble.com.au

>To: veronica@bumble.com.au

>Subject: RE: Dad's moving out!!!

>Sent: 16 February, 10.47 p.m.

Oh, my God, Vee!!! That sucks about your mum & dad. I don't remember a thing about when my dad left. I'm really sorry about everything. It's not 2 cool, but you'll b OK. - & just think, u can now get away with heaps of stuff. Like, if your mum says u can't do something, then u call up your dad & he might say yes. & if your dad says u can't have something, then u go & ask your mum & she might say yes. So it's kind of cool-as. Don't u reckon?

You won't believe. There's a new girl & she's in our class & her name's Veronica. She's moved over from America. Also, Mr Woolsley quit. There's a rumour he got the sack! The new principal's cool-as. Her name's Agnes Treacle, & we're allowed 2 call her Agnes. All the parents r complaining about her, though.

I'll call u 2moro night. I have so got 2 tell u about John Landy. He is so 'dur' & pathetic. I can't believe I had the hots 4 him. Hopefully he'll get the message when he sees Steve picking me up from school on Friday. (He's catching the train out.) Talk 2 u soon. Your best-est buddy & blood sis. XXOO Suzie-Suze

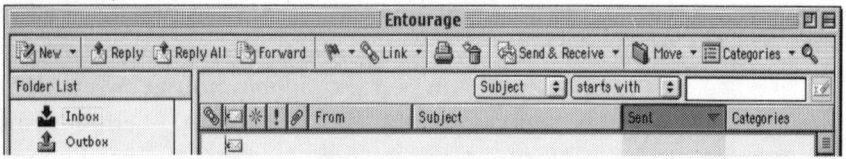

>From: veronica@bumble.com.au
>To: susie@bumble.com.au
>Subject: Mitchell River!
>Sent: 17 February, 8.41 p.m.

Hi. Suze. I've just tried calling your house, but the phone rang out, & then I remembered that Pony Club Committee meeting is 2nite - so that's probably where u r. Anyways, maybe we can talk 2moro night. Things r still kind of crazy around here. Penny moved home, but then she & Mum had a huge fight about Freako Nick still being her boyfriend. So Penny moved back 2 Lisa's house. Mum was super-upset & cried. Also, Penny refuses 2 stay at Dad's.

Dad's apartment is across the road from the Botanic Gardens. U have 2 ride a lift 2 get up 2 his apartment. Mum says if there was a fire, we'd be trapped. I told Dad, & he didn't think that was funny. I've kind of worked out not 2 talk 2 Dad about Mum, & not 2 talk 2 Mum about Dad. Dad's apartment is OK. U can c the trams going in2 the city & the boat that goes 2 Tasmania on the Bay. But there's no home stuff on the shelves or photos or anything. & he doesn't have any food in the fridge. I scanned some photos 4 him. A couple of them r of the family, when we went 2 Sovereign Hill. (You're in those. Do u remember when we went a couple of years ago? & how, when we were driving back, we got the giggles when we tried 2 c how many lollies we could fit into our mouth. & then u choked so Dad had 2 pull over, jump out of the car & whack u on the back so u could breath again!)

Mitchell River was wicked! We saw this huge fish jumping in the river, so Dad made a bet - if I caught it, I got 2 spend $10 at the milk bar, & if he caught it, he got 2 throw me in. As soon as I threw my hook in, the fish grabbed it. I pulled back really hard bcoz I was so excited, but instead of hooking the fish, the hook went flying out of the water. It made this really loud, flinging noise when it flew past my head, & then it got stuck in a tree. Dad had 2 climb up & get it out. He said the idea of fishing was not 2 pull the face off the fish. Dad kept pretending he was the fish & talking like he didn't have a mouth. My gut hurt bcoz we laughed so hard (I almost peed my pants). We slept in swags & we got 2 c the stars.

Miss u. I know this sounds boring-as, but I gotta go & finish my homework. Your best-est buddy & blood sis. XO - Vee.

Four months had gone by. I'd made zero friends.

It was lunchtime. Although the sun was out, we were banned from sitting on the oval. The rain hadn't let up for two days, the drainpipe was blocked and puddles had formed on the ground. We were allowed to sit on the stone wall that was the border of the grounds. I sat in my usual place. I'd twice read the April issue of *The Australian Horse Magazine*, and we still had half an hour before the bell would ring. *At least it's Easter break the day after tomorrow*, I thought, *and that means a four-day weekend . . . And Dad's promised to drive me out to Yarra Valley on Sunday.*

I bit into my apple. I hadn't heard from Suze for ages. These days, we spoke on the phone sometimes and emailed each other now and then. The last time we'd spoken by phone was three or four weeks ago, and the conversation hadn't gone too well. She'd asked me, 'What've you been up to?'

And I'd said, 'Nothing.' I mean, I'd just been doing the usual stuff, like going to school, going home and sometimes staying over at Dad's.

'Don't you do anything?' she'd asked, and then she'd blabbed on and on about her and Steve, and how she'd snuck away to go camping with him on the weekend . . . 'Then the ranger saw us,' she'd said, 'and told us to put the fire out. The dumb-ass told us, "Bonfires are illegal!" He had this really dumb voice that was croaky *as*, and a huge-as nose. So Steve told him we couldn't see any signs that said we couldn't light a fire. "Where are the signs?" Steve'd asked him. "There *are* no signs!" the ranger had said. Then he saw our tent – like, big deal – so he told us to get lost. We had to hitch a lift to Bells Beach, and there was a "NO

CAMPING" sign there, so we ended up camping in this paddock at the back of someone's place . . .'

By then, I'd drawn a huge scribble on the cover of the 'A-to-K' White Pages and coloured in half the segments. I decided to change the subject and butt in: 'Did you go riding after school?'

'Nah,' she'd said; 'Sam's lame: he knocked his leg when we were showjumping last weekend. But I'm teaching Von to ride.'

I hated how she called the girl from America 'Von' – and I couldn't stand that the girl and I had the same name.

'Von's thinking about buying a horse,' she'd gone on. 'Mum said she could ride Tige until she buys one . . . blah-blah-blah.'

'Cool,' I'd lied.

'What did *you* do after school?' she'd asked.

I hadn't wanted to tell her I'd been hanging out with Amy after school. 'Not much,' I'd said. 'I ate heaps. We've got an account at the milk bar. Mum says we're meant to buy bread and milk – like, as *if*! She cracks it when she gets the bill and it's chips and chocolate and ice cream. After that, I hung out. There's this place Amy and I go.'

'Place?' she'd asked. 'What place?'

'Hr-hrm; well, Amy calls it Paradise.'

'Para-what?'

Me and my big mouth. 'Paradise,' I'd said again.

'*P-AAA-radise*! Oh-la-la! Sounds fancy *as*.'

'Shut up: you make it sound stupid, and it's not. It's really cool. It's this house at the end of our street. It backs onto the lane, and we jump the fence to get in. The owners don't come home till late, and they've got a trampoline. The garden's huge. There's ferns everywhere – and a creek.'

'Crap,' she'd said: 'a creek? in the city?'

'I'm not kidding you. They've got this tennis court, and it's raised on stilts. And there's this statue, of a man's head, by the pool.' Suze'd gone quiet, which was a dead giveaway that she didn't believe me. 'When it gets dark,' I'd continued, 'we go home.'

In the background, I'd been able to hear her tapping on something. Then the tapping had stopped.

'How's school?' she'd asked. The tapping had started up again.

'Boring,' I'd answered. 'I spend recess, lunchtime and frees sitting by the oval. I've read the *Lord of the Rings* trilogy, *Star Wars*, *Watership Down*, 4 collections of *Calvin and Hobbes*, and –'

She'd burst out laughing. *'Bookworm!'*

'I know – but get this,' I'd said: 'the librarian subscribed to *Hoofs and Horns*, *Eventer* and *The Australian Horse Magazine*!'

'Hey, I've gotta go!' she'd suddenly said: 'Mum's calling.'

Yeah: right – as *if*. 'Okay,' I'd said. 'See ya.'

'Maybe we can –'

And that's when I'd hung up. Then she'd called me back, only to hang up on me.

Thinking about that little episode, I looked up from the magazine and threw the apple core into a puddle. I did miss her – and I swear she missed me. And I wasn't just thinking that to try and make myself feel better – because it only took about five minutes for her to call me back.

'What's up?' she'd asked.

'Not much,' I then added, 'I was trying to unplug the phone, but obviously I wasn't fast enough.'

'But Vee, I love you – you're my best-est buddy.'

'I thought Von was.'

'"Von"? She's dumb. She worries about her hair all the time.'

'Sounds like someone I know,' I'd said.

'Get stuffed. Steve likes it when my hair's really messy. I haven't brushed it for a *week*.'

Not Steve again, I'd thought. 'Are you sorry?' I'd asked.

'Sorry for what?' she'd asked back.

'For hanging up on me.'

'*You* hung up on *me* first!'

'Oh: sorry,' I'd admitted.

Then we'd laughed and become the best-est of buddies all over again . . .

I tossed the magazine aside. A bunch of girls were hanging out on the other side of the oval. Anthea Tsouracus was the roughest and toughest of the 'Wogs', and was picking a catfight. When she was really mad, she'd grab the front of a girl's hair and tug really hard; she called it a fringe-ing.

The other girl in the fight pushed Anthea back, and that's when I saw who she was: Debbie Forshaw – *the* most popular girl in Year 8. About a month before, she'd made out she was my best-est friend, and then turned everyone against me. We'd been in the lunch yard, and all I'd said was I'd rather ride my horse on the weekend than have a boyfriend to hang out with. And she'd said, 'Veronica: the horse kisser – watch out!' Then she'd backed off, like I had a super-contagious disease. Now, every time she passes, she says, 'Hey, farmer: how's your horse?' I'd love to see her as the new girl at Yarra Valley High: the cricket-pitch chicks would give her heaps.

The girls who spoke Italian and had big, boofy 80's hair with stacks of gel in it – now gathered around Anthea. Everyone else – the 'Rowers', the 'Skips', 'Team Nike', the 'Smokers', the 'Teenie-boppers', and even the lesbian 'Tuff Muffs' – gathered around Debbie. Anthea yelled at Debbie in Italian; Debbie screamed back. Then everyone *hisssssed*.

The crowd split. And then for some reason, most people on Debbie's side changed their mind: they shuffled to stand behind Anthea and the Italians, so Debbie and the 'Deb-ettes' were then outnumbered: about 10 Deb-ettes to 100-plus Wogs.

A couple of nuns ran towards the fight, notebooks and pens in hand. Everyone *hissssssed* again. The Deb-ettes *hisssssed* back. Then someone from Anthea's side spat. Then Debbie fell, flat on her arse.

I felt like cheering. *Hah: serves you right,* I thought. *Not so popular now, hey?*

'You're wise not to get involved,' a gentle voice said.

I jumped about three inches in the air. '*Oh*, Sister Frances! Sorry: you gave me a fright.'

She smiled at me. 'Do you have a minute?'

'Yeah, sure,' I replied. Oh, God, what had I done? Was she gonna ask me the dreaded 'How are you settling in: are you making friends?' question *again*?

'I was hoping to have a chat with you about your IRP,' she said then smiled to let me know I wasn't in trouble.

'Oh, sure,' I said – even though I wanted to scream, '*Nooo!*' I'd been dreading the compulsory Religious Education Individual Research Project from day one. Every Year 8 girl *had* to keep a journal for the whole year. It was a stupid, self-development, 'increasing self-awareness' project, presented in the format of each student's choice. Some girls were keeping a diary, others were making an autobiographical website, and yet others were editing videos to make a short film. They were really into it. My IRP sucked: so far, I'd submitted the Melbourne photos, which I'd taken at Dad's work, and basically that's as far as I'd got.

'I think your photos are excellent,' Sister Frances said. 'And the montage idea is extremely creative. However, I must say –' I could tell she was choosing her words carefully – 'the idea of the project is to present and express *yourself* as the subject; your photos are snapshots of your environment, not of you.'

'But they *are* of me,' I answered in defence. 'I've moved to the city, and the photos are of what I see.'

'Certainly,' the sister assured me. 'And how about extending that idea and including photos of yourself within your environment? and of the people around you – family? friends? You've told me about your horses, and how you visit them most weekends.'

Liar-liar; pants on fire! I thought.

'You could even set up your camera on a tripod,' she continued. 'Does your camera have a self-timer?'

'Ah, I guess,' I replied; 'most cameras do.'

'Great! Keep it up: it's coming along fantastically.'

With that, she bent over to pick up the apple core I'd thrown in the puddle earlier.

It didn't feel right, having Sister Frances pick up my garbage, so I bent down and grabbed it before she could get to it.

'Thanks,' she said. 'You're a dear.'

I looked back at the fight, which by now had broken up. 'That's okay,' I said, and stepped away as if in search of a rubbish bin.

Sister Frances suddenly straightened her back and frowned. 'Veronica, I'm very sorry to have to do this,' she sighed, 'but I'm going to have to confiscate your necklace – you know the rules.'

'No! You can't!' I protested. 'I'll take it off!' I clutched my hands to my neck and covered the locket.

'We don't have special rules for individual students,' she said.

'But sister, I'll take it off, and I promise I'll never wear it again.'

However, she held out her hand. 'Confiscated property is claimable at the end of term.'

'But sister!'

'I'm sorry,' she added firmly; 'it's the rules. Can you tell me a good enough reason why I should think otherwise?' She paused. 'Is there something sentimental about the piece?'

'No, I just –' I thought about the photo, of Mum and Dad, that I'd stuck inside the locket, and my lucky clover. I'd taken out Mum's letter: the 'trial year' didn't mean anything now. The only thing that meant anything, anymore, was the clover but it's not like my wishes came true anyway. 'I promise,' I begged. 'I won't wear it again.'

But she took the locket. 'I'm sorry.' Then she smiled. 'I'm really looking forward to seeing the progress of your IRP. As I said, keep up the good work; quite a few members of staff have mentioned your outstanding test results across all subjects.'

I looked away. I pressed the flesh of my lips firmly against my teeth. 'Fine,' I said.

As she walked away, I wanted to yell, 'Hey, sister, *wait*! I've got a seventh wish, and I'm gonna use it: I *wish* I had the guts to yell like Penny – 'cause I'd yell, "Hey, you – you *and* your stupid prison: *You can all go and get stuffed*!"'

Ding-ding-ding.

. . . But I didn't. Something in my guts told me to save it: it was the last week of April, and I only had four wishes left to last me till the end of the year – even though there wasn't any such thing as a trial year, now Mum and Dad were divorcing. Still, there were heaps and heaps of other, way cooler things I could wish for – like having the power to make myself invisible . . . or blinking my eyes to transport myself to another century . . . or:

shooting through the solar system in a rocket ship – *Vrrrooooooom!!!* If I could just make it through the year, then I could move back with Dad when the Wilson's rent contract ran out. Then being me would be fun again.

No way was I going back to class. I walked off, jumped the concrete ledge and ran as fast as I could down the driveway. I was out of there: gone; never coming back . . . *Then again,* I thought, *I could pretend I have a really bad headache and spend the rest of the day in sickbay* . . . I turned back, cut across the lawn and headed towards the administration entrance.

A smelly old nun was on nurse duty, and proceeded to ask me heaps of questions. The first was 'Are you menstruating?'

I went bright red. 'No; it's a headache.'

'"No; it's a headache,"' she repeated. 'So you're *not* menstruating.' She made a note in her book.

I nearly walked out, but within a minute I was lying in bed with a cup of tea and a Gingernut biscuit. I stayed in sickbay for the rest of the day. Then, rather than walk Amy to Mum's place, I took her to Dad's work. He was really nice, and believed me when I said I felt sick. I knew Mum wouldn't have, because she was a nurse. He took me to his apartment and set up a little TV for me, on a table at the end of my bed. He called Mum and said Amy and I were staying the night at his place.

When he went out to pick up Chinese takeaway for us, I jumped out of bed and connected to the 'Net. I was wrapped to see an email waiting in my Inbox:

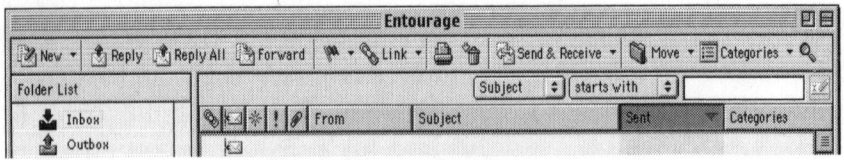

>From: susie@bumble.com.au
>To: veronica@bumble.com.au
>Subject: CONDOMS!!!
>Sent: 27 April, 7.06 p.m.

Hi, Vee. I've just caught Mum in MY bedroom going through the drawers! She said she was looking 4 cigarettes & alcohol! They've been cracking down on me ever since Steve & I were busted trying 2 get in2 the pub with fake ID. She went on & on about Dad & how he used 2 drink. I was mad as that she'd been snooping! And what did she find?! CONDOMS!!! that I HAVEN'T used – obviously EMERGENCY!!!!!! & USELESS, bcoz I'm no longer going out with Steve!!! So she's gone & told Morris, & now they both think I'm doing it & want me 2 come downstairs for a SEX-ED lecture. I'm thinking of going down with a pillow stuffed down the front of my T-shirt - preggas me!!! I can't phone your place 2nite (2 suss) bcoz I was going 2 ask if u wanted 2 wag. We could meet up 2moro & hang out. I need someone 2 laugh with me about this CONDOM FIASCO. Hope u get my email b4 it's 2 late 2 organise something!!! Write back ASAP!!! Don't call my place (2 suss) - just email YES & where 2 meet. Your best-est buddy & blood sis. XXOO Suzie-if only-losing-it-was-true-Suze

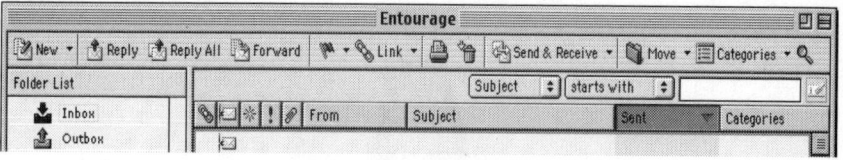

>From: veronica@bumble.com.au
>To: susie@bumble.com.au
>Subject: RE: CONDOMS!!!
>Sent: 27 April, 7.18 p.m.

YES! YES! YES!

I've got a plan. I'm staying over at Dad's 2nite, so I'll steal his Cabcharge & meet u at the Igloo at 10.00 a.m. I don't think it'll take any longer than that 4 a taxi driver 2 drive me out. And thanks - I didn't plan on going 2 school 2moro anyway. I was thinking of chucking a sickie. I spent this arvo in sickbay & made it really obvious 2nite that I still felt sick.

Can u do me a favour? Can u call Lagilla 2moro & pretend you're my Mum & say I'm staying at home 4 the day bcoz I'm sick? Do u want me 2 call YVHigh 4 u?

Can't wait! Your best-est buddy & blood sis. XO - Vee

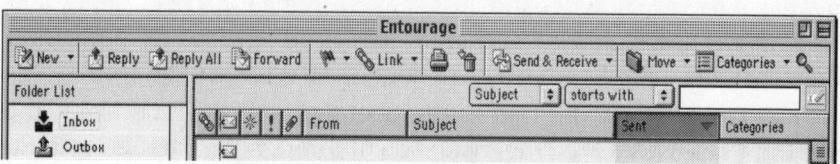

>From: susie@bumble.com.au
>To: veronica@bumble.com.au
>Subject: RE: CONDOMS!!!
>Sent: 27th April 8:56PM

COOL AS!!! No probs about calling Lagilla. But thx, I'll call YVHigh myself (no offence, but u r a crap liar). C u 2moro. Your best-est buddy & blood sis. XXOO Suzie-Suze

4

That night, before I went to sleep, I *wished* for Suze and me to wag together and not get caught. I fell asleep, and rather than have wish number seven happen when I woke up the next morning, I had it happen during the night, in my dream.

This is how wish number seven happened: I dreamt I was sitting in the kitchen at Dad's place. To prove I wasn't sick, I ate two bowls of Vita Brits and smiled a lot. Dad was convinced. I put on my uniform, hitched my bag over my shoulder and, just before leaving for school, snuck into Dad's room and stole his Cabcharge. "Bye, Dad!' I called from the front door. '. . . No – thanks anyway; we don't need a lift: we can walk.'

Amy and I walked out Dad's front door and rode the lift down to the ground floor. We crossed the road and cut through the park: everything as usual – except when we got to the front gates of Lagilla, where, rather than drop Amy off at the prep school and cut across the grassed area towards the main building, I dropped her off and doubled back, straight out the front gate.

'*Taxi!*' I yelled to a passing cabbie.

He turned out to be a madman, who turned his cab in a super-fast U-turn to pull up beside me.

I opened the back passenger door. 'Do you take Cabcharge?' I asked him, holding up Dad's card.

'*Yars,*' he replied.

'Can you drive me out to Yarra Valley?'

'*Yars; yars,*' he answered; '*Get in.*'

I glanced around to make sure no nuns were around, and jumped in.

I kept dreaming. The driver drove super-fast in the direction of Yarra Valley. We didn't talk much. I wasn't sure he could speak English, except for '*Yars; yars,*' and lots of grunts and groans about the traffic. I was happy to stare out the window. The traffic was peak hour, heading into the city, but not as bad the way we were heading. And it didn't take long before paddocks and gum trees rather than building developments and shopping strips were lining the side of the road.

The driver sped the whole way. At one intersection, I had to hold my bag down so it wouldn't fly forward and into the front seat – we'd hit a pothole in the road, and the wheels had lifted off the ground. '*Whoa!*' I shrieked.

'*Sarry; sarry,*' he said.

Then I heard this weird noise, kind of like a loose, 'rolling-around tinny' sound, like an empty barrel shifting in the boot.

'What's that noise?' I asked.

'*Gars tank; gars tank,*' he explained.

'What?!' I could picture the taxi exploding and how it would take weeks for Mum and Dad to realise it was me splattered into a thousand tiny pieces across the street. What had I been thinking: that I could get away with this? Of course Sister Cecilia was gonna be suss: she was suss about everything – that's why the girls had nicknamed her SS, after the Nazi secret service.

I realised I'd planned everything wrong: what if Suze forgot to call the school and say I was sick? I should've pretended I still felt sick this morning – then Dad would've called the school, and then – when he'd left for work and the coast was clear – that's when I should've phoned for a taxi.

'You feel si*arc*k?' the driver asked me, noticing my pale face in the rear-view mirror.

'No; no; no: keep driving,' I said, and forced myself to smile, to prove that the freaked-out schoolgirl in the back seat was A-OK. 'We're turning right up ahead, at that street – see there?' I told him, in a voice like Mum's: cool, calm and confident.

'*Yars; yars,*' he answered, nodding his head.

Maybe Suze *had* remembered and pulled off one of her convincing, movie star acts. She'd better not have used her English accent . . .

The taxi skidded to a halt out the front of Suze's place.

In my bed, I tossed and turned . . . The dream kept going.

'*Buuuumble!*' Susie squealed, crushing me in a huge hug. 'I didn't think you'd make it! I thought you'd pike!'

'As *if!*' I said. '*Oh:* look how long your hair is!'

'I had it straightened – you like?'

'It's wicked!' I said.

'*Doi!* Look at you in your uniform!' she laughed.

We both looked at my dress. 'I know,' I said; 'it's ridiculous.' I threw my bag onto the ground.

Suze undid the bag's zipper, and pulled out riding clothes and heaps of junk food.

'Wait up,' I said, and held her back from following me as I crawled into the Igloo to change. 'A bit of privacy, if you don't mind!'

'Still a prude,' she teased, and hovered impatiently. 'Come on,' she said; 'I haven't seen you for God knows how long – then, when you do get here, you nick off and hide!'

'I'm coming,' I said, and hopped around as I put my jodhpurs on. 'Did you call Lagilla?'

'No – shit: I forgot!'

I could tell she was joking. 'Wanna ride to the pine plantation?'

'Yeah: cool,' she said. 'We'll have to take Eb and Maje. Sam's leg's better, but not as good *as* – not enough to ride; is that okay?'

'Yeah: fine,' I agreed.

We ran over to my place and saddled the horses. The Wilsons weren't around, but I could see they'd hung a clothesline across the courtyard. 'It makes the place look junky,' I said, 'don't ya reckon?' Suze agreed.

She pointed to a tiny item hanging on the line and said, 'She wears G-strings.'

'Wears "what's"?'

'G-strings, you know, butt floss: undies that wedge up the crack of your arse.'

'Are you for real?' I asked, as I jumped up on Eb.

'Dead set,' she said. 'Come on: race you to the back gate.'

The fastest way to the pine plantation was the path that started at the back of my place, cut across the Gibbses', and then went up and over the ridge.

'*Wait up!*' Suze yelled when she saw me and Eb overtaking her.

'*Suffer!*' I yelled back, squeezing my legs to make Eb run faster.

'Slight advantage!' she yelled. 'Eb's way faster than Maje . . .' Her voice faded as Eb sped up.

We had to pass Nick's property, and that thought gave me the heebie-jeebies, so I made Eb gallop and held my breath. As I passed his driveway, a statue out the front of the house caught my eye. I'd ridden past his place often enough to realize that I'd never seen that statue before. I pulled Eb back to a walk so I could take a better look. The statue had, what looked like, a horse's body, but the head was a man's. Eb pranced on the spot, spooked by the movement and the sound of the wind chimes. I looked around some more: at the bones and feathers hanging from the trees, glanced quickly at each window, the front door and either side of the house. I couldn't see anyone, but it felt like someone – maybe Nick? – was watching me.

Suze cantered past. '*Suffer,*' she yelled, and kept going.

I was glad Suze was close by and kicked Eb to canter on. It didn't take long for Eb and me to catch up, then edge off the track and overtake them. I took the lead, turned right off the track and scrambled up the bank and through the scrub towards the ridge. I could feel the branches brushing against my face, so put my elbows up as a shield. When I got to the ridge's highest point, I made Eb halt. He rubbed his head on his leg and puffed out his gut. Foam was frothing at his bit.

I could see the Yarra River twisting and turning down the valley, the criss-cross and dot patterns of fruit and vegetables growing on working properties, and instead of a black scar where the bushfires had charred the grass, I noticed baby grass and new trees. Halfway down the other side, to the right, I could see the pine plantation . . .

I turned around. Suze and Maje were trotting towards us. I wasn't going to mention the 'statue' thing to Suze either. She hadn't noticed as she'd cantered past Nick's house, and if I'd told her, she'd probably say it was *really cool and exciting* and want to go back and have a look. 'Is Maje okay?' I asked. 'He normally bolts heaps faster than that.'

Maje put his head down and coughed.

'He's probably unfit,' Suze replied, 'which isn't anything surprising – what else do you expect, now you're so busy city slicking?!'

'Get lost!' I said, and poked out my tongue and blew her a raspberry: '*Pluutthhh*! It's not like it's *my* fault.' I kicked Eb on and leant back in the saddle as he scrambled down the bank, towards the creek. 'But I'm not gonna go on about it,' I called out to her, over my shoulder. 'I mean, like, in RE, we study World Vision issues. My life's cushy compared with how some people live – did you know that globally, one-third of children suffer from hunger and malnutrition? and 250 million children between five and 14 are forced to work to support their families?' Eb stopped at the creek and plunged his head into the water. 'And – hang on,' I continued; 'I think – yeah, that's it: 16 out of 20 –'

Suze laughed.

I turned around and gave her a cross-eyed, long-faced ugly. 'What's so funny?' I asked.

'Oh, nothing,' she replied.

I guessed I *was* going on a bit. 'Yeah: well – *whoa*! I hung on as Eb jumped the creek in a giant leap. My boots slid out of the stirrups.

'*Novice*!' Suze yelled out to me. 'Go back to Level Z!'

Level A was the highest, and Suze and I were Level C. Acting as if I hadn't heard her, I cantered off and pretended my boots hadn't slipped.

When we got to the pine plantation, we tied the horses to a tree. I set my camera to the self-timer so I could take a photo of Suze and me; then, I balanced it on a tree stump. 'Is the green light flashing?!' I yelled out to her.

'No!' she yelled back.

'Now?'

'Noooo!'

'Damn it!' I cursed, and pressed the button harder.

'It's flashing!' she shouted.

'*Argh*!' I scrambled towards Suze and dived into frame.

'*Cheese*!' we shrieked, grinning from ear to ear.

Suze shoved a handful of potato chips into her mouth and puffed her cheeks out like a chipmunk's. I clenched a fist behind her head and made the 'rabbit ears' shape with two of my fingers.

'*CHEEEEESE!*' we shrieked even louder – and this time, the camera flashed. '*YEEEAAH!*'

I wasn't about to admit I was glad she wasn't going out with Steve any more, so I just said, 'what's with, anyway? I thought you said Steve was great.'

'Yeah,' she said; 'that was, until he dumped me: he said I was too young and he didn't want to go out with someone he'd have to babysit.'

'*Oh*, harsh – sorry.'

'*Doi!* Tell me about it. Doesn't matter – I'm over him.'

I laughed. 'I didn't want to say anything,' I said, 'but he *was* a bit old.'

'Vee, you're such a prude.'

'I am *not*: He *was* 17.'

'*Eww*: "17"! How dare *me*? Susie-scandal!' She swatted my head with the book *Every Woman*, which her mum had given her after she'd found condoms in Suze's drawer. I'd seen the book at Lagilla's library, but only quickly looked at it during one of my frees. I was embarrassed looking at it on my own, never mind having my parents give it to me.

'*Ouch, Suze!*'

'Serves you right,' she said, and turned away to flick through the book's pages . . . '*Doi!* Check these out!' she said, and held up a picture of what looked like a photo of dicks and balls with hair and . . .'

'Oh, *Suze*: that's disgusting!' I pushed the book away.

'Can I borrow your glasses?' she asked, clicking her fingers to reinforce the point.

'N.O.' I replied. 'You're such a despo – *stop it*: you're freaking me.' I grabbed the book and threw it into a bush.

'Hey – I was looking at that!' she yelled.

'Yeah – well: you've got a serious problem . . . What the hell was that, anyway?'

'*The* 10 stages of erection, from limp to blowhole.'

'Orgh: that's disgusting!' But I *was* kinda curious . . . 'Okay. Show me.'

Suze ran over and grabbed the book. We huddled together against the stump.

At first, I didn't get it: I just thought each photo was of a different dick. 'Hoh,' I gasped then: it *was* the same dick, but I didn't know what to say.

'Which one do you like best?' she asked me.

'Get lost! You can't be serious, can you? None of them.'

'I like *that* one best,' she said, and pointed at photo number six.

'Gross.' It looked the one in the dirty magazine Suze'd stolen from Morris's study. 'It's huge . . . Look at the veins: it's about to pop.'

'It's Popeye!' she screamed. '*Haaaaaaaaaaar . . .*'

We rolled around and laughed till we ached. It was ages before we could sit up with a straight face.

After we'd caught our breath, I thought about what I'd said to her earlier. 'Hey, Suze,' I said.

'Yeah?' She snuggled closer and curled her left arm around my waist.

'Well, you know,' I began, 'how I was saying before, about how so much has changed?'

'Yeah?'

'Should I be worried?' I went on. 'I mean, I used to be able to picture everything. But now my parents are divorcing, and we're not moving back to YV, well, does that mean you and I – well, do we stop being friends?'

'Haven't you got new friends to replace boring old me?' she asked, half seriously.

'Well . . . There was *one* other group,' I began, 'but seriously, they were *so* daggy: if it wasn't choir, it was chess club, and if it wasn't chess club, it was jazz ballet, and if it wasn't jazz ballet, it was archery. And they wore their dresses down to here,' I added, chopping my right hand across my ankle. 'Oh, *Suuuuze*, what am I gonna do?'

'Don't worry,' she said. 'I'll buy you a crystal ball for your birthday.'

'Oh, yeah: right,' I said. 'And, like, that's meant to help! Even if I could see the future, what if I didn't like it? I can't change anything.'

'That's what fate is,' she said, raising her eyebrows thoughtfully like she was super-smart.

'"Fate."' I thought about the word. 'Don't you mean more like "jinxed"?' I flopped back and closed my eyes. 'What am I gonna do? What am I gonna do? What am I . . .? What am I . . .?'

. . . I tossed and turned. My sleeping bag was clinging to my sweat-soaked skin. My seventh wish had turned from a cool-as dream into *a total nightmare!*

Beep! Beep! Beep! Beep!! Beep!!!

I sat up; rubbed my eyes; blinked; flicked my legs over the edge of my bed; stood up; yawned and stretched; shuffled across the carpet; opened the door; stepped out into the hall . . . *Oh: that's right – I'm at Dad's place,* I thought.

I could hear the sound of spraying water coming out of the shower in Dad's en suite. If I stole his Cabcharge now, I thought, he'd never know, and then I could put it back when I came back later. Dad didn't know it yet, but I was gonna ask whether I could sleep over a second night.

I crept across the hall. I could hear Dad whistling as I tiptoed across his room. His wallet was lying on the bedside table. I stood there for what seemed like an eternity, Dad's wallet in my hand, freaking out that he was about to turn off the shower any second.

I fumbled through the wallet's leather compartments. The Cabcharge was hidden behind the Visa card. I slipped it out, and counted the money in the wallet: $340 in total. I figured it was okay to take a $50 note. I took it, and placed the wallet back on the table – exactly how I'd found it, with the Spirax phone-message book balanced on top of it – and bolted out of the room . . .

I leant against my wardrobe. My heart was pounding inside my chest. *Pu-thump; pu-thump.* I looked at the Cabcharge and the crisp $50 note. Beads of sweat were dripping from my armpits; even the underarms of my pyjamas were wet.

Surely the bank would open at nine o'clock: I *could* withdraw the last of my savings. I could still meet Suze by 10, and I knew, from the last time I'd checked, that I had $40 and five cents in my account . . . Or maybe Suze could lend me some money – I'd loaned her some in the past . . .

I tiptoed across Dad's room again. The shower water stopped running. I quickly opened the wallet and stuffed the Cabcharge in.

'Veronica.'

'Argh!' I said, and jumped.

Dad was standing in the doorway of his en suite, a towel wrapped around his waist. 'What are you doing?' he asked.

'*Ah* . . .' I began, looking at the wallet. '*Ah* . . . cleaning up,' I lied, and screwed the money up, to hide the evidence.

'Do you know how naughty that is?' he asked; 'taking money that's not yours?' He wiped the water from his nose.

'I wasn't, honestly – I was just . . . borrowing it. I was putting it back – see?' I put the money back. 'All fixed.'

He shook his head, marched across the room and took his neatly ironed pants from the heat panel of his trouser press. Without turning around, he raised the index finger of his right hand. 'I don't care how sick you say you are,' he said: 'if you're well enough to steal, you're well enough to go to school.' He turned to face me. 'Now get changed!' he ordered. 'I'm leaving in 10 minutes, and I want you to be *dressed* and *ready*! And *that's* an order!'

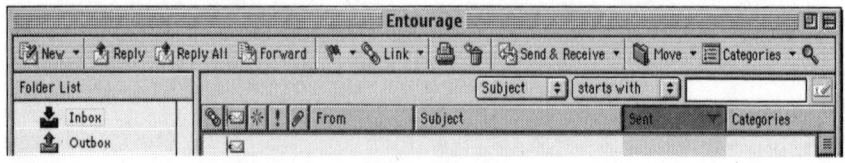

>From: veronica@bumble.com.au
>To: susie@bumble.com.au
>Subject: EMERGENCY!!! ABORT PLAN!!!
>Sent: 28 April, 7.59 a.m.

Suze, I'm sorry!

I've just tried calling your place but your Mum said you'd already left. Yikes! I'm in BIG trouble. Dad's caught me stealing his Cabcharge & now he's making me go 2 school. Oh, God, I hope u don't wait outside the Igloo 4 hours & hours. I'll call u later.

I'm sorry-sorry-sorry. PLEASE don't b mad. Your best-est buddy & blood sis. XO - Vee

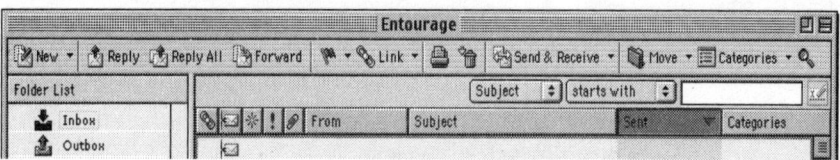

>From: <u>veronica@bumble.com.au</u>
>To: <u>susie@bumble.com.au</u>
>Subject: #8: R we still best-est buddies?
>Sent: 1 May, 6.34 p.m.

Suze, this is my 8th email, & I've just made my 5th phone call. I didn't mean 2 stuff up, & I didn't mean 2 b caught stealing. So even though I never turned up that day, it's not like I'd deliberately planned it that way. SO, PLEASE don't ignore me!

Mum & Dad have grounded me 4 the Easter break. Bcoz Mum's working, I have 2 stay at Dad's. He's been super-strict - so it's not like I can surprise visit u 2 tell u how crappy I feel & how important u r as a friend. I'm trapped in his stupid apartment, & I can't even watch TV, & I've had 2 sneak in2 the kitchen 5 times 2 make 5 phone calls that u won't take. AS IF every time I call, you're out.

So if u haven't already guessed, I'M MAD NOW. At least write me an email 2 let me know if u do, or don't, hate me.

Sometimes your best-est buddy & blood sis. XO - Vee

I clicked on the Send button, and then clicked back to the Newbury Girls' School website. Why hadn't I thought of going to a country boarding school before? Horse riding and stud management were compulsory subjects at those schools – and you could stable your horse on campus, *and* two Newbury students had ridden for Australia in the Olympics.

I read the website for the fourth time and clicked back to the home page. It featured a photo of a girl and her horse jumping. *They could easily be me and Eb,* I thought. Even though Suze and I weren't talking, I knew she'd agree it was an unreal idea for both of us – and she wouldn't have to put up with Morris being a creep. And if Mum and Lisa had been allowed to board, *I* was allowed to as well.

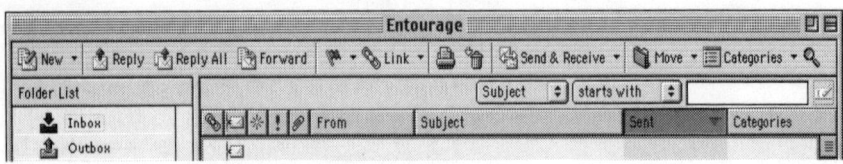

>From: veronica@bumble.com.au
>To: susie@bumble.com.au
>Subject: #9: R we still best-est buddies?
>Sent: 1 May, 6.59 p.m.

Suze! Write me an email. I've so got 2 tell u the most BRILLIANT-BLITZER of an idea!!!!!!!!!!!!!!!!!

Your best-est buddy & blood sis. XO - Vee

As I crossed the hallway, I kicked Amy's teddy bear out of the way. I wasn't mad at *her*, though: I was mad at everything else. As loud as I could, I stomped down the hallway and into the kitchen. I knew Dad was around the apartment somewhere. It wasn't fair: he could've given me a chance to come up with something better than 'cleaning' – because I was returning the money, and I am worried about Major: the Wilsons had sent us a photo of him, and he looked as if he'd lost weight.

I pushed the laundry door open and threw my uniforms into the washing machine. Then I shook in a handful of detergent. I had to do Amy's, Dad's *and* my washing. I switched on the normal–cold cycle and stomped back to my room. 'Maybe I *am* bad!' I yelled to no one. 'Maybe I'm just as bad as *Penny*!' I slammed the door and sat down at my desk. I was bored stiff; Amy hadn't even come into my room to annoy me. I drummed a pen against the desk.

I thought about it, and realised that I had to write Dad a card and tell him that I was sorry. I hated that he thought I was a thief and that it seemed like I didn't give two hoots about it. I took a piece of paper from the printer tray and folded it in half. Then I wrote:

Later that night, before I went to sleep, I left the card on his bedside table.

1

The Easter break was over, and so was my grounding.

Mum usually slept in after a night shift, but this morning, when I walked into the kitchen, she was sitting on a stool, dressed in her pyjamas, the paper spread out in front of her. A pot of porridge was bubbling away on the stove, and the kitchen smelt as yum as a bakery. 'Morning,' I said, and dumped my school bag at the back door. 'How come you're up?'

'Permanent shifts start today,' she said. 'Ten till six, weekdays.'

I gave the porridge a stir. Two packed lunches, for Amy and me, were next to the toaster. I turned around to face Mum. 'Does that mean you got the promotion?'

'Yes,' she answered. 'And that means we can buy lounge chairs for the lounge room.'

'Wicked!' I said. 'What about beanbags?'

'Lounge chairs first – then beanbags.'

'Great.' I put my lunch in my bag. 'Thanks for the lunch. Is it still the Mercy Hospital?'

She stretched her arms and yawned. '*Oh*, excuse me . . . Yes.'

'Hey, don't move.' I grabbed my camera from my bag. 'I have to take a photo for my IRP. Hold still, or else Sister Frances –'

'Veronica,' she interrupted, flapping the paper, 'don't! My hair looks like a bird's nest.'

I pushed the paper away from her face. 'Come on, Mum: *smile.*'

She gave in.

I took three more photos, each of her reading the paper and trying her best to ignore me. 'Where's Amy?' I asked. 'I want to take a photo of her doing a fish face on the glass.'

'Out the back with Dad,' she replied. ' And *no* fish faces: I've just had the window cleaner come and clean the glass – it cost me a fortune; you'll leave smudge marks.'

'What?! Is Dad here?!'

'Mmm,' she replied, and snapped the paper straight.

'How come – are you guys getting back together again?' Ever hopeful me.

'No!' she said; 'he's fixing the pool filter – that *green pond* at the deep end smells like a rubbish tip.'

I slumped into the nearest chair. 'That'd be right,' was all I could add.

The phone rang. I was about to get up and answer it, but the ringing stopped. I could see Dad and Amy outside, by the pool. Dad had taken the filter apart. He was barefoot, and he had his pants rolled up to his knees. I pushed the window open. 'Dad! Amy!' I yelled. I held the camera up. 'Smile!'

They both looked at me.

'I said "*Smile!*" I'm taking a photo!'

The garden looked like crap. Where flowers should have been, there were weeds. The tiling wasn't finished. And the green water at the deep end did look pretty yuk. But so what? Dad was here, and things were like how they used to be; we were a family again.

The phone rang out. I took one more photo and then raced over to answer it. 'Hello – the Bees's,' I said. Suze's voice was recognisable straight away. 'Suze! Finally! I thought you'd been abducted by aliens. *Hey, Suze*, what's up? How come you're crying?'

I couldn't believe what Suze told me. I raced up to my room, wedged the chair under the doorknob, dived into bed and covered my head with my 'Bumble' blanket.

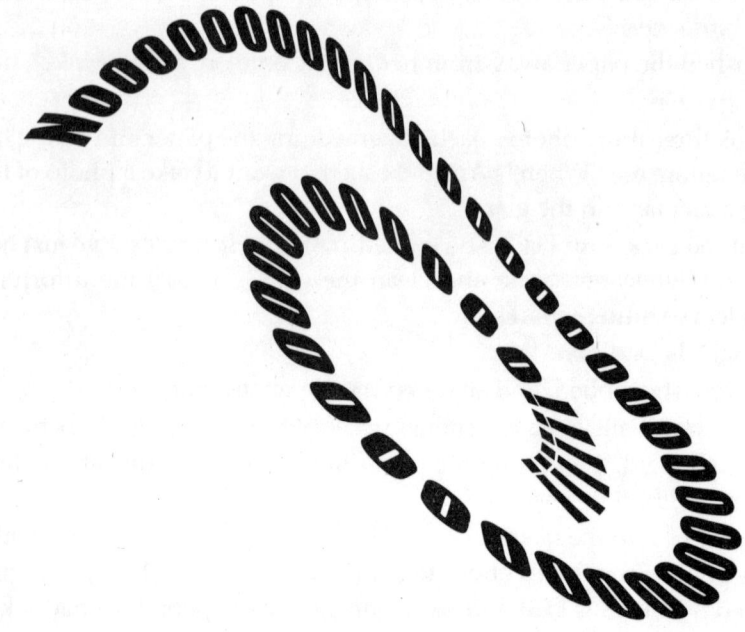

How could she? I wouldn't do it to her. I kicked off my shoes and threw them onto the floor. Just when I'd been thinking Mum and Dad were getting back together, Suze goes and tells me this.

'Veronica.' It was Mum.

'Go away,' I said.

I heard her rattling the door handle. 'Veronica, open up.'

The chair budged. I turned to face the wall as Mum walked in. The mattress tilted as she sat down on the bed. 'Take the cover away from your face,' she said, and pulled at the blanket.

'No,' I insisted, and clenched my fists to hold the wool tighter around my face. 'Ooh, Muuum: she's *leaving*.'

'Who? Sit up.'

'Suze. She said not to get mad, but she said she was gonna go and live with her grandmother in England – and that she was flying out next Wednesday; that's, like, in seven days, she said. *Orgh, Mum*: how can she do that – to me?'

'*Sshh*,' she said. 'This isn't about you; it's about Susie, and what she wants.'

'It's always about what everyone else wants: I'm *jinxed*, Mum – why can't you and Dad be together, and why can't Suze stay?' I got out of bed and put my runners on: I had to get away. 'If she calls,' I said, 'tell her I don't want to go to the airport – and there's no way I'm gonna change my mind!'

'Where are you going?' she asked.

'School.' I didn't waste any time: I ran quickly out of the room, down the stairs and through the kitchen, grabbed my bag, and doubled back out the front door.

As I was crossing the main road, a cyclist swerved and just missed me. 'Sorry!' he yelled, and then stopped to watch me cross the road.

'Watch out!' I yelled back, and kept running, annoyed that the stranger was just standing there and staring.

I couldn't wait to get to school. I couldn't wait to be anonymous and lost amongst all the laughter, shrieks, holiday gossip and chaos. There was a certain comfort to the anonymity I craved and missed. A part of school life I'd come to expect; a certain shrinking to the edges; a total state of ignorance

I was no longer Veronica Bee, the new girl; I was Veronica Bee, the girl from Year 8 who liked, and wanted, to be left alone.

Ding-ding-ding-ding-ding!

That week, I spent recess, lunchtime and frees slouched on a beanbag in the reading corner of the library. *STOOOOOOOOOOOOP!* Hah: gotcha! *STOOOOOOOOOOOOP!*

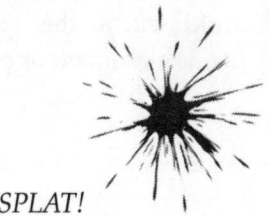

SPLAT!

I'd made a game up and called it the 'Stop! Splat!' game: all I had to do was block out bad thoughts so that then, I only thought about good stuff. It was Friday, 1.05 p.m. – and I'd made it through the week. Every time I'd thought of something bad, I'd blocked it out by imagining I was chucking a big, black blob at it. *STOOOOOOOOOOOOP! SPLAT!* Lately, it seemed that if I didn't play the 'Stop! Splat!' game, I felt like I was gonna spontaneously combust.

Orange lava, and huge balls of gold and red were gonna shoot across the librarian's desk – or even worse, the library roof was gonna blow *off*! Watch out: red and blue flashing lights! Watch out, Lagilla! Watch out, Melbourne! Huge balls of fire were gonna land as far away as the Dandenongs. And the cows at Yarra Valley were gonna cough up volcanic dust.

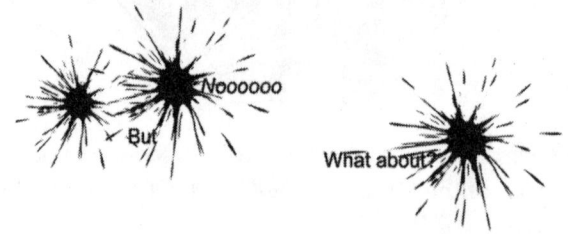

STOOOOOOOOOOOOP! I could win at this game; I *could* imagine every crappy moment in my life as a moment of bliss.

Watch out!

SPLAT!

Watch out, Year 8!

Ka-pow!

Watch out, world!

Incoming . . .

What was happening to me? I used to be happy; my thoughts used to be as sweet as fairy floss. And now, when I got home, I was grumpy *as*. I was running up to my room and locking myself in; otherwise, I was getting mad at Mum and Amy, over absolutely nothing. Then Mum would come up and knock, and I'd tell her I was studying – which was *so* not true: I hadn't done any homework that week. Not only that, whenever I was sitting in the library, I couldn't read – I couldn't keep my eyes on the page for long enough; like today: I'd read every paragraph 10 times, and every time I'd tried, my head had filled up with thoughts about bad stuff.

Your parents are divorcing.

Your best friend's moving overseas.

At night, you hear your Mum cry.

And what about the lipstick on the wine glass at your Dad's place?

Penny's a nutcase –

Always running away.

And now you're running,

So does that make you a nutcase, Vee?

Yes, you are; yes, you are:

You're just as bad,

As bad, as bad, as bad as Penny.

Excuse me, ladies and gentlemen: if I could have your attention, please? I'd like to introduce the new *Veronica Bee! This one doesn't think bad thoughts; this one doesn't care about the detention Sister Frances gave her for wearing runners – because this Veronica Bee is just like Penny!*

Ding-ding-ding!

Lunchtime was over . . . I'd nearly made it through another day. *And hah!* I thought, slumping further into the beanbag. *So what if I didn't go to class?*

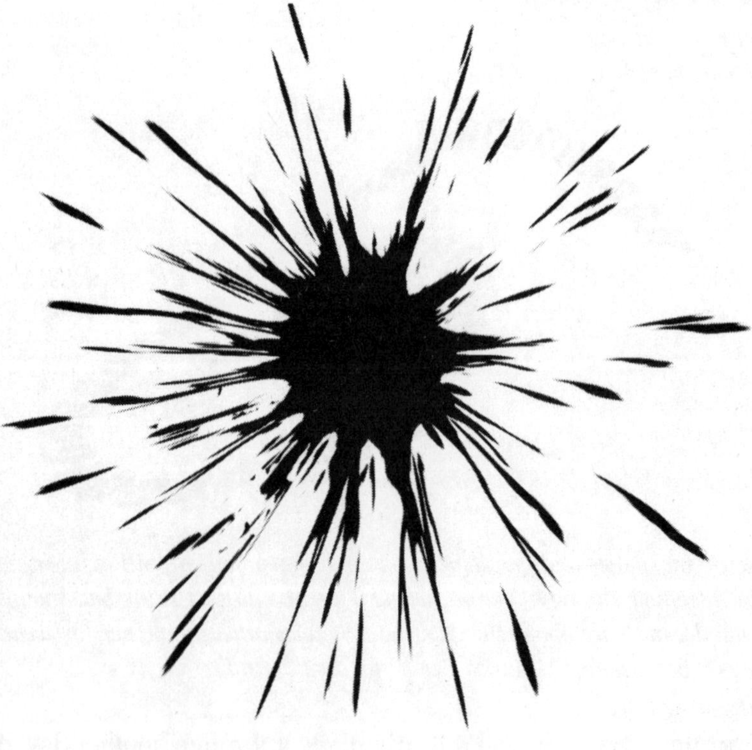

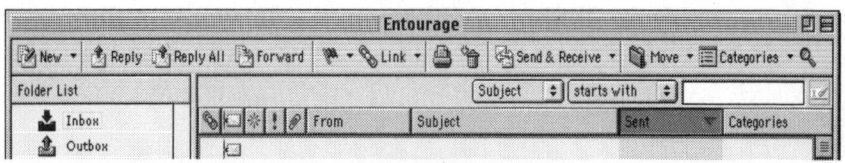

>From: susie@bumble.com.au
>To: veronica@bumble.com.au
>Subject: No matter what!!!
>Sent: 6 May, 10.46 p.m.

Vee, at last!!! I thought you'd never talk 2 me again - & that's fantastic that you're coming 2 the airport. It's QF 193 International. It leaves at 7.40 in the morning on Wednesday the 10th. (Doi! Only 4 sleeps!!!) Loved your email, & yeah - we r lucky 2 have each other as friends. But don't xagger8 & say you're xstatic about me living with my Nan. I know she breeds Warmbloods - which r the best-est breed 4 eventing (Doi!), & that she competed in the Olympics 4 GB. I'm lucky as! But no matter if she breeds the most amazing horse in the whole wide world, if I can't ride as good as, I don't make the team. So don't b jealous - & don't 4get I'll miss u 2, & I can't wait 2 c u! XXOO Susie-always your-best-est-buddy-&-blood-sis-Suze

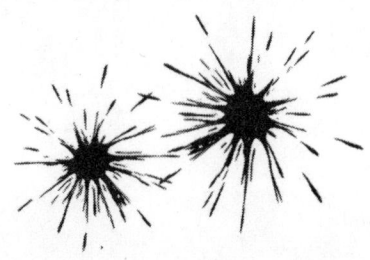

I didn't write back to her: I was tired, and had nothing to say. I turned the computer off and jumped into bed. She'd really believed I was looking forward to going to the airport to see her off.

See if I care, I said to myself . . .

I rolled over. I liked the new me: it was easy to pretend everything was hunky-dory. But no matter how hard I tried, I couldn't sleep . . . And then the bad thoughts started up again:

He said it was a 'break', not a 'break-up',
And you believed,
And don't forget the lipstick on the wine glass,
And how many business meetings does a dad have?
Bet the president of America's not as busy as that –
Maybe he's lying:
Whatcha reckon 'bout that?
Penny's a nutcase –
Always running away,
And now you're running,
So does that make you a nutcase, Vee?
Yes: you are; yes, you are:
You're just as bad,
As bad, as bad, as bad as Penny.

I tossed and turned: I was back to being a total worry-wart.

On Monday, after my detention for wearing runners rather than school lace-ups, I picked Amy up from after-school care. But rather than hang out together at Paradise, we caught the number 48 tram to Richmond. The night before, I'd looked up Lisa's address in the White Pages, and then checked Mum's *Melway* to find Charles Street.

On the tram, I kept an eye out for street signs, to make sure we didn't miss our stop. The tram rattled over the bridge that crossed the Yarra River.

'When do I get my ice cream?' Amy asked me, yanking on the sleeve of my blazer.

'In a minute,' I said, yanking back on the sleeve of her blazer. I pulled the cord. 'Come on: this is our stop.'

As we walked down Bridge Road, I felt bad thoughts pinging like pinballs inside my head. I couldn't make them stop! What if Penny wasn't home? Mum had told me she was still living at Lisa's – but would she be home when I knocked?

'What about my ice cream?' Amy asked again.

'Stop bugging me,' I answered. 'You'll get one: there's a 7-11 up there, see? I'll buy you an ice cream – I said I'd get you one, didn't I?'

She did the zipping sign on her lips.

'Good,' I said; 'that's better.' I walked faster, Amy skipping along beside me. What if Penny wasn't home? *Whatever. Shut up. Stop it. STOOOOOOOOOOOOP!*

I bought Amy a Paddle Pop at the 7-11, and then grabbed her hand and crossed the road to Charles Street. I recognised Lisa's house straight away: it was the only one among a row of five that was painted purple and orange; all the rest were painted a creamy colour, and had either 'federation' green or red window frames.

I lifted the brass rapper on the door of house number 17. The knocking sound echoed down the street. Across the road, I saw an older woman look up from her gardening. She eyed us suspiciously, as if I could be a burglar and Amy my accomplice. Amy sat down on the top step and bit into her Paddle Pop. I turned back and gave the rapper a knock again. If Penny wasn't home, was it worth waiting for her? No way was I gonna leave a note: the wind might blow it away – and anyway, I really wanted to speak with her.

Still no answer. 'Bugger.' I turned and took Amy by the hand. 'Wanna catch another tram?' I asked her.

'*Yes!*' she said, and jumped up. 'Are we –'

'*Sshh*,' I whispered, and clapped my left hand over her mouth: 'zipped lips, okay? I've got a headache; we're going home.'

She nodded her head and licked the ice cream.

We walked back to Bridge Road and waited for the next tram. Some of the cars coming out of the city had their headlights on.

'Bugger,' I said again, this time under my breath. I really wanted to speak with Penny, but I couldn't come back on Tuesday morning: I had to be at school at 7.45, for a Biol excursion. I'd come back the next afternoon, after school, after my detention for not handing my book report in – and if she wasn't home then, I'd come back on Wednesday morning *and* afternoon, and . . . *Damn*, I thought: *Wednesday I can't – Suze is flying out that morning*! 'We'll come back tomorrow,' I told Amy; 'after school.'

'Do I get another ice cream?'

'*Sshh*; yes – but only if you don't mention to Mum that we came here, or I'll give you *the worst-est, most "killer"* Chinese burn!'

She dropped the corners of her mouth to a frown.

'Is that a deal?' I asked, and put my hand out for her to shake.

She nodded her head, then we shook hands.

The next tram was ours. We had to stand in the aisle, our bags at our feet because the older style 48 was packed. Rain splattered against the windows. Passing cars' windscreen wipers swished. The air was stuffy. I squeezed Amy's hand; she squeezed mine back.

No matter what, I knew I had to speak with Penny – and this time, she wasn't gonna get away with telling me to nick off: I'd refuse to leave Lisa's house unless she answered *all* my questions; I'd even packed my bike lock inside my bag, so that if she did tell me to nick off, I'd chain myself to Lisa's letterbox.

I had to know what Penny had said that day by the pool. I reckoned it had something to do with Dad's business meetings *and* the lipstick on the wine glass. I couldn't ask Dad whether he'd been seeing someone else because if he said no, I wouldn't know whether to believe him – and no way was I gonna ask Mum. If it were true, I'd prefer Penny to be the one who told me.

When we got off the tram, the rain was even worse. We lifted our blazers over our heads, in the shapes of a hood, and ran down the street. By the time I opened the front door, we were dripping wet. I thought we were going to get into huge trouble for being late, but luckily Mum wasn't home. She had, however, left a note for us on the kitchen bench. I read it out:

'V and A, I've got a meeting with a lawyer. I shouldn't be home any later than 10, and my mobile is on if you need to call. There's lasagne in the fridge – heat it up in the microwave for eight-plus minutes. I'll be back about 10. All my love, Mum'

I put the lasagne in the microwave and went upstairs with Amy, to change . . .

When Mum came home, she opened my bedroom door, poked her head in and then went off to bed.

7

That night, I couldn't sleep. The tossing and turning went on for hours.

2.11 a.m.

3.28 a.m.

4.04 a.m.

5.18 a.m.

'Oh, God: come on.'

The birds outside were awake and were making heaps of noise. I pressed two pillows to my head, one to each side, to cover both ears. Finally, I drifted off into the strangest dream . . .

I tossed and turned, dreaming that Dad's ute was stuck to a cliff, like a magnet stuck to the door of a fridge, and that Dad was sitting in the driver's seat. He had his hands on the steering wheel, and looked like he was driving: turning left and right and shifting the gears, even though the car wasn't moving.

I was standing in the car park above the cliff. Behind me, I could see a steep hill. And between me and the hill, I could see a sandbank. I called out to Dad, and waved to him: 'Get out of the car! Quick! The car's gonna drop!'

But he couldn't hear me – or if he could, he was ignoring me.

I saw waves pounding against the cliff, and chunks of rock crumbling and splashing hard into the ocean. 'Dad!' I yelled again . . . And then I realised why he couldn't hear: no matter how loud I yelled, nothing was coming out. 'Dad,' I continued yelling, 'get out of the car!'

But it was no use.

The waves were crashing higher and higher, almost to the point of touching the back tyre of the ute. Then the strangest thing happened: the ocean shrank back, until only sand remained, like in a desert. And that's when I saw the town – raised up out of the sand, where the water had been – like a huge sandcastle. A deep groove had formed in the sand where a river had twisted and turned: a horseshoe-shaped ridge, a general store . . . it was Yarra Valley! But the store was upside down in the pine plantation, and the pine trees were scattered everywhere, like pick-up sticks. I shouted and waved: 'Dad!' Again, my mouth was open but no sound was coming out . . .

Then, out of nowhere, a huge wave crashed against the cliff. The car park was too high up to get wet, but I was thrown back from the impact of the force. I fell down against the concrete . . . I rolled onto my side, to see whether I could see the ute – but it was gone: the ocean had sucked and swallowed it, and now there was nothing . . .

'Bumble!' I swore I heard someone calling out my nickname . . . And that's when I saw our house at Kew, sliding down the hill, heading straight towards me. I tried to get up, but my legs were wobbling, like they were made of jelly. Huge chunks of glass shot up into the air. My bedroom wall caved in . . . And then, *Crrrrrrrrrrrrrr!* The whole house screeched and skidded into the sandbank . . .

I could feel glass shattering all around me. Small pieces were stabbing into my skin. I screamed: '*Help! Stop it!!* STOOOOOOOOOOOOOP!'

Finally, it did.

'Bumble!' I heard again, and looked up. I could see Mum, Penny and Amy, standing in the upstairs part of the house, behind a triangle of glass that hadn't cracked. They were waving and yelling: 'Quick! *Hurry!*'

But I couldn't move: I was paralysed from the waist down – and even if I could've got up, I knew that once I'd scrambled up the bank, I wouldn't be able to tell them that Dad's ute had slipped and that Dad might've drowned.

Was I to blame for everything that'd gone wrong?

But Mum had given me a mobile phone, in case of an emergency. I could have called a rescue team: *STOOOOOOOOOOOOOP!*

'Mum! Penny! Amy!' I yelled. This time my voice shot out across the scene. I took my hands away from my eyes – but when I looked, the three of them were gone: there was only me . . . and somewhere, submerged deep beneath, thumping his fists against the windscreen, trying frantically – desperately – to break the glass, was Dad.

'Hoh,' I gasped, and sat up to wipe my wet forehead with my pyjama top. The clock beside my bed was ticking so loudly, I felt like it was inside my head.

5.53 a.m.

I rocked back and forth, slowly, catching my breath . . . waiting . . . wondering whether I'd ever stop feeling the pins and needles inside my arms and legs. I stood up and stamped my feet. I shook my arms above my head. Then I stepped out of the folds of my blanket.

Dad's old bedroom door was closed. I turned the handle, pushed the door open and switched on the light. The room was empty – Mum still used the study as her bedroom – except that some of Amy's colouring books and pencils were scattered across the floor.

I switched off the light – and stood there. This time, bad thoughts weren't pinging around inside my head; instead, my thoughts leapfrogged. *Dur: I'm such an idiot – Dad was the creep!* I knew that when I asked Penny about what I'd thought he'd done, she'd agree.

I changed out of my PJs and into casual clothes, happy to get out of wearing school uniform to the Biol excursion. I shoved my camera, my folio, a pen and a notebook into my backpack and crept down the stairs.

I sprinted all the way from our place in Kew to Charles Street in Richmond. When I got to the beginning of Charles Street, I slowed the pace to a jog. My breath was visible in the early-morning fog. I hadn't worked out whether I'd knock on the front door or try to guess which window was Penny's – but what if her window was too high up for me to reach?

I picked up a stone and stood in the middle of Charles Street, outside number 17. The upstairs front room was most probably Lisa's room. I jumped over the gutter to get out of a taxi's way as the driver headed towards me. He slowed down. I shook my head at him and stepped back towards the house, to let him know I hadn't ordered the cab.

He wound his window down. 'Are you 17?' he asked me.

'Seventeen Charles?' I asked back.

'That's it. Someone –' he tapped his clipboard – 'from 17 Charles phoned on a landline and ordered a cab.' He double-checked the monitoring device beside his steering wheel. 'That's the one.'

'I don't think so,' I replied. Then Lisa's front door opened. 'Hang on,' I told him.

A suitcase tumbled down the steps, followed by Penny's hessian shoulder bag and a tube of PVC pipe. I shoved my hands into the front pockets of my tracksuit. My breath puffed into the fog . . .

She got a shock when she saw me, and ran down the steps. 'How come you're here?' she asked. 'Is everything okay?'

I burst out crying. 'I know about Dad,' I said. 'He's been cheating on Mum.'

When she didn't say anything, I scuffed the toe of my right runner along the bottom step. I thought I knew what the secret was, but wasn't 100 per cent sure.

She turned to the driver. 'Give us a minute,' she said to him.

He put her things in the boot and waited in the car.

Tears were sliding down my face and plonking onto my tracksuit top. I wanted her to tell me I was wrong.

But she didn't. She bit her nails and then lit a cigarette. When she puffed on it, the air looked whiter from the smoke. 'Who told you?' she asked. And that's when I knew there was no hiding from the truth: Dad *was* cheating on Mum.

'*You* did,' I told her. 'You said something by the pool that day about whoever it was. You said her name – it was "Paully" or something – and how you'd known for years, and that Dad had made you not tell Mum you knew.'

She flicked her cigarette into the garden. 'Shit,' she said, and came over and gave me a hug. 'Are you alright?'

'No,' I said; 'I'm not – and if Mum knew, why'd she let Dad do it? And how come you guys kept it a secret?'

'Mum asked me not to tell you,' she explained.

'That's not fair!' I yelled. 'How long's Dad been doing it? You said "years". And I've been nice to him all that time – and because of that, I hate him now. He lied: he said it was a "break", not a "break-up". He said the "separate room" thing was only "temporary". And when he said that, he knew the whole time that he and Mum were getting a divorce – didn't he? I think it's disgusting . . . And now, what am I gonna say to Mum when I see her tonight?'

The cabbie wound the window down. 'Do you want the taxi?' he asked Penny.

She lifted her hand. '*Yes*: you can start the meter, if you want – don't get your Y-fronts in a knot.' She sat me down on the front step. 'Dad's a prick,' she said. 'I can't stand him. That's why I moved out. And I'm glad they're getting a divorce.'

I was glad too. 'Where are you running away to this time?' I asked her.

'I'm not.'

'What are the bags for, then?'

'It's my art stuff,' she said. 'I'm installing a sound-scape for the foyer of the uni library. I'll be back later tonight. You can come, if you want.'

'I've gotta go to school,' I said, and checked my watch. 'We're going to the zoo – there's this baby elephant –'

'Maybe you shouldn't go,' she said.

'But I want to.'

'She chewed on the inside of her cheeks. 'Okay. Look, why don't you come over on Sunday? Lisa's been wanting to invite you over – we could talk about it more then.'

'Yeah – okay,' I said.

'Will you be alright till then?' she asked.

I nodded my head. It felt good having the nice Penny back. 'Thanks,' I said.

She dropped me off at the tram stop. Before I got out of the taxi, she scribbled her mobile number on my hand. 'Call me if you need me,' she said, and gave me a reassuring smile.

I read the number back to myself, and then got out and waved . . .

The tram took ages. Three trams passed me going the other way, into the city, but none of them were going my way. I couldn't believe that Dad had been going on about "lack of parenting" and "absence": he was the one who'd said parents should be there for their kids. If I'd been a teacher and I'd had to give him a mark for 'family', I'd have written:

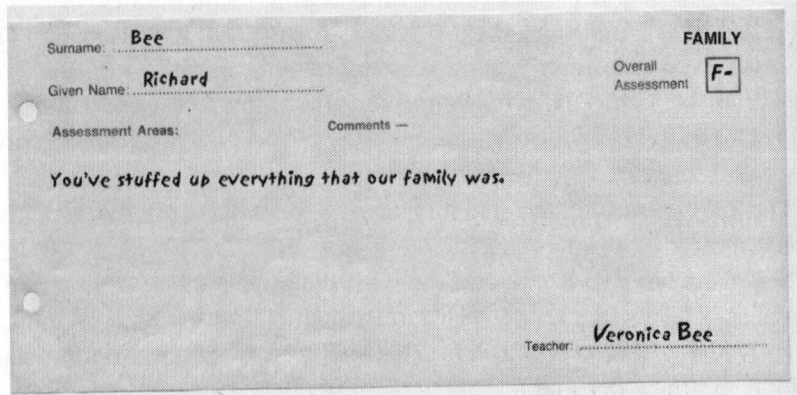

Surname: **Bee**

Given Name: **Richard**

FAMILY

Overall Assessment **F-**

Assessment Areas:　　　　Comments —

You've stuffed up everything that our family was.

Teacher: **Veronica Bee**

As I was getting off the tram, the excursion bus was turning out of the school's front entrance. I chased after it, but no one noticed me. It'd be two hours before Mum would be leaving for work. I didn't want to go home until she'd left: if I'd seen her, what would I have said?

I walked back, and sat down under the tram shelter. Rain splattered onto the concrete. I pulled my sleeves over my hands. The weather wasn't good enough to hang out at Paradise today, but there was always the library . . .

I went there and sat down in my usual place – the reading corner – and proceeded to hide behind a hardback copy of *The Macquarie Dictionary*. The librarian passed by a couple of times, but was too busy to notice me. During period three, Sister Frances came in to look something up on one of the computers – which happened to be right next to my reading corner. I held the book up so only the legs of my tracksuit were showing . . .

Sister Frances left when the recess bell rang, and most of the other girls left then as well. Seeing her reminded me of my locket and my lucky clover, and I thought about how I had three wishes left, and how I could wish to be as far away from Kew and all this crap as possible. Too bad I couldn't get my locket until the end of term, but maybe it was best to save the wishes, just in case – like, what if things got worse? . . .

'*Pssst.*'

I looked over the top of the *Macquarie*.

'Whatcha doing?' the student asked. It was Cas, the Chinese girl.

Isn't it obvious? I thought, and closed the dictionary. I chose not to say anything back.

'Are you okay?' she asked.

'Fine,' I replied, and held up the dictionary. 'I'm looking something up –'

'What?' she asked, enthusiastically.

Talk about nosey! 'Pagan,' I answered.

'"Pagan"!' She laughed out loud.

'*Sshh!*' The librarian gave us a look of warning to cut it out.

Cas came over to me. 'A pagan's a heathen,' she said.

We'd never really talked before, although she'd waved now and then. I'd seen her carrying a guitar case, and on it she'd stuck magazine cut-outs and stickers of pop and rock bands. She didn't hang out with the 'Chingas' – the other Chinese girls; she hung out with Sam Porcello.

'A heathen's someone who doesn't believe in God,' she told me. 'You know: like people in cults. How come?' She spoke so fast I barely had time to process what she'd said.

I closed the *Macquarie* and put it on the floor, to give myself time to think. 'I guess my sister's a pagan,' I remarked. I'd seen 'pagan' written on one of the photos in Penny's room – it was the only word written in English.

'*Doo-doo-doo-doo.*' Cas hummed the theme from *The Twilight Zone* and wiggled her fingers. 'I'd love to be in a cult,' she said. 'I wouldn't do the blood-sacrifice stuff – no way. But I'd do the other stuff – you know: like dancing on the top of a hill when it's a full moon, making music with drums and sticks.' She sat on the beanbag beside mine. 'I've seen you in the library,' she said. 'Actually, I've seen you in here a lot. Don't get me wrong: if I've seen you, that means I'm here a lot too – and *I'm* not a nerd . . . So, whatcha doing?' She seemed to speak everything she thought – it was kinda funny.

'I'm working on an assignment.' I went for an outright lie.

'Your IRP?' she asked, looking at the folio on which 'IRP' was written, lying on the floor, beside the dictionary.

'*Um* . . . yeah,' I said, scratching my ankle, even though I didn't have an itch.

'Can I've a look?' she asked, and grabbed the folio before I had the chance to say no. 'Wow! They're really good!' she said, and turned another page. 'Did *you* take them? How'd you do *that*?' She was pointing at the collage.

'Mmm. In Photoshop.'

'I wouldn't even have a clue how to do that,' she admitted. 'They're fantastic . . . Is that your mum?'

I nodded. 'And that's my sister Penny – the pagan!'

She held the folio closer to her face. 'Yep,' she said: 'she dresses like the drummer in *Aniseed* – and *they're* into cults.'

'Mmm,' I said in response.

She twisted one of the gelled spikes of her short, brown hair. 'I'm recording a song for my IRP,' she said. 'It's meant to be *a* song, but it's turned into an *album*. Once I'd started, I just couldn't stop. Lagilla's got *the* best recording studio – that's why I'm going to school here; I won a music scholarship: not a Junior Burger, but a Big Mac. I can't believe how lucky I was. SS called the principal of Weddell High, which is the school I went to before here, and she asked me to try out. She'd heard me play at a concert. Weddell's music resources aren't too good, so I thought, *Why not?* Mum was so excited. We're not poor, but we're not rich either. Mum and Dad get a lot of people eating at their restaurant. But I've got two brothers, so we'd have to feed the whole of Melbourne for an entire year to be able to afford for the three of us to go to a school like this.'

'What do you mean by a "Big Mac"?' I asked her.

She tapped her forehead: 'Sorry – there's two types of scholarships. A Big Mac's a full scholarship,' she explained. 'And a Junior Burger's a half scholarship. I'm a Big Mac, which means all my expenses are paid.' She looked at her watch. 'I was gonna ask –' she stood up and grabbed her guitar case – 'do you wanna hang out at lunchtime? Sam's on lunch-order duty this week. Do you know Sam Porcello?'

I nodded. I knew her from class.

'Remember when Sam ate that note?' she asked. 'We were writing to each other, and Sister Frances tried to take it from us, and Sam ate it before sister could take it. Because of *that*, Sam has to do lunch-order duty for the rest of the week. And get this: Sam can't stand Debbie Forshaw, and they have to do lunch-order duty together.'

'What did Debbie do?' I asked, suddenly interested.

'She got into trouble for lying about the hedge burners: she said Anthea Tsouracus's cousin was one of them – and Debbie dobbed *him* into her Dad, and her Dad's a QC, and they were gonna press charges.'

'Was *that* what Anthea and Debbie were fighting about that day by the oval?'

'Yes,' she said excitedly. 'Did you see it? I was at guitar practice. But Sam told me all about it.' The bell rang. We looked at our watches at the same time. 'So, wanna hang out?' she asked me again.

'Ah . . .' I began. *If Sister Frances catches me walking around in casual clothes,* I thought, *I'll be in huge trouble.* I shook my head. 'No thanks,' I said.

'What about lunchtime tomorrow, then?' she asked. 'Do you wanna meet up at the bottom of the music-hall stairwell?'

'Ah, well: I've actually – well, I'm kind of busy.' I didn't want to tell her I was going to the airport 'cause then I'd have to explain about Susie.

'How about Thursday lunch, then?' she suggested. 'Go on! Sam gets to ride the service lift, in the nun's old dormitory, when she takes the food trolley to the different floors. I'm gonna meet her, before the lunch bell rings. I've got a free fifth. It'll be *so* cool: it's one of those old lifts, with the pull-down door. I know you've got a free fifth – I've seen you in the library.'

Talk about persistent, alright. 'Okay,' I said.

'Cool! See you then – sorry: I've gotta go! I've booked the studio.' Then she moved off. 'I'm Cas, by the way.'

'Veronica,' I said, and gave a little wave.

'Yeah, I know,' she called over her shoulder, and walked quickly out the door.

I put the *Macquarie* away and ran the whole way home. While I was watching TV, I found that the photo of the family, staring down at me from the mantelpiece, was giving me the creeps. I went into the kitchen and grabbed the scissors from the drawer. Then I went around the house and cut Dad's head out of *all* the photos.

Later on, I picked Amy up from school. When Mum came home, she didn't say anything about me not going to class, whether SS had called, or about the evidence that Dad's head had been cut out of all the family photos.

I went to bed early and set my alarm clock.

Rain bucketed down. Then came hailstones the size of Kool Mints that made the Tullamarine Freeway look like it was covered in snow.

'Don't worry,' Mum assured me. 'We won't be late: there's no way they'd allow a plane to take off in this weather.'

Our car lurched forward, along with the other trillion vehicles in the bumper-to-bumper, airport-bound traffic. I wanted to say something about Dad, but didn't want to yell above the hailstorm. As we turned off at the airport exit, the hailing stopped. 'Hey, Mum, I've been over to Lisa's,' I announced.

She didn't say anything. She had a puzzled look on her face.

'So don't go hiding anything,' I continued: 'I know about Dad, and I'm glad you're getting a divorce – I think it's disgusting he's seeing someone.'

She pulled up beside the boom gate, rested her arm on the head of my seat and stared across at the scene confronting us. The driver behind us beeped her horn. 'Can you grab some change?' Mum asked me. 'My wallet's next to your feet.'

When we'd parked, Mum held me back from getting out. 'Are you okay?' she asked.

'I'm never staying at his place again,' I said. 'I don't care who she is – I never want to meet her. And I can't believe Dad chose *her* over us: I thought *we* were his family. And how come you never told me?'

'Veronica,' she began, 'when we were living at Yarra Valley, I didn't want you to know. I was hoping your father would stop seeing her, and that he and I could keep it a secret –'

'Why do adults have so many secrets?'

'Well: sometimes adults do have secrets, or rather, sometimes not everything needs to be told. I was protecting you. I didn't think it would come to this. I'm sorry – I know it hurts. It hurts everyone, I'm still seeing the counsellor – and now that you know, I think you should talk to one as well; Penny's seeing a nice lady – she's –'

'No!' I cut in. 'There's nothing wrong with me – I'm not a nutcase.'

'I'm not saying you are,' she said. 'A counsellor would help you talk about your father and the divorce. It's a time, and a place, for you to talk about how you're feeling.'

'You can't make me,' I said. 'Let go of my arm. We have to go now, or we'll miss Suze's plane.'

I jumped out and walked ahead, in the direction of the departure lounge.

Once inside, I didn't know where to go. Mum caught up to me, read the flight monitor and worked out we had to go to Gate 3.

Suze spotted us and ran over. 'My flight's delayed,' she said. For her, that was a bummer.

For me, though, it was great news: 'Maybe it'll be delayed forever,' I said.

'It'd better not be,' she replied, widening her eyes.

Her Mum waved us over to a lounge chair. 'We're over here!' she called to us.

'Hi, Jeanie,' Mum said to her, and went over and kissed her on the cheek.

Jeanie's eyes were red. 'My little girl's leaving me,' she said.

'They grow up fast, don't they?' Mum said.

Suze and I rolled our eyes.

The four of us talked for a while, and watched through the window as the attendants loaded the bags onto the plane. I didn't ask where Morris was, but I wasn't surprised that he wasn't there: he'd never gone to Suze's school or pony-club stuff, unlike the other dads.

'There's the food,' Mum said, pointing at a silver trolley being loaded onto the plane.

I stood up and grabbed Suze by the hand: I wanted to spend some time alone with her, without our mums.

'Don't go too far!' Jeanie called out to us.

We hung out at the far end of the departure lounge and pressed our faces against the window. Sixteen planes were lined up at the end of the runway. The tarmac was flooded from the rain. Suze puffed on to the glass, and leant back and drew a smiley face on it.

I changed the smile into a frown.

'Von wanted to come to the airport,' she admitted. 'But I said no: I just wanted it to be you and me.'

'Thanks,' I said. I'd promised myself I wouldn't cry. I tried thinking about happy stuff, but couldn't help blurting out, 'Suze, I'm sorry.' I wiped a tear from my right eye. 'It's just –'

She gave me a hug.

I couldn't hold it in any longer. 'Why do you have to go *now*?' I asked.

'My new school starts next week,' she explained; 'I don't want to miss out.'

'I don't mean like *that*,' I said. 'What I mean is I saw Penny yesterday, and she told me Dad was seeing this other woman – that's what the secret was.'

'Yikes – are you for real?' She stepped back. Her jaw dropped.

'It wasn't just because of the fire,' I said. 'And now Mum says I have to see a counsellor.'

'You don't *have* to,' she said: 'just say no.'

'I did say no – I don't want to talk to someone I don't know; I'd rather talk to you. Do you *have* to go?'

'Vee, we can write emails and talk on the phone.'

'It's not the same,' I said.

She grabbed me by the shoulders. 'You know that day we were meant to meet up at the Igloo? And how you didn't come?'

'It wasn't my fault – I told you –'

'Yeah: Cabcharge fiasco – I know; I know,' she said. 'But you know how Mum says gifts are wrapped in strange packaging? Well, that's what that day was for me. I sat in the paddock for ages, and thought about everything. I thought about you, me, Mum, Morris, Steve, and how I wanted to ride in the Olympics. Then I went back and told Mum how unhappy I was. So we talked about stuff. And after a while, we came up with the idea of me living with Nan . . . So if that day hadn't happened, I wouldn't be here – *doi*! Vee, maybe *this* is like a gift in strange packaging for you. Now I'm gonna live overseas, you never know what's gonna happen to you.' She took a parcel from her bag. 'I made you a present – go on: open it,' she said, placing it in my hands.

I fiddled with the bow and managed to force a smile.

'Come on!' she said, and pulled the wrapping paper back. 'I'll have lived in England for a *year* by the time you've opened it.'

Inside the wrapping was a snow dome. I shook it, and the snowflakes fluttered to the ground. Miniature horses were glued to the base. They galloped around a framed photo of Suze and me. 'Thanks,' I said. 'How'd you get the photo in?'

'Magic,' she said, and rolled her eyes.

I gave her a hug, and then – before I had a chance to stop myself – I gave her a huge kiss on the lips. She was my best-est friend and I was going to miss her so much. It wasn't a lover's kiss; it was a friendship kiss. Suze stepped back and then both of us couldn't stop laughing. 'But I didn't get *you* anything,' I said, wiping the tears of laughter from the corner of my eye. 'Oh, Suze, don't go – or can't I go with you?'

'Maybe you could visit,' she said.

'That's like *the* best-est idea!'

We ran over and asked our mums if I could visit Suze overseas.

'Can I?' I asked Mum. 'Can I? *Can I?*'

Mum gave Jeanie a look of uncertainty.

'I could work weekends at Lisa's flower shop,' I begged. 'And save up heaps of money. Come on, Mum! You know I would. I picked apples and saved enough money to pay for half of my saddle.'

'We'll see,' she offered, and smoothed a crease from her top.

Suze and I jumped up and down together: to us, "we'll see" sounded like a yes.

Over the PA, passengers were advised that Flight QF 193 was now boarding. The four of us jumped up out of our seats. Suze hugged me, her mum and my mum, and then hugged her own mum a second, third and fourth time. I'd brought my camera, so Mum took photos of the two of us striking silly poses and then a couple of serious ones. Then our mums left us alone so we could say our final goodbyes.

'If you don't ride in the Olympics,' I said to her, 'I'll come over and give you a big kick up the bum!'

'Oh, yeah,' she threatened. 'I'll kick your bum even harder if *you* don't.'

'Yeah, but truly, I'll miss you,' I said. 'You're my best-est buddy.'

'Same, blood sis,' she said. 'Always and forever.'

We hooked pinkies and shook on it.

Then she and her mum spent one last minute on their own. It was weird how Suze was so excited about her life and I was bummed out about mine. I waved one last time, as the sliding door to the walkway closed.

We stood by the window and watched the plane taxi down the runway. Then:

She was gone.

Absentmindedly, I pressed my lips against the window, and blew out a breath. The pressure resulted in a *huge* fart noise. Heaps of people turned around to see who the rude person was. Mum was horrified, but Jeanie laughed – which made my mum laugh. The three of us ended up laughing, hugging, crying and laughing again as we walked back to the car park.

Jeanie walked us to our car. 'Thanks for coming,' she said.

I showed her and Mum the snow dome.

'It's beautiful,' Mum admired.

Compared to some of the presents Suze had made me – like the rock with the painted pebbles of the cricket-pitch chicks stuck on it, having an orgy – it *was* great. 'I told Suze I'd send her a photo,' I said. 'Maybe I could make a collage out of the ones we took today.'

'She'd love that,' Jeanie said. 'And if you happen to have a spare copy, I'd love you to send me one, too.'

'Sure,' I said. 'I'll email the file when I've finished.'

Mum beeped the horn as we drove off.

'Can I fly over and visit Suze?' I asked her. '*Please*, Mum.'

'We'll see,' she said. 'We'd have to ask your father.'

'What's he got to do with it?'

'He'd have to help pay.'

'Forget it,' I said; 'I'd rather save up the money myself.'

'Does that mean you don't want him to contribute towards your schooling, your clothes, your health insurance, the roof over your head, the horses?' she asked.

Nothing seemed fair, I thought. I crossed my arms and stared out the window.

'I've taken the day off work,' Mum announced: 'we could drive to Yarra Valley and visit the horses, if you'd like.'

'Are you for real?!' I said. 'What about school? *Oops.*' I clapped my left hand over my mouth.

Mum smiled. 'I don't think one day would set you back too much.'

'Wicked,' I said. 'Can I go for a ride? I can ride in my jeans, and I've got boots on – and my gear's in the shed.'

'I'll drop you off at the holding yard,' she said, 'which gives me a chance to catch up with the Wilsons. Then I'll read the paper and have a coffee at the general store. That'll give you – let's see – at least a couple of hours.'

'Yeah.' I hadn't felt this happy for a long time. 'Thanks, Mum.'

We took the Ring Road turn-off. The drive took exactly 56 minutes.

I couldn't wait to get out of the car. The rain had stopped, and the sun was peeking through a break in the clouds; they were dark grey and sitting low over the ridge. The spur was covered in mist. Just in case more rain was on the way, again, I put on my Drizabone. The autumn leaves crunched under my boots as Mum and I walked towards the holding yard . . .

Eb looked great – his dark coat was wet from the rain, and shone like black satin. But I was right about the photo Cathy had sent: Maje *had* lost weight.

'Maybe it's old age,' Mum suggested.

'Dunno – I hope nothing's wrong.'

She gently rubbed my shoulders. 'He looks happy enough. And he *is* eating grass – so it's not as if he's gone off his food.'

'I guess,' I said, and called out to them: '*Eeeeeb! Maaajor!*'

Eb's head shot up, and the whites of his eyeballs flashed. Maje turned and whinnied.

'*Eeeeeb! Maaaje!* Come on!'

They ran when I blew my whistle.

Months had passed since I'd last seen them. I jumped down from the top rail and ran into the yard. Eb nipped Maje on the bum as they circled around me. I could've run circles around them. They hadn't forgotten me.

'Whoa!' I said. 'There's a boy!'

They skidded to a halt.

'Hey, there! Look at you!' I fussed, and wiped the mud from Maje's coat. 'Dirty *as*, hey? Whatcha been up to?'

Mum called out to me: 'They look good, don't they?'

I waved back. My eyes started stinging from the tears that had been welling up in them. I hugged Eb and buried my face in his mane. 'You been a good boy?' I asked him. 'Miss me? *Hey*? I miss you, too.'

They nipped and nudged me.

'Come on,' I said, but I had to push them apart to stop them from fighting for my attention. 'I love you *both* just as much.'

Mum went off to talk to the Wilsons while I gave my boys a brush, oiled my saddle and cleaned the trough. I still had plenty of time for a ride . . .

It didn't seem fair to leave Maje behind, but I couldn't ride two horses at the same time. Maje neighed, and trotted back and forth along the fence of the holding yard till Eb and I were out of sight. I'd left him a biscuit of hay so he'd have a treat to munch on while we were gone.

We cut across the Gibbses' and then cantered around Neilson's Reservoir. Over the hill towards the Hendersons', I could see that the apple trees in the family's' orchard had lost their leaves. We cantered down the hill and then turned left and right around the tree trunks, like we did in flag and pole races at pony club. The smell of the damp leaves on the ground reminded me of the cinnamon smell of Dad's pancakes. I rode on past the Hendersons', taking the track that zigzagged to the top of the ridge. When we got to the highest point, I stopped and looked out: the vineyard leaves were various shades of yellow, red, orange and green; and emerald green river grass bordered the chocolate brown potato fields.

Eb pricked up his ears when he saw a rabbit hop past. We bolted after it and followed it till it managed to disappear inside a log. The scrub on the other side of the log looked level enough, so I kicked Eb on. He jumped the log and scrambled down the spur, towards home.

We had to pass Nick's place. No goths were out the front, but I could see a pile of burnt wood in the paddock, where they must have had a bonfire. And some mud bricks were lined up, like Freako was planning to build an extension onto his house, or maybe even build a second house. Someone screamed, and then the front door of the house swung wide and banged against the wall. A girl – about my age – came running out. I didn't recognise her as one of Penny's goth friends because her skin wasn't covered in tattoos and her hair was naturally brown rather than dyed. Following behind the girl was Nick – they were playing a game of chase. I slowed Eb to a walk, so I could take a better look. *Yikes!* The girl was Karen Tools – the leader of the cricket-pitch chicks – and her shirt was ripped at the shoulder. Nick wrestled Karen to the ground and pinned her shoulders down, then poured wine from an opened bottle into her mouth.

Eb pranced, but I reined him back to make sure that Karen *was* okay. She was kicking her legs and trying to buck Nick off from on top of her. Karen spat the wine onto Nick's face then laughed like she was enjoying herself. Nick took a swig from the bottle, then leant over and dribbled the wine, from his mouth, into her mouth, and then leant closer and kissed her. *Gross*, I thought, *I always knew Nick was a creep*. Whatever *was* going on, there was no way I was ever going to mention *that* to Penny. She wouldn't believe me, plus I didn't want to hurt her – that certainly wasn't what I'd want my boyfriend to be doing! Hopefully, soon enough, Penny'd figure it out for herself.

I kicked Eb on and cantered off without a backward glance.

Mum waved when she saw us coming. I could see she'd bought the horses a bag of apples – Pink Ladies: yum! – and she was holding one of them up to show me. She had no idea Maje was behind her and that he was stretching his neck over the top rail. Most of the pony-club mums, Suze's included, were confident around horses and rode them as well, but not mine: she freaked when Maje cheekily decided the apple was his and pinched it from her hand. I laughed out loud.

Mum stood with her back against the wall of the shed keeping a safe distance. 'Good ride?' she asked.

'Wicked! Eb had heaps of go in him.' I brushed Eb and Maje down and checked their hooves for stones. Then I put my saddle in the shed. As I was walking out, I stopped and grabbed my diary from the box by the door. I had this idea of scanning some of the entries I'd written, and then cutting and pasting the words into my IRP.

'How's Maje?' Mum asked, stepping sideways to stand beside me by the gate.

We watched as he chewed contentedly on the Pink Lady, the juice frothing at the corner of his mouth.

'He seems okay,' I replied. 'Maybe he's lost weight 'cause it's almost winter.'

'Winter!' Mum said, and shook her head. 'Is *that* all? It seems like five years since the move, not five months.'

I rolled the rest of the apples into the horses' yard. Some of the larger ones were too big, so I stomped them in half so the horses would be able to chew them more easily – they didn't mind about dirt.

'Maybe we could find some agistment closer to the city,' Mum suggested. 'The Board of Works leases paddocks along the Yarra river; I think there's some in Ivanhoe – which is only a bus ride from Kew.'

I leant back against Eb's left shoulder. 'We're never moving back, are we?' I just knew it.

'Honestly,' was all she said in response – she didn't have to say no: I knew. 'But I doubt your father would ever sell the property.'

It didn't matter now, anyway: even if Dad did move back I wouldn't live with him, and Suze had moved overseas.

'I can understand you're angry,' she went on. 'Sometimes life doesn't seem fair – but you have to go on.'

'Mum! Nothing changes what Dad did.' Why did I have to state the obvious – especially to her?

'You're right,' she answered, 'and it's okay to be mad – but you can't be mad forever.'

'Can we not talk about it, please?' I asked. 'I'm here with the horses, and I don't want to wreck my day.'

'Fine,' she said; 'I understand.'

As we were driving back along the Eastern Freeway, she asked me whether I'd thought any more about seeing a counsellor.

'No,' I replied. 'And don't ask me again.'

'I'm a little worried,' she went on, and changed lanes to get off the freeway at the next exit. 'I've seen the photos around the house.' Then she started to laugh, but stopped herself. 'Hr-hrm. I'm sorry,' she said: 'there were times I could've cut your father out of those photos as well.'

I felt weird: my mother was talking to me like I was an adult. 'Are the paddocks nice?' I asked her.

'The what?' She'd forgotten about her own suggestion.

'The paddocks at the Board of Works, where we could agist the horses?' I reminded her.

'Oh,' she replied, but was obviously lost in another world. 'Yes: Jeanie said they were very nice – and there's a pony club there too.'

'Well,' I said, 'I've thought about it – and I think it's a great idea.'

'There might be a waiting list,' she added. 'But I'll call and find out, when we get home.'

That night, I opened my diary to a blank page and wrote:

I haven't written for ages. Susie's gone to live with her Nan. I'm not mad at Mum. I'm mad at Dad. And the more I think about moving the horses to Ivanhoe, the more I like it. Mum's put my name on the waiting list.

I think it's disgusting that Dad's cheating on Mum. I've always thought Dad was cool. But now I can't stand him. I don't know who SHE is, but I think she's disgusting. And I thought SCHOOL sucked!

Opinion Poll

Tick who I'd rather spend time with

☑ SS (Sister Cecilia)

☐ or Dad

I'm meeting up with a girl called Cas tomorrow. I'm not really looking forward to it. But I guess she's NOT Debbie Forshaw.

Anyways, gotta go. Way tired.
See ya
XO Vee

I closed the diary and pulled the doona around my face. *The plane's prob'ly in England now,* I thought. I shook the snow dome and watched the flakes flutter down. The horses inside it bucked and kicked. I fell asleep before the flakes had settled on the ground.

1

I met Cas at the bottom of the music-hall stairwell.

'I left my guitar in the studio,' she said; 'saves me carrying it. I told Sam we'd meet her at 11.55 – oh: it's 11.55 *now!*'

We sprinted across the lawn between the music hall and the sporting complex. As Cas ran around the corner, she bumped into Father Curry. 'Whoops!' she said to him. 'Sorry, father.'

I ran past. 'Whoa! Sorry!'

'Always in a hurry, you young ones,' he called after us.

We ran up the steps to the administration-building entrance. Once we were inside the building, we could hear our shoes squeaking down the corridor: past the admin office, sickbay, the lounge, the student–teacher conference room, and SS's office. But rather than go straight ahead – through the double doors leading into the chapel – we turned right, ignored the 'NO ENTRY' sign and climbed up the narrow staircase in front of us.

We passed the first level, where Year 7 and Year 8 classes were held, and then the second level, where Year 9 and Year 10 classes were held, and finally the third level, where Year 11 and Year 12 classes were held.

'Cas,' I said to her, as softly as I could, considering how fast my heart was racing.

'*Sshh!*' she whispered. 'This is the nuns' old dormitory.'

'But Cas, what about Debbie?' I asked. 'She'll say something if she sees us.'

'Nah,' she replied; 'they take it in turns. Sam's delivering the lunch orders today – and Debbie's helping out in the kitchen.' She led the way down a narrow hall. Along each side of it, doors led off to tiny rooms. Some of the rooms were empty; some had a bed and chest of drawers. 'The nuns used to sleep here,' Cas explained, 'before they built the retirement home. They say it's haunted.'

I could feel a chill go up my spine. 'They look like prison cells,' I said.

We turned left down another hall . . . more rooms. One of them had a music stand in the middle of it and chairs lined up against its walls.

'Before they built the music hall,' Cas explained as part of her guided tour, 'they used these for lessons.' She made the hooting sound of an owl, and the echo bounced off the walls. 'How bad are the acoustics?!' she observed. 'I'd never have accepted a scholarship if my lessons were in here; this is way worse than Weddell High.'

We came to a door at the end of the hall, and Cas turned its handle. '*Sshh!*' She pointed her thumb backwards over her shoulder, for us to back away.

I nodded in response: I'd heard the strange noise as well.

'Hang on,' she said, and grabbed my right arm.

Then we heard another noise, but instead of a thud, it sounded like laughter.

Cas opened the door, just a crack. 'Sam, is that you?' she asked.

'Cas!' Yes, it was Sam, and she threw the door open. 'Check this out!' she said to us, and kicked up her legs into a handstand. One of the walls had heaps of black marks on it, where her shoes had hit. She let her uniform drop over her head. I couldn't help but notice she was wearing bike shorts rather than undies.

'Sam, *you're crazy!*' Cas whispered to her friend.

Sam lowered her legs, came closer and faced Cas. 'You don't have to whisper!' she yelled. And then, turning to me, '*Oi!* I know you: You're that chick from Thoroughgrove – 'VB', like the beer. I know your sister Penny: talk about a bad-arse; we had a tonne of detentions together last year. I'm Sam – you gotta try this: it's shit-hot fun.' She took her shoes off, sprinted down the hall and slid 10 metres in her socks. 'I got as far as *here* last time!' she yelled back to us, and motioned for us to join her.

Cas pushed me forward. 'Why me?' I asked.

'*Because*,' she said, 'you guys are gonna have to catch *me* when I fall!'

I took my shoes off and gave it my best shot . . . I passed Sam's mark. She gave me the thumbs up. 'VB! Not bad!' she yelled.

I didn't like the nickname, but I wasn't about to tell her that: she was taller than me, and a lot stronger. I'd read in the newsletter that she was a wicked rower, which was probably why she had blisters on her hands. Even though she was Italian, her curly, dark hair wasn't gelled up like the Wogs' – it was pulled back, loosely, into a ponytail.

'Cas, come on!' Sam yelled.

Copying Sam, I flapped my elbows as if I had chicken wings.

'*Beurk*! *Beurk*!' Sam squawked.

Cas gave in, and joined us in the on-the-spot chicken dance. Then she ran down the hall in an awkward style. She wasn't a natural athlete: her elbows stuck out and her knees jerked up to her chest. She went for the big slide . . . and only got as far as *three* metres.

'*That* was shithouse!' Sam remarked.

I tried my best to hold my laughter in.

However, Cas heard me snorting: 'I'd like to hear *you* play the guitar,' she said.

'I guess I'd be pretty crap,' I admitted.

'*Oi*, I'd like to hear Cas play a country-and-western song,' Sam said, 'to go with her barn-dance running style.'

Sam and I cracked up.

'Are you done?' Cas asked us, pretending she was cut. 'And anyway, aren't we here to ride the lift?' She led us back to the lunch-order food trolley, which was standing beside the lift.

'Anyone hungry?' Sam asked.

Cas's jaw dropped. 'You can't *eat* the food!' she said, nervously. 'Don't! Sam!'

'Says who?' Sam dared. She tore open a paper bag and took out a Mars Bar. She tore the wrapper and took a huge bite.

Cas squealed.

'*Mmm*, yeah!' Sam was egging her on, taking another bite and smearing some of the chocolate around her mouth. 'I didn't do it, SS!' she protested, pretending she'd been caught. 'I promise: I wouldn't steal – I swear on the Holy Bible.' She shoved the rest of the bar into her mouth and chewed.

We heard the lift door clunk. Cas grabbed my arm: it was okay for Sam to be there, but Cas and I were definitely out of bounds.

Sam opened the door of the fire-hose storage box. 'Quick: shit!' she said. 'Hide in here!'

'We won't fit,' Cas squealed. She was panicking, jumping around on the spot.

'Bloody oath, you will,' Sam ordered, and pushed both of us into the box . . .

It was dark in there. I heard the lift door open, and then Sam talking to someone.

Cas whispered to me, 'Sam's still got chocolate smeared all over her face!'

We held in a giggle.

We heard footsteps go past the storage box. Sam and whoever it was talked some more, and after a minute or so, everything went dead quiet. Cas squirmed, and jabbed her elbow into my rib.

'Ouch!' I said, and poked her back.

The door of the box flew open.

'Coast clear!' Sam yelled to us.

I don't know about Cas, but I had nearly crapped my pants.

'It was that Katherine Cook chick,' Sam explained, pointing to the second food trolley, which was standing beside the lunch-order trolley; 'you know: that crazy chick who's repeating Year 8? She's coming back – in a minute. She takes the lunches to the nuns in the retirement home. Can you believe? She volunteers to do it every day – talk about a suck!'

We climbed out and checked out the other trolley: instead of paper bags, it had plates with metal lids on them.

Sam lifted one of the lids and studied the sandwiches, like a scientist in a laboratory. 'Mmm,' she said: 'cucumber sandwiches.'

'No; *no* – Sam, *don't*!' Cas pleaded, and pulled her back.

'Relax,' Sam said: 'I just wanna mix it up a bit.' She grabbed a paper bag from the lunch-order trolley and took out a pie. 'Sister Goddard would be most delighted to dine on the traditional beef pie – Four 'n' Twenty, of course – accompanied with a drizzle of delectable tomato sauce.' She swapped the pie with the sandwich. 'Ah, Sister Bermesda: a Big M for you today, a bag of popcorn *and* a Mars Bar.'

The thought of it was too funny. Sam made us form a production line so we could quickly swap the lunches from one trolley to the other. I couldn't believe we were doing it: if we got caught, we'd be in huge trouble . . .

When we were done, we wheeled the lunch-order trolley into the lift and somehow managed to cram ourselves in as well. The lift clunked and whirred down to ground level.

When the lift door opened, I fell backwards, and Cas flopped onto the ground beside me. We were both spreadeagled, in the middle of the hallway, laughing so hard I nearly peed my pants.

'See you lunchtime,' Sam said, and passed us each a Big M.

'I'm not taking *that*!' Cas said and passed hers back.

I was about to give mine back too, but Sam called out, 'Wuss!'

'Alright,' I said; 'give us a coffee scroll as well.'

'You are dead cool,' Sam praised, and passed me two donuts and a coffee scroll. 'Here: and this!' she added, and tossed me a sausage roll.

'Thanks,' I said. 'See ya.'

We waved to her as the lift door closed. Then snuck off down the hall, turned into the corridor . . . and ran – *smack-bang*! – straight into SS.

Cas's donut rolled across the floor.

'I *beg* your *pardon*!' sister said. 'Miss Bee and Miss Chen, shouldn't you be in class – and what is this, eating indoors?'

'Ah . . .' was all I could think to say.

'Yes, Miss Bee?' she asked. 'I don't have all day: is there something you'd like to say?'

'Ah . . .' again.

'I thought as much! Pick up that rubbish – then, outside my office, thank you. I'll be along shortly. Actually, Cassandra, you come with me: I'd rather you two were separated – that would *certainly* eliminate any attempt to concoct a story as to your whereabouts.'

I found myself sitting in the chair opposite SS's desk. The curtains were closed, and the only light was from the desk lamp. And because the lampshade was green, SS looked a bit like ET. Heaps of books were on the shelves. And there was a weird smell, kind of like lentils – like the dhal Mum occasionally made.

SS wrote notes as I tried to answer her questions convincingly. 'And *where* exactly *were* you coming from?' she asked.

'Well,' I began, 'I don't know – I was lost . . . and then I saw Cas –'

'We've been over *that*,' she cut in. 'Very well: that will be sufficient, but certainly not the end. Take a seat in the corridor and ask Miss Chen to come in.'

As I passed Cas outside, I whispered to her, 'We were lost; you found me –'

'Miss Bee!' SS glared from behind her desk. 'Bite your tongue: you're in enough trouble as it is!'

Half an hour passed by. I could picture Cas, crying and admitting to everything; SS's notes stacking up, the pile of paper in front of her getting as thick as the *Macquarie Dictionary*. *Bugger*! I thought: *Mum's gonna kill me*! I couldn't afford to get another detention. That morning, Mum had said she'd take my name off the Board of Works waiting list if I got into trouble once more – and that meant *not* wearing runners, handing in all my homework, and definitely *not* being sprung out of bounds . . .

Ten more minutes went by. Finally, Sister Frances came strutting down the hall, Sam beside her. My stomach was churning: if SS didn't already know what had happened, she was about to put two and two together and cotton on to our lunch-order scam . . . Mum was probably gonna *sell* the horses now.

SS answered the door when Sister Frances knocked. The two nuns then stood to one side of the corridor and whispered between themselves. Then SS ordered the three of us girls to sit in separate corners of the student–teacher conference room. The two of them then stood at the door and began whispering again, shook their heads, tut-tutted and started whispering all over again.

Another nun then appeared at the door. I didn't recognise her, or the girl who was standing beside her.

'Miss Katherine Cook!' SS exclaimed, and ordered the girl into the conference room. 'Now *that is* a disappointment,' she remarked. 'Take a seat in the far corner. Hurry along – and not a peep.'

The three nuns whispered among themselves, and raised their palms.

SS tut-tutted again, and turned and pointed at Sam. 'Very well,' she said to the other two nuns, and then dismissed them. She turned around, entered the conference room and closed the door. 'Samantha Porcello, Veronica Bee, Cassandra Chen and Katherine Cook!' She looked at each of us in turn. 'Quite the dire situation, isn't it? I am assured your parents will be as suitably unimpressed as I am when they hear the grave report of today's adventures. Lunch orders certainly do not get muddled up on their own.' She paced the room. 'Samantha Porcello: you are a continuous exasperation to the Sisters of Lagilla. It seems a week of lunch-order duty has had no impact. We are exhausted by your pirating ways. I believed your conduct would radically improve as a result of Amanda Reilly's move to Perth – she was quite the troublemaker; however, it seems your constant rebellion is an ingrained trait. We do not accommodate ringleaders – it leaves a principal with only *one* choice.' She took a deep breath before continuing with the dressing down. 'Veronica Bee,' she announced, shaking her head: 'a self-conducted guided tour of Lagilla Convent might be the way of the bush; however, your walkabout ways are not welcome within my historically classified establishment. The Code of Conduct is printed at the front of your diary for a purpose – are you aware it is your duty to read and memorise those rules?'

I nodded.

'I thought as much,' she said: 'as wayward as several other members of the Bee family.' She tut-tutted again, and moved on. 'Cassandra Chen: if it were not for the charity of your music scholarship, I imagine your parents would be "paying through the nose" to afford the privilege of having their daughter attend a school of such standing – lest you forget. This is your first year of many at Lagilla Convent. Let it be said that a waltz through life will advance a young girl only as far as the dance floor. I firmly advise that you address your ways sooner than later.' Finally, she turned to the other girl. 'Katherine Cook: Well, I *am* surprised! What will your grandmother say?'

Katherine, to our surprise, spoke up. 'Sister Therese Cecilia, . . .'

'Yes, Miss Cook?' came the response.

'Could I have a word with you in private?'

SS took off her glasses and folded their arms over the lenses. 'Very well,' she said.

The girl and the nun went out into the corridor. We couldn't hear what they were saying, but we could see them through the open door. After a minute or so, they came back in. Katherine sat down in her chair again.

'Miss *Bee* and Miss *Chen*,' she began, pacing the room and then stopping to put her glasses back on, 'Lagilla Convent is richly endowed with a legacy of honour, tradition and ceremony. Year 7 students, on their first day, are inducted into the convent with a ceremonial mass followed by a tour of the tower. Miss Cook was kind enough to inform me that, because Year 8 is your first year, neither of you received such an induction – a matter that we shall rectify immediately. As for Miss Samantha Porcello, I advise you to gather yourself and accompany us to the tower, and be re-inducted into Lagilla Convent with a clean slate.'

Cas jumped up. 'Thank you,' she said to SS. 'Sister Therese Cecilia, thank you – I thought we were gonna be expelled.'

'Miss Chen, gather yourself, young girl: outbursts are most detestable.'

Cas sniffled. 'Yes, sister – sorry.'

We took the staff lift – which was a lot bigger than that service lift – to the third level. At the end of the corridor on Level 3 was a narrow spiral staircase. A metal-screen gate had been erected to section it off from the rest of the school. SS rattled a set of cast-iron keys. She opened the lock of the gate and pulled the sliding door sideways. One after the other, we climbed up the staircase. At the top, the five of us had just enough room to squeeze on to a platform. The wooden floor creaked underneath us.

'Miss Porcello,' SS said to Sam, pointing to a trapdoor above us, 'a strong rower such as yourself should be capable of opening such a door.'

'Yes, sister,' Sam replied. She climbed up the ladder, gave her shoulders a heave and pushed the trapdoor upwards. Light suddenly flooded the platform, and dust circled around in the musty air. Sam climbed back down. 'After you, sister,' she said to SS.

SS reached down and hitched her skirt above her knees. We could see the hem of her petticoat. As she was climbing up the ladder, Sam, Cas and I pushed and poked each other . . . Then her navy shoes disappeared.

'We could lock it now,' Sam dared us, pointing at the keys in the lock.

Cas's jaw dropped. 'No!' she said.

'Lagilla's prison enough,' I added, 'let alone the real thing.' And that's where we'd end up if we did lock the door.

We climbed up the ladder, one after the other. The tower was the same width as my bedroom. You could walk all the way around it and see a panoramic view of Melbourne: north, south, east and west. We had a bird's-eye view of the city.

'Look: the Shrine of Remembrance!' Cas said. 'And there's the Entertainment Centre!'

'There's the rowing shed!' Sam pointed out. 'And the roller coaster at Luna Park! And my Mum's house! . . . There's yours, Cas!'

'Where?' I asked. I leant forward, my skin pressing cold against the brick ledge.

Cas showed me. 'See? Over there – right next to Mannix.'

'What's Mannix?' I asked.

Sam laughed as if I were a complete idiot. '*Dur*! Fred! It's our "brother school" – like, you know: lots of –' and she pumped her hand back and forth, like she was wanking a dick.

Gross, I thought, but I pretended she'd said I'd qualified for the Olympics and said, 'Unreal.'

Katherine, who'd been very quiet up till then, rolled her eyes. They were blue, and she had her brown-blonde hair pinned back with what looked like chopsticks.

'Girls! That will do!' SS brought us back to reality, and proceeded to herd us, like a flock of sheep, to the tower's west side. 'St Patrick's Cathedral,' she pointed out to us. 'See? There: the spire. Do not forget, girls, your body is your temple: treat it with the utmost respect, like it is the house of God.'

Even Katherine turned away on hearing that one, and covered her mouth.

'Now, now, girls,' SS said.

Sam decided to read aloud some of the names scratched into the brickwork. There were hundreds, probably thousands. Each name was handwritten in a different style – lots of the names had symbols and pictures beside them. Then we took it in turn to scratch our own names into the lower corner:

The moment felt important – like when Suze and I pierced our thumbs and became blood sisters. Sam and Cas seemed pretty cool, so it wasn't the worst thing if they accepted me as their friend. Now that Suze had gone away, I figured I needed a new friend. Two new friends would be kinda fun – kinda like a gang.

Then Sam knelt down and added the date.

'That's yesterday's date,' Cas pointed out.

'Shit a brick!' Sam whispered under her breath. 'Too late now, though.' She offered Katherine her house key so she could scratch her name beside ours.

'No thanks,' Katherine said.

'What?!' Sam's mouth dropped wide open, and I could see a big glob of chewing gum on her tongue. 'Give up a chance to graffiti school property?! You *are* whacked!' She offered SS the key instead.

'Good Lord, no!' SS replied, and twitched her lips. 'Miss Porcello, you do test my boundaries.' She took a deep breath. 'Come along, now.'

We closed the trapdoor, climbed back down the ladder and rode the staff lift down to the ground level.

'Girls, that will be sufficient,' SS said. 'Katherine, report to Sister Frances for a late pass. And as for you remaining three, Father Curry expects your assistance in the chapel for the remainder of the day. Make up your studies in your home time. Dismissed.'

Katherine walked off in a hurry.

'Stuck-up bitch,' Sam commented when Katherine had disappeared. '"No thanks." *I wouldn't want to write my name next to yours.* Dur. Does she think we have leprosy?'

'She might be really nice,' Cas put in.

'Are you kidding?' Sam asked.

We took our time getting to the chapel, slipping and sliding down the corridor towards it.

'Splendid!' Father Curry announced. His face was glowing red, and he was obviously out of breath. 'I'm short of helpers, and I've been racing around.' He showed us the cushions in the corridor. 'Arrange them nice and neatly along the seats,' he advised: '12 a pew. Shouldn't take too long. And a prayer wouldn't be out of the question: God is our guide, and heavens above, you young girls need guidance. I'll be back when the final bell rings.' He rubbed his palms together and shuffled off through a secret door behind the organ.

'Anyone got a wheelbarrow?' Sam joked.

But I realised she wasn't kidding. 'More like a forklift,' I replied.

Cas spread her arms out. 'Look how many there are! It's gonna take forever!'

We made trips back and forth, each working on our own section. At first, I arranged the cushions neatly: a foot apart, with the school emblem facing up. Then I saw that Sam was way ahead of Cas and me: her cushions were at odd angles, and she wasn't worrying about which side was facing up – and some of her pews had eight or 10 cushions rather than 12 . . .

A cushion went sailing past my head. 'Hey!' I yelled, and ducked. Another one went flying past . . . and then another. 'Sam!' I jumped up and threw two cushions back. 'Take that!' I yelled at her.

Then it was on for young and old: Cushion World War Three. Sam fired cushions at Cas and me, and Cas and I ganged up on her. Then it was anybody against everybody . . .

I sprinted down the aisle and took a flying leap, only to be whacked in the back by a cushion. 'Argh!' I shrieked. I ducked behind the altar, grabbed the cushion and threw it back.

'"Your body is your temple!"' Sam yelled. She switched the lectern microphone on and cleared her throat like how SS does. 'Come on, girls: hurry along!'

We laughed so hard we couldn't stand up. It felt good to laugh hard. I decided right then and there that Sam and Cas were definitely my new best friends.

It took us ages to tidy everything up. When we heard the final bell ring, Father Curry appeared from the secret door and waved us over. 'Jolly good job,' he told us. We bunched up together and made a human wall so he couldn't see we hadn't finished. 'I'll let Sister Cecilia know how impressed I am. Now, run along – the fresh air will do you good. Oh – and girls, I trust you remembered to say a prayer.'

Cas, looking guilty *as*, quickly kneeled.

Father Curry rubbed his palms together, excited at the thought of leading us through a prayer. 'At the altar,' he suggested: 'that would be nice.'

I didn't dare look at Sam or Cas; instead, I closed my eyes and focused on the prayer. We said the 'Hail Mary' and the 'Our Father'. Sam prayed extra loud, like she was really into it. It was only on the last bit of the 'Our Father' that I had to mime the words. I swore Father Curry added an extra bit I'd never heard before.

'Off you trot,' father said, and pushed himself up to stand.

'I feel very cleansed and pure,' Sam said, and shook his hand. 'Thank you, father.'

'Splendid!' he replied.

We raced back to the locker room and grabbed our bags. 'See ya,' I said, and backed out of the room.

'We're going to my house,' Sam offered: 'wanna come?'

'Ah bum, I can't,' I admitted: 'I've gotta pick up my sister from the prep school – but thanks.'

Cas smiled. 'See you tomorrow, then?'

'Yeah, sure: cool,' I answered. 'That'd be great.' I waved to them. Then, with a hop, I turned and left the school day behind.

2

It was Sunday night, and Mum, Amy and I went to Lisa's for dinner. Penny cooked homemade pizza and set the coffee table, rather than the kitchen table, with placemats, cutlery and a big, lavender-scented candle. We sat on the floor, with cushions under our bums.

'What *is* this music?' Penny asked Lisa.

Lisa cleared her throat. 'It's the '80s,' she replied: 'the best of.'

'You can't be serious,' Penny scoffed, and got up to change the CD.

'Hold it right there!' Lisa demanded. 'I put up with *your* music all the time – and I happen to like this.'

'Like it?!' Penny just couldn't see the attraction. 'It's daggy!'

'If you think it's so "daggy",' Lisa went on, 'why don't you show us, and dance. Go on!'

Penny put on her best 'bored stiff' look and mimed along to the lyrics.

'Come on,' Lisa suggested to Mum: 'Show the kids your funky-dance moves.'

'Go on, Mum,' we cheered, not expecting she really would.

'Okay; okay,' she agreed. She went and chose a song, and then turned her back to us, her legs apart. Instead of music, though, we heard only sound effects: the creak of a door hinge, the tap of heels on a floor, a bolt of lightning – and then, a howling wolf. Mum tapped her left foot as the beat to a Michael Jackson song started up. I was about to burst out laughing, but then she turned around, and, like a robot, did *the funkiest* dance – and when she was singing 'Beat It', she knew all the words.

'Whooo!' Penny shouted. 'Go, Mum.'

I couldn't believe it either.

Lisa grabbed the remote control and turned the volume up. We all clapped along to the bass beat. Mum spun around, flicked her head from side to side and did *the coolest* moonwalk, sliding backwards just right, like she was on a conveyor belt. And when she reached the wall, she spun around twice and did a body wave. It was as if she'd learnt the dance moves off by heart.

'Hot damn!' Lisa said. 'That girl can dance.'

When the song was over, the four of us huddled together to decide on a score.

'And the winner is,' Lisa announced, 'with a perfect score of 10, "Wacky Jacquie"! Come on, down, Jac!'

Mum acted all 'cool cat' when Lisa awarded her a Strawberry Freddo.

'Where'd you learn to dance like that?' I asked her.

'Your mother used to know *all* the latest moves,' Lisa said on her behalf. 'We'd sneak out to the clubs, with the other boarders from school, and dance in a group, doing a special, choreographed routine that your Mum had taught us. And the guys would go crazy! We were pretty smooth.'

Penny and I rolled around on the floor and laughed our heads off.

'Come on, Jac,' Lisa said to Mum. 'What would *they* know? They're just try-hard dags!'

She and Mum stuck their noses in the air and moonwalked out of the room, to the kitchen.

'"Smooth"!' Penny yelled out after them.

Lisa poked her head around the corner. 'Losers clean up,' she said, matter-of-factly, and disappeared back into the kitchen.

'Did you know Mum could dance?' I asked Penny.

'Nup,' she said, and laughed. 'And next time you get into trouble, remind her that *she* used to sneak out of the boarding school.'

'Whoa!' I said. 'That is *the* wickedest idea.'

We cleaned up, put our jackets on and went out to the backyard, where Mum and Lisa were sitting on the back step.

'It's a Princess-land,' Amy shouted. She took off, ran around the garden, and flapped her arms like a butterfly . . .

Fairy lights were strung up everywhere, and there were lots of smaller paths leading off the main path. We helped Lisa light some lanterns and hung them from the branches of trees. Then we floated some 'ceremonial' candles in the pond. There were all different types of trees and flowers, including a bonsai garden.

I decided to hold up a lantern in front of me and take one of the smaller paths that twisted and turned. It led down to the back of the yard. 'Hey, there's a tepee!' I yelled back.

Lisa came over to where I was standing and held up her lantern. 'It's for yoga,' she explained. 'Here: have a look.' She pulled back the flap of the entrance to the tepee. Inside was a circle of candles, and in the centre of the circle was a purple mat shaped like a star.

'You've got this thing about purple,' I said to her.

'You could say that. What's *your* favourite?'

'Colour?' I asked. 'Mmm . . . I like blue, 'cause there's lots of different types of blue . . . But I reckon Eb looks better in red – his rug and saddle blanket are red . . . But Maje looks really good in blue.'

'Horses; horses,' she said. 'You're obsessed.' She put the lantern down. 'Here: you sit on the cushion, with your legs crossed.'

'I know,' I said. 'I'm not a brickhead: I've seen them do it on TV. But I reckon it's dumb. Why don't they just go to bed and take a nap instead?'

'Not a bad point,' she replied, with a bit of a laugh. 'But have a go – you never know what you're missing out on if you don't try.'

'No way,' I said, and stepped back. I suddenly remembered what Cas had said about cults. I wondered whether Lisa, like Penny, was a pagan . . .

Amy came along and ran around the tepee. 'Whoo-whoo-whoo!' she cried, like an Apache.

I ran out and chased after her.

When we got puffed out, we rejoined the others. They were now sitting on the mat inside the tepee, facing outwards, their backs up against each other's. The candles were lit, flower petals were scattered on the floor. 'Are you guys pagans?' I asked.

'Hark!' Lisa yelled in response. Her face screwed up, like a witch. 'It's salt-dipped bats' wings we eat for dessert tonight!'

Amy giggled. 'There's bats that poo and stink,' she said, 'in the park near Dad's house. Pauline said they –'

Penny grabbed Amy, and shoved her hand over Amy's mouth to stop her from saying what she was about to say. 'That's not *all* that stinks around *there*,' Penny said.

'Now; now,' Lisa said. 'Let's cleanse this air.' She lit a stick of incense and waved it around. Her bangles clinked, Gypsy style.

I sat down next to Amy, remembering what Penny had said ages ago. 'Hey, Lisa,' I asked, 'were you *really* expelled?'

She squinted her eyes. 'Not *that* again!'

'You were! What did you do?' I asked.

'Ah, nothing,' she replied. 'I don't think it's very hard to get expelled from *that* school.'

'Come on, Auntie Lise,' Penny said. 'Tell us: we wanna hear it again.'

Lisa rolled her eyes and looked over at Mum. 'Okay,' she said. 'But only to clarify my innocence. I was in Year 10, and my Biol prac was a glasshouse experiment. The first part of the prac was to dry the seeds. I put them inside some stockings and hung them from the roof of the gardener's shed. Then, about two weeks later, the gardener set up his ladder and helped me take them down. Sister Bermesda was the principal back then, and she happened to be walking past and nearly had a heart attack. She saw me . . . the gardener . . . stockings.'

'Whoo!' Penny flicked her tongue out.

'He was *helping* me with the experiment,' Lisa went on, 'so you can put that tongue back inside your mouth. It was all *totally* innocent: *Sister Bermesda* was the one who thought we were –' she covered Amy's ears – 'having *sex*. Sister grabbed the broom and threatened the gardener, "Get back! Get back!" she said, and whacked him. And then –' Lisa couldn't stop laughing.

'Then *what*?' I asked, dying to hear.

Finally, she managed to sit up. 'Sister Bermesda fainted. They called an ambulance – and sent her *and* me to the hospital. It took our parents three hours to drive from their farm to the city . . . so while I was waiting, I walked around the hospital and saw there were hardly any flowers. I told the head nurse they should open a flower shop on the ground level, plus design some sort of disposable vase. I drew some pictures for her. She thought it was a great idea, and she introduced me to the director of the hospital. And he liked the idea so much he said I could set up a flower shop when I finished school. The next day, I was expelled – so I went back to the hospital and said to the director, "Guess what? I've finished school!"'

'Did you tell him why?' I asked, rapt.

'Of course not,' she replied: 'I'm not a "brickhead" . . . And now I've got a chain of flower shops – it's hard work, but I love it.'

Mum got up and walked out.

I looked at Penny, then Lisa. 'Where'd Mum go?' I asked.

Lisa squeezed my arm. 'Wait here,' she said. 'I'll go and check.'

Penny held Amy back from following.

'What's up with Mum?' I asked. 'Did I say something wrong?'

'Didn't you hear?' Penny asked.

'Hear what?' I didn't have a clue.

'What *Amy* said?' She leant closer and whispered: 'Pauline.'

'Oh,' I said. I had no idea what she'd meant – but I went along with it and pretended that I did. 'Mmm . . . Pauline.' And then it clicked: 'Pauline! – from Dad's work! Is *she* –' And then I remembered: the fish; the cracked glass; how she'd chucked an absolute barney – and the lipstick on the wine glass at Dad's place! 'Oh, yuk: it's Pauline, from Dad's work, isn't it? That's who 'Paully' is – that's disgusting!'

'I thought you knew,' Penny said to me. 'Oh, shit: Mum's gonna kill me. Please don't say anything! I just thought Amy's met her, and you stay over at Dad's, so I presumed you'd met her too.'

I burst out crying. 'I hate Dad! I hate him!'

Penny hugged me. 'Sshh,' she said. 'Imagine how Mum feels: I bet she wants to murder him. Please don't say anything. I'll show you my room; you can even have my Silver Brumby collection – you can have *anything* . . . Come on.'

She grabbed Amy and me by the hand and led us through the garden. We tiptoed across the balcony, through the kitchen, down the hall, past the lounge room – where Mum and Lisa were sitting.

I could hear Lisa talking in there, and Mum crying.

'Sshh,' Penny said to us.

The stairs creaked as we tiptoed up them. Amy didn't say a word: she thought the 'tiptoe-spy game' was a great idea for right now.

Penny opened the door to her bedroom and turned the light on. She'd cut holes into the lampshade, so it now looked like the oil burner she'd given me, and the light shining through the holes made the room look like a galaxy.

'Wow!' I said. 'This is way cool.' I reached up and tapped a wind chime. It was like the ones Nick had hanging from the trees outside his house – but instead of animal bones, these had crystals. 'Nick's got those,' I said, but was immediately sorry that I'd mentioned him. All I could picture was him kissing Karen Tools. I still wanted to protect Penny from the truth 'cause I didn't want to upset her or ruin our time together. But maybe there was a chance that they'd already split up: 'Are you still going out with him?' I asked. Ever hopeful me.

'As if I'd tell *you*,' she said, then thought twice. 'But yeah: I will – *if* you promise not to say anything to Mum . . . Amy!' She went over to Amy and held her down on the bed. 'Stop bouncing!' she ordered her. 'Why don't you sit up at the desk and do some colouring in?'

'No,' Amy complained.

'Well, don't jump!' She turned to me. 'Come on,' she said. 'Alright: I'll tell you . . . I'm not going out with him – he's a dickhead; he smokes too much pot. Besides, he got so high one night he pissed his pants. And I told him he was an arsehole to sell drugs to the high school kids, but he wouldn't listen to me and then the police caught him, so now he's gotta go to court. Now, get off my case, and *promise* not to say *anything*!'

I was relieved to hear Penny and Nick had split up: that made the 'Nick kissing Karen Tools' secret not that important anymore. 'Okay: I promise not to tell Mum. But *only* if you promise to move back home.'

'Okay,' she said. 'I was gonna move back anyway.'

The three of us sat down on the bed.

'Have you met her?' I asked Penny.

'Who?' she asked.

'Pauline – *dur*!'

'Oh – she used to come to the house, years ago.'

'You mean, at Yarra Valley?'

'Yeah – don't you remember? She'd work with Dad on designs together. One night I saw them in the vineyard; I was coming back from Nick's – and they were holding hands.'

'Orgh! That's disgusting!' I said.

'I know – that's what *I* told Dad . . . But you can't let on to Mum that you know: she wants to tell you herself . . . so when she does, act like it's the first time.'

I stood up. 'I *promised* – and I don't break promises, so I won't.'

'Good,' she said. 'You'd better not.'

I sat with Amy at the desk and helped her colour in.

'Do you know Sam Porcello?' I asked Penny. 'She says she knows you.'

'Sam?' she said, chewing on a fingernail. 'Yeah, I do know her. She's Year 8, but she knows a lot of the older girls 'cause she rows with them and 'cause she's always at detention, which is how *I* know her.'

'We hang out at school,' I said. 'Her, me and Cas Chen.'

'Cas Chen?' Nup – can't say I know her.'

'You wouldn't,' I said; 'she's new this year. She's really good at guitar – not that I've heard her play – but I'll hear her at the end-of-semester concert. It's in two weeks – wanna come?'

'Get stuffed!' she answered. 'I *hate* that place. As if I'd step foot in that school ever again!'

And then I remembered the present I'd made her. 'Hang on!' I said, and ran downstairs to grab my bag.

When I came back, she had her head stuck out the window. 'Close the door,' she said.

I could smell burning tobacco and noticed the cigarette in Penny's hand. I closed the door and took the dartboard out of my bag. 'I made you this,' I said, holding it up. 'Wanna play?'

She butted her cigarette out and came over. In the centre of the dartboard was an enlarged photo of Dad's head. 'That's satanic! Hang it there, on the wall,' she said. 'Let's play.'

She went first, and then we took it in turns. She scored the bull's-eye when she hit Dad's nose. We cheered and jumped. Amy didn't know why, but was happy to join in the fun.

Mum knocked on the door. 'We're going,' she called through it.

'Here, cover it up,' Penny said, and stood me in front of the dartboard. 'What?' she asked Mum casually, and opened the door.

Mum came in. 'It's late,' she said to us. 'We've got an early start.' She picked Penny's jumper up off the floor and folded it. 'Your appointment's at 8.10 – I'll pick you up at quarter to.'

Penny turned bright red. She grabbed the jumper from Mum. 'Fine,' she said. 'We've already talked about that, haven't we?'

I kind of guessed it was the counsellor they were talking about.

'True,' Mum said; 'we had – I just wanted to check you remembered.'

We went downstairs and thanked Lisa for having us. On the way out, she gave Amy and me a Strawberry Freddo each.

By the time we got home, it was after midnight. I followed Mum as she was carrying Amy upstairs. It was hard not to say *anything* about Pauline – I wanted to: if Eb nicked off and let someone else be his best friend, *I'd* be super-mad . . . I'd spent so much time with him, and I'd get such a shock when I'd found out, but I guess, I'd still want to know. ''Night, Mum,' I said to her. I'd figured out enough on my own – especially since the 'Nick and Karen Tools' incident – and realised that sometimes keeping secrets is easier than dumping the truth on someone.

'Don't forget,' she said: 'winter uniform tomorrow.' She stretched her arms above her head. 'Ooh, I'm tired . . . I'll have to leave early tomorrow. Are you and Amy right to catch a tram?'

'Yeah, that's fine,' I said: 'I'll set the alarm clock a bit earlier. 'Night.'

I didn't brush my teeth – I went straight to bed. But I couldn't sleep: I kept thinking about 'Pauline', and my Dad.

I couldn't *believe* how much stuff I had to wear: undies, shirt, tie, stockings, tunic, jumper, shoes, blazer. And it was raining, so I had to chuck on a raincoat as well – it was clear plastic, and made me look like a granny. But that was what we had to wear.

Amy was dressed exactly the same. She was lying on the kitchen floor, scratching her legs. 'My stockings are itchy,' she said. 'And my tie hurts.'

'Here, I'll loosen it.' I lifted her onto the bench. '*Ooh*, you *are* getting heavy . . . Is that better – can you breathe?'

'Mmm: yep,' she replied. 'My toast got stuck-ed.'

'In your neck?' I asked her.

She nodded.

'Do you want me to cut it into quarters – just like kindergarten squares?'

'No,' she answered; 'I'm a big girl now.'

'Yes, you *are*,' I said. 'Come on: I'll wrap your toast up and we'll take it with us.'

We ran through the rain to the tram stop. Because Amy took four steps to every one of mine, I decided to stop and give her a piggyback. I couldn't run as fast then – what with carrying her and our two bags. But we were faster than we would have been if she'd kept running on her own. When we got to the tram shelter, heaps of people were waiting there: girls from other schools, guys from Mannix College, older people dressed in business suits. Usually it was just Amy and me and only a couple of other people.

'The tram's held up,' a woman announced. 'We've been waiting for 40 minutes *plus*. An inspector drove past, about 20 minutes ago, and said it'd be here in five minutes.' She looked at her watch, impatiently.

I looked at my watch as well: we were definitely gonna be late, but I didn't care: I thought the rain was cool.

We shuffled under the shelter to join the other people waiting. The rain got heavier and splashed onto our stockings. Then the wind blew sideways and splashed the water onto our faces. I pulled our hoods over our heads. If Suze had been with us, she'd have loved it: she had this thing about being outside when it rained, and on the weekends, when she thought it was gonna rain, she'd call me up and say we *had* to go for a ride . . .

I hadn't heard from her since she'd left. But I'd sent her an email plus attached the photos of us at the airport. I'd stuck the best photo – of us pulling a silly face – on the wall next to my bed, and made a collage of the rest of the pictures for my IRP.

'Tram!' a man yelled.

The rattler finally appeared and stopped in front of us. Everyone piled in.

It rained all that day and the rest of the week as well. By Friday, the school oval was looking like a lake. On the weekend, the weather was too wet to do anything, so Amy and me lay around and watched DVDs.

On the Saturday afternoon, Mum came into the TV room. 'Your father's on the phone,' she announced. 'He wants to talk to you.'

I paused the movie. 'Tell him I'm busy,' I said.

'"Busy"?' she asked. 'With what?'

'With watching a movie, and babysitting Amy.' I looked over at Amy, but she'd fallen asleep. 'Tell him I'll call him back, when it's over.' Not that I was going to – I was still mad about the 'Pauline' thing.

'*You* tell him!' she said, then huffed. She'd already told Dad, three times that week, that I was "busy".

'Do I have to?' I asked. 'The movie's nearly finished – it's on a really good bit.'

She picked up a cereal bowl lying on the floor. 'I'll tell him,' she agreed. 'But after you've spoken to your father, I want you to take Amy to the park.'

'It's raining,' I protested; we'll get soaked!'

'Well, no eating on the new couches,' she insisted: 'we've got a perfectly good kitchen bench.' Then she left us alone again.

I watched the rest of the movie and never called Dad back.

That Monday, the morning was super-foggy. When Amy and I walked to school, we could only see as far as a couple of metres in front of us. She screamed when I ran ahead of her and hid. After that, I had to hold her hand the rest of the way. At lunchtime the sun came out, and because we were dressed in winter uniform, we were boiling hot. Cas had 'band camp' that week, so Sam and I hung out. We sat on the wall around the oval and ate our lunch. Most of the rainwater had sunk into the grass, but there were still heaps of puddles.

'Dare me to cut our stockings into socks,' Sam offered.

'Mum'll kill me,' I replied.

'Go on!' she said, and took some scissors from her pencil case. 'I'll cut them high enough – so then, when we go back to class, we can hold 'em up with elastic.'

I wasn't keen on the idea. 'Cut it higher,' I said. 'Oh, my God: Mum is *so* gonna kill me.'

When she was done, we paraded back and forth in front of each other.

'That's heaps cooler!' she said, and wrapped the waist part of her stockings around her neck. 'Like my scarf?'

'Mmm: great colour!'

'Thanks, *darling*!' she said, and sat down to cut the feet part out of her stockings. 'Look,' she said, holding up the feet part covering her hands: 'matching gloves! Quite the outfit, isn't it?'

I couldn't *believe* she'd done it: now her stockings weren't even socks – they were leg warmers. I burst out laughing. 'Let me guess,' I said: 'designer French?'

'*Oui*,' she said, and leant forward to kiss my cheeks. '*Moi-moi!*'

We took turns to parade up and down the catwalk.

Sam was pretty funny at it. She pretended to twist an ankle and fell headfirst.

When it was my turn, I took my jumper off – super-sexily, like a model – but my head got caught . . . and I didn't mean to, but I tripped. 'Ouch!' I said; 'that hurt.' I rubbed my butt. Then I noticed Katherine Cook on the other side of the oval. 'How come she gets to leave the school at lunchtime?' I asked.

Sam looked over her shoulder to see who it was.

'Katherine Cook goes into that house,' I said. 'See, there: through that gate on that back fence? Then she comes out when the bell rings.'

'She lives there with her gran,' Sam explained. 'She's such a suck: she's allowed to leave 'cause she's SS's pet.'

I'd wondered about that house. 'It's huge,' I said; 'they must be loaded.'

'No shit,' Sam replied; 'it's a bloody mansion. Her dad's a film director and lives in Hollywood. And 'cause her mum died of cancer last year, she lives with her gran . . . Hey – check it out: she's smoking!'

We jumped up and watched.

'How come she's repeating Year 8?' I asked.

'She missed heaps of school last year,' Sam replied; 'I guess she's making up for the study she missed from being away for so long. I wouldn't have a clue what she said to SS that day we got in trouble – whatever it was, it bloody well stopped us from getting expelled.' She took off and sprinted across the oval, dodging the puddles left and right.

I chased after her. 'Where are you going?' I called out.

'I'm gonna ask!' she yelled back.

But I didn't hear the rest: she was too far ahead of me.

We eventually caught up to Kath. 'Thanks for the other week,' Sam said to her.

But Kath just ignored us and walked on.

'*Oi*! You can't just walk off like that!' Sam yelled after her: 'we wanna know what you said to SS that day!'

Kath stubbed out her cigarette butt and flicked it into a bush. 'I told SS that Sister Bermesda ate her meat pie. She never eats her lunch, and she never gets out of bed. That day, she asked me to put her chair by the window, so she could eat her pie and look at the garden – so now SS lets the nuns order from the tuckshop, that's if they want to.'

Sam jumped up and down. 'We've made history!' she yelled. 'History – *yeah*!'

'See ya,' Kath said, and backed away before disappearing through the gate of her Gran's house.

Sam and I walked back across the oval together. 'We should ask her to hang out with us,' I suggested.

'Nah,' Sam replied; 'I asked her once – she said, "What for? It's not like I'm desperate for a friend." She's so stuck up. When her mum died, the year level had a special mass, and she didn't even come. Amanda wrote this special prayer for it.'

'Amanda – she's your best-est friend, isn't she?'

'*Was*,' she replied. 'She got into some big shit, but: she got pregnant, and the guy was a total arsehole and bragged about it to everyone.'

'Whoa!' I said. 'That's full on.'

'I know,' she said. 'But get this: SS heard she had an abortion, so she asked her to leave.'

'SS can't do that!' I said. 'There was this girl at Yarra Valley High, and she was preggas, and she was allowed to keep studying.'

'*Newsflash*!' Sam announced. 'Lagilla's Catholic?! . . . anti-abortion?!'

'Oh – yeah: that's . . . Well, it's full-on, and it sucks,' I replied. 'But hang on, what's she doing getting pregnant? She's our age!'

Sam looked like she wanted to punch me. 'I couldn't give a shit what you think!' she yelled. 'And what would *you* bloody well know? It's not like *you're* Amanda! Imagine what it was like for *her*!' She stormed off to a spot a short distance away.

I waited a while and then went over to her and sat down. 'Sorry,' I said. 'I miss my best mate too: Suze moved overseas about a month ago.'

She didn't say anything; she just kept staring at the ground.

Finally, I said, 'You could always go and visit Amanda.'

'She doesn't want me to,' Sam admitted. 'She doesn't want *anything* to do with *anyone* from here. Maybe that's her way of pretending it never happened, but it hurts *me* which is so stuffed up 'cause I'm the one who stood by her.'

'Why don't you just go and surprise her?' I persisted. 'We're on holidays next week.'

'I can't,' she said; 'Dad and I made plans to go away, and I've already invited Cas to come along.' She pulled a handful of grass from the ground. 'You're right, though: maybe I could – at the end of the year.'

'I bet she really does want you to visit.'

'Yeah, maybe.'

The bell rang, and we grabbed our stuff. As we ran off, our stockings bunched up around our ankles. 'What about our stockings?' I asked Sam.

She showed me how to hold them up using my hair elastic.

'But now we'll get into trouble for having our hair out,' I said.

'So what,' she said. We laughed, and ran into the locker room . . .

When the final bell rang, Sam came over to my desk. 'I was thinking,' she said: 'I go round to Dad's tonight.'

'Don't you live with your dad?' I asked.

'Nah – my parents are divorced; I live with my mum . . . But I was gonna say, "Do you wanna come with us, when Cas and me go away?"'

'Oh bum, I can't,' I said; 'I'm moving my horses – I just found out last night I got some agistment, in Ivanhoe – but thanks anyway . . . Where are you going?'

'Disneyland!'

'Are you serious?!'

'Nah – only shittin' ya: we're dirt-bag poor; we're going to Wilson's Prom for the week.'

'Whoa! It's winter! It'll be freezing cold.'

'We've rented a cottage, so it's not like we're camping,' she replied, then gave me hug. 'Sorry about getting mad at ya.'

'No probs, I've forgotten about it,' I said. 'Don't worry.'

'"Don't worry?" You looked like I'd stabbed you in the guts.'

'Seriously – it wasn't a big deal. I think you and Cas are cool, it's not like I'm gonna get upset about a little thing like that.'

She smiled. 'So, I'll see ya tomorrow?'

'Yes,' I reassured her. 'It's not like I'm about to change schools or run away!'

I picked Amy up. Before we went home, we hung out for a while at Paradise. It was Dad's birthday and he was going to be taking us out, so I wasn't in a huge hurry to get home.

Dad phoned as soon as we got home. 'I've booked a restaurant,' he said: 'can you make sure you and Amy wear something nice?'

'A restaurant!' I said. 'How come?'

'I thought it'd be a nice treat.'

For you, not us, I thought. 'What time are you coming over?'

'About seven, say – will you make sure you're ready?'

'Sure: okay,' I replied, and hung up.

Mum came into the TV room, where we were watching the end of a show. 'What about getting ready?' she asked. 'Your father'll be here in a minute.'

'I *am* ready,' I said. 'All I've gotta do is go to the loo. I'll go in the ad break – it's only 10 to 7.'

'"Only?"' she asked, giving me one of her deadly, out-of-the-corner-of-the-eye looks. 'I don't think your father will be very impressed – not when he sees what you're wearing.' She walked out of the room.

Rather than let himself into the house, Dad rang the doorbell. Amy raced down the hall, opened the door and jumped up for a hug. She'd changed from her favourite pink tracksuit into a floral pink dress, and because she'd asked me to, I'd plaited her hair. I'd put on my standard gear: jeans, jumper and runners – and tied my hair back in a ponytail.

'Daddy! Daddy!' Amy squealed.

I leant back against the wall and stuffed my hands into the front pockets of my jeans. 'Hi, Dad,' I said, casually. 'Happy birthday.'

'Thanks, Bumble,' he said, giving my clothes the once over. 'Haven't you got something other than jeans to wear? I did ask – and I've booked a swishy restaurant.'

Amy squirmed for him to put her down. 'Come and see!' she said to him. 'We've got beanbags! *Daddy*, come and *see*!'

'Ames, not now,' he replied; 'another day.' He shifted her onto his other hip.

'But we've got *beanbags*!' she persisted.

'Not now, honey – *sshh*.' He turned to me. 'Haven't you got a shirt? and shoes other than runners?'

'What about your tan pants?' Mum asked me. She was standing at the top of the stairs, too far up for Dad to see. But she'd obviously been listening: '. . . the ones we bought for Christmas, and the leather sandals.'

'The pants don't fit,' I said: 'they're too short. All I've got is sports stuff, riding clothes and jeans – and I'm not wearing my uniform.'

'At least put the sandals on,' Dad suggested.

I wanted to yell, 'No!' But I clomped up the stairs to do as he'd said. When I stood in front of my full-length mirror, I couldn't help but screw my face up: the tan pants looked ridiculous. They were okay everywhere else, but the legs ended above my ankles, half mast. I guessed I'd grown since Christmas.

A knock came on the door. It was Mum: 'Your father's waiting in the car.'

'Do I *have* to go?' I begged.

She came in and sat down on the bed. 'What's wrong?' she asked.

I pretended I was looking for something in the wardrobe and quickly wiped my tears away. 'I hate him, Mum. He can't make me go. And there's no way I'm wearing these clothes.'

'No one's forcing you to go,' she said. 'But it is his birthday – and Penny's going.'

I didn't want to tell her what I was really thinking, because then I'd have to tell her I knew about Pauline. 'Can't we go to the Pancake Parlour, not some posh restaurant?'

'You can go to the Pancake Parlour – when it's *your* birthday,' she replied. 'It's only for a couple of hours: it won't kill you.'

'Yes it will!' I shouted at her. I closed the wardrobe door and burst into tears. 'Pauline might be there.'

'Who?' she asked.

But I knew she'd heard. 'Pauline,' I repeated, and sat down on the bed. 'I know it's *her* – Penny didn't tell me; I worked it out when Amy said something about Pauline the other night, when we were at Lisa's. And I've met her: when I was working at Dad's office, at the start of the year. She was horrible. And I reckon she's going tonight. Dad's never taken us to a posh restaurant. If it was just us, we'd be having a barbecue or going to a movie . . . And he's never cared about what we wear.'

'There's not a snowball's chance in hell of that,' she said; 'I gave him strict instructions not to allow something like that to happen – and he agreed.'

Dad tooted the car horn.

'Do I *have* to?'

'You don't *have* to,' she replied, 'but I'd like you to go downstairs and at least explain why.'

'Can't you?'

'No – he needs to know how *you* feel about it. He was going to tell you tonight, so it's a chance for you to talk about it. You don't have to go – that's fine.'

He honked the horn again, longer.

I knew Penny would kill me if I didn't go. 'Alright,' I decided: 'I'll go – but I'm not wearing these pants . . . And if *she's* there –'

'She won't be,' Mum confirmed.

'Well, she'd better not be.' I quickly changed out of the pants and back into the jeans, and then gave her a hug and ran downstairs.

He'd left the front passenger door of the ute open. I jumped in. Amy was looking all pink and pretty in the back seat.

'What took so long?' he asked.

'I don't know,' I replied. 'I had to put my sandals on.'

'Well, giddy up, slowcoach; close the door or we'll be late.'

'Giddy up, slowcoach!' Amy repeated.

I leant over and gave her a horsy bite on the knee.

'Don't!' she cried, but laughed when I did it again.

We picked up Penny and headed for the city.

'Are we there yet?' Amy asked. 'Where's the *restedrant*?'

'Wouldn't you like to know?' Dad teased her. 'It's somewhere special – somewhere up very high.'

She was that excited she kicked her sandals against the back of his seat.

The underground car park Dad chose to leave the car in was a spooky kind of place. Our shoes tapped eerily as we walked towards the lift. Amy ran ahead to push the lift button, which was always her job . . . After a minute or so, *ding!* The doors opened. Dad lifted Amy up so she could push the top button in the lift. It was bigger than all the other buttons and had fancy writing on it.

'"*La Ville des Lumieres*",' Penny read, in a super-posh voice.

The lift glided up towards the top floor. The inside of the lift was mirrored. I could see Dad and Penny's reflection. Penny had her arms crossed and was chewing on a nail. Amy held onto the leg of Dad's pants. Her shoes danced on the carpeted floor. Dad cleared his throat. The only sound then was the lift whirring up the floors. Then *ding!*

We stepped out into a huge room. It had a bar and lots of lounge chairs, and people sitting around talking and drinking, and a band playing classical music. A woman wearing glasses was playing the violin, a bald-headed man was playing the cello, and a girl the same age as me was playing the guitar. She was Asian, and I thought for a minute she was Cas – but when we got closer, I could see it wasn't her: her hair was too long.

We waited till the song had finished and then clapped along with everyone else.

'Come and see the view,' Dad said to us.

We walked over to a wall-length window. The sky was black, but down below we could see heaps of bright lights; I could tell that the white ones, all in a row, were roads. We could see different-coloured signs on building tops, and whole floors of offices lit up with no one in them. And when a helicopter flew past, the flashing red light on its tail was level with us.

'That orange light over there is the lookout tower at the Dandenongs,' Dad pointed out. The light was higher up and all on its own. 'And left of that is Yarra Valley.'

'I gotta go to the loo,' I announced; I didn't really need to, but I wanted to talk to Penny on my own. But when I stood behind Dad's back and waved at her to come with me, she didn't see: she was too busy looking out the window.

217

'That was quick!' Dad said when I came back two seconds later.

I'd walked into the loo, turned around and walked straight back out again. I shrugged my shoulders. 'I don't know,' I replied; 'that's just how long it took – I can go back and take ages if you want.'

'Cute,' he remarked. 'You wouldn't last five minutes: you'd get too hungry.' He looked at his watch. 'The restaurant's up those stairs.'

As we walked into the restaurant, a waiter came over, dressed in a black shirt and pants, and a stiff, white apron that reached down to his shoes. '*Bonsoir*!' he said.

Dad winked at Amy. 'We have a booking for four,' he said; 'under the name of Bee.'

'Ah, *oui*,' the waiter responded. 'We are expecting you. I trust you are well this evening, Mr Bee?'

'Yes, thank you,' Dad replied. 'The girls and I were admiring the view.'

'The lights are superb, are they not? *C'est magnifique*!' Then he took our jackets and hung them up on a coat rack. 'Follow me,' he instructed. 'You will like your table: it is right by the window; it is possible you may admire the view some more?'

'Thank you,' Dad said. 'The girls would like that very much, I'm sure.'

Heaps of old people were sitting at the tables, and they now turned and stared at us – especially at Penny and her hair. When we sat down, the waiter made a big deal about unfolding our napkins: he flicked them into the air and then put them down on our legs. Amy got the giggles when he did it to hers. Then another waiter came over and gave us each a menu and filled our glasses with water.

'Hey, look,' I said, and pointed at the table: the top part of it was made of glass and had lots of triangle-shaped pieces joined together, exactly like the wall of our old and new house. 'Did *you* make this?' I asked Dad.

'*Oui*,' he replied, and smiled. 'You like, *ma'moiselle*? Do you not think that La Ville des Lumieres is a special restaurant?'

I nodded: it *was* pretty cool, and maybe *that's* why he'd taken us to it. The more I looked around the more I noticed how familiar the architecture was. The water feature in the middle of the restaurant had spotlights that reflected a ripple pattern onto the walls. *And dur*: even the chandelier above each table was exactly like the chandelier in the lounge room at home.

Penny got up. 'I gotta pee,' she said.

I jumped up as well: this was my chance. 'Me too,' I said.

Dad gave me a funny look. 'I swear you just went,' he said to me.

'I know; I gotta go again.'

'Why don't you order first,' he asked, 'then go?'

'But we have to go *now*,' Penny replied. 'And anyways, I'm not French, so I can't read the menu.'

'Okay: go – I'll order for you. But don't be too long.'

As we walked off, he waved us back to the table. 'Take Amy,' he said. 'She says she needs to go as well.'

We went down the stairs to the bar. 'I'll wait over here,' Penny said, taking up a lounge chair next to the bar.

'How come?' I asked. 'I thought you said you needed to go.'

'Just take her,' she said.

When Amy and I had finished, Penny was standing waiting by the loo door. She had our jackets bundled up in her arms.

'Let's split,' she announced.

'We can't leave,' I said.

'Fine,' she replied. 'If you don't wanna come, I'm going anyways.' She marched off towards the lift.

I ran after her. 'That's not fair!' I said. 'I wasn't gonna come tonight – I only came 'cause I knew you'd kill me if I didn't!'

Ding! The lift door opened.

My face screwed up.

'Bloody hell!' she said, and dropped our jackets onto the floor. 'Alright: we'll stay – but you gotta turn off the waterworks.'

We went over to the bar and sat on three high stools. Amy laughed when I spun hers around. 'Again!' she cried. 'Again!'

'No – you'll vomit,' I warned her, and turned around to face Penny. 'What if he gets married: does that mean Pauline's our mum?'

She lit a cigarette, took a drag on it and blew out the smoke away from us. 'Get stuffed,' she said. 'That's not how it works: she's only our *stepmum* if we call her that, and we can hate her if we want.'

'Good,' I said. 'I thought she was coming tonight.'

'Yeah: right,' she said. 'I'd have given her a fat lip if she did.'

'Me too,' I added, not that I really would have . . . 'Hey, where's Amy?'

Penny pointed to where Amy had wandered off. 'Over there, by the band.'

The woman playing the violin stood up and played it extra loudly, and Amy responded by dancing around even more. When the song finished, everyone clapped for the ballerina in the floral pink dress.

'We'd better go back,' I said.

'Stuff that,' Penny said – but stood up and butted out her cigarette.

When we sat down again at the table, we found Dad in *the* worst-est mood. I knew he was about to tell us off for being away so long, but luckily a waiter came over and put bread rolls on our plates. When he'd gone, Dad cleared his throat and said to us, 'I want you to know I love each and every one of you.'

Penny pushed her chair back and turned it on an angle. 'Yeah: right,' she said. 'Divorcing Mum is a funny way of showing it.'

He smiled as two other waiters put our dinners on the table.

After they'd left, Penny asked him, 'Is Pauline gonna live with you? If she does, I'm *never* coming to your apartment!' She stood up, and I stood up as well.

'Sit down,' Dad said.

Penny held out her hand. 'No – we're going. And we'd like some money for a taxi.'

'Sit down, please,' he insisted. 'People are staring.' He stood up, came over to me and plonked me down on my chair. 'Let's talk about it.'

'I don't want to,' I put in. 'I want to go home. And forget about coming to my end-of-semester concert – I only want Mum to go.'

'No matter what,' he began, looking straight at me, 'I'll always love you. And I do want to come to your concert. Christ, I pay the school fees. And I've told your mother I'll pay for the Board of Works agistment. Just because I'm not *with* your mother doesn't mean I stop being your dad. And it doesn't mean you stop being my daughter.' Maybe that's what *he* thought but I was thinking differently.

'What about me?' Penny asked. 'You couldn't give a rat's arse. The only reason I can't get Austudy is because it's 'means tested' against your income – and because you earn too much, I get nothing.'

'I didn't know that,' he replied. 'Have you talked to me about it?'

'What's the use?' she asked. 'You don't care.'

'I *do*. I'll organise a certain amount, equal to Austudy, to be paid into your account each week. All you have to do is let me know how much it is.'

'Forget it,' she answered. 'I don't want your money.'

'Yes you do,' he replied; 'you wouldn't have mentioned it otherwise. I'm offering.'

She looked at him. 'Well, if you're offering,' she said, 'I'll take it.'

'Good,' he said, and dabbed his napkin across his brow: 'starts as of Monday.' Then he waved a waiter over. 'We'll have the bill, thanks.'

And as quick as that the dinner was over.

On the way home, we dropped Penny off first. ''Bye,' she said. 'And happy birthday – hope it was perfect. And don't think giving me money means I have to like *her*.'

'That's entirely your choice,' he said. 'I'm not forcing anyone to do anything they're not comfortable with.'

Penny grabbed her jacket and got out of the car. 'Thanks for the money, anyways,' she said. 'It does help.'

'If there's anything else,' he began – but she'd closed the door.

He didn't say a word all the way home. When he pulled into the driveway, he turned the engine off. 'What time tomorrow night?' he asked me.

I wanted – needed – to let him know I was for real about what I'd said earlier. 'I only want Mum to come to the concert; a lot of my friends don't even have their parents going.'

'Bumble!' he said, with a hurt look.

'I'm not your Bumble!' I said, and got out of the car. 'And I've only got *one* mother. 'Night. Thanks for the dinner – and happy birthday.' As I ran in past the front door, I burst out crying.

Mum must have heard Dad's car pulling up in the driveway. She was sitting at the bottom of the stairs and put her arms around me and rocked me back and forth. When Amy came in, the three of us went upstairs together.

I didn't even bother brushing my teeth or putting my PJs on. Mum tucked my doona around my face and asked me heaps of questions about Eb and Maje.

'I *wish* I didn't have a dad!' I said. 'I *wish* he'd go away – forever! And I *wish* I wasn't me!' Poof! – my last three wishes used up.

Mum sat down on the beanbag and lifted Amy onto her lap. 'You'll feel better in the morning,' she said, quietly. 'Your father's been very good to you.'

'No, he hasn't.'

'He's helped you with the horses . . . gone to all your shows . . . built the horse shed – and the holding yard.'

'I don't care,' I said. 'None of that means anything. And I'm never going to his place again if Pauline's there.'

She squeezed my hand.

I squeezed hers back, and wouldn't let go . . .

When I woke up, the room was dark. It was 3.24 a.m. Mum had fallen asleep on the beanbag, and Amy was curled up tightly beside her. I spread my Bumble blanket over them, and jumped back into bed. The pocket of warm air under the doona felt good. I closed my eyes and slept.

Mum kissed me on the forehead. 'Wakey; wakey!' she said. 'You've slept through the alarm. I called the school and told them I'd drop you and Amy off by 10. It's the most beautiful day today.' She pulled the doona back. 'I've cooked you scrambled eggs.'

'Mmm, I can smell them,' I said, 'and I'm starving.'

She left so I could get dressed. The sky *was* the most beautiful colour, and there wasn't one cloud. While I was waiting for the computer to connect to the 'Net, I went off to the loo. On the way back, I heard the computer beeping. I ran in and clicked on the Inbox.

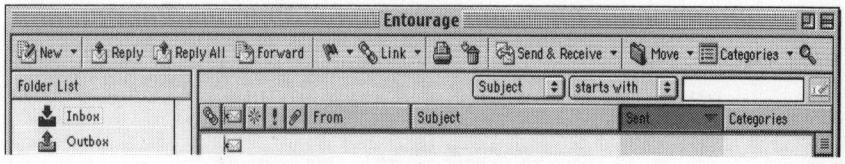

>From: susie@bumble.com.au

>To: veronica@bumble.com.au

>Subject: THANKS!!! U R ACE-AS!

>Sent: 14 June, 5.12 a.m.

Hi. Vee. Thanx 4 the email & prezzies!!! I've put the photos on the wall in my bedroom & ate (OINK!) ALL the chocolates that u posted. They don't sell Crunchies or Freddos here, so u r ace as!!! Nan's house is near this village called Ainsbury, & all her friends remember me, but I don't remember them. The house is small as. But how cool is this? My bedroom's in the attic & there's little windows. It's tiny as but cute as. I live with Nan & 3 others who help out with the horses. There's Jenny. She's 18. Sonya's 24 & Pen's 19. We muck around heaps & all of them have done IT. We've got 24 horses & 11 of the mares r about 2 have foals. I can't wait! Nan looks EXACTLY like the Queen & is so STRICT! You're not allowed 2 say Yeah & Yep! U have 2 dress up 4 dinner. U have 2 put the cutlery the right way up in the drawer when u unpack the dishwasher! & we have 2 get up early as. I'm talking 5 o'clock! & there's heaps of stuff 2 do. The stable has 2 b perfect. Nan marches around & says SPIC & SPAN! SPIC & SPAN! & if u break the rules u have 2 shovel a wheelbarrow of horseshit. Nan said if I want my own horse I have 2 work 6 months without pocket money. But the best part is I'm riding heaps! & hopefully getting better. Nan is the best rider. She can do Piaffe, Piaffe-Pirouette, single & tempi flying changes & she rides dressage 2 music. She says I have 2 get at least 4 A's at school b4 she'll give me riding lessons. I've cheated on 2 tests & got 2 A's so far. School is OK, but not as cool as YVHigh & ALL the spunks have already got girlfriends! Mum's coming next week & she's staying 10 days! She's taking me 2 London. Miss u heaps as & can't wait 4 u 2 visit. Your best-est buddy & blood sis. XXOO Suzie-Suze

PS Nan has pink hair!!!

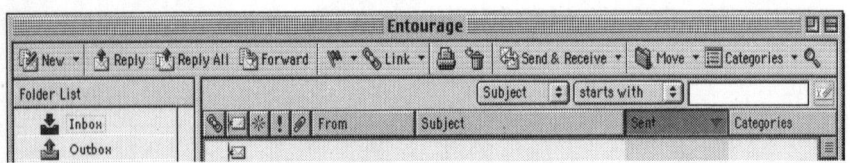

>From: veronica@bumble.com.au
>To: susie@bumble.com.au
>Subject: RE: THANKS!!! U R ACE AS!
>Sent: 14 June, 8.36 a.m.

Hi, Suze. It is so cool 2 get your email. And I've got the photo by my bed as well.

Guess what! 2day's the last day of school b4 mid-year break. WICKED! I'm moving Eb & Maje 2 a paddock in Ivanhoe, which isn't far from home. And Audrey said she'd come & give me lessons on Tuesdays after school. Also there's a pony club, so I'll check it out & if it's any good I'll join.

School's OK - a lot better than when it sucked at the start of the year. I hang out with a couple of girls. Sam's a wicked rower & wants 2 b in the Olympics. Cas is like u, well kind of - she's obsessed with guys! She's been going out with her boyfriend 4 ages. She plays guitar & she's doing this song at the mass/concert thingo 2nite. Hey, I saw Craig Berton on TV! He was singing in this band. I couldn't stop laughing. He had this huge pimple on his nose that was about 2 explode. The band was called Flat Out Jesus. They sounded really cool, but u can't tell ANYONE that I told u that.

Penny's moving home 2moro. She's heaps nicer than how she was. She's stopped going out with Freako. & Mum's a lot more relaxed. She never used 2 sit on the beanbags & now she loves them. She even fell asleep on one last night. Anyways, I found out more stuff about Dad. That woman's name is Pauline. & remember when I told u about the fish at Dad's office, & how this woman chucked an absolute barney when the fish spilt on the floor? Well, guess what? That's her. Yuk!

I don't care if we never move back 2 YV. I kind of like it here & I like Sam & Cas. That doesn't mean I don't miss u heaps & heaps. So I'll ask Dad if I can visit & I'll let u know. Your best-est buddy & blood sis. XO - Vee

At afternoon house-room roll call, Sam made up the daggiest song. 'Go on,' she said to Cas, trying to release the buckles of her guitar case: 'I won't break it – let me play, and we'll all sing along.'

Cas gave in and took her guitar out. Sam made up a country-and-western tune, and the whole class sang along. We got louder and louder:

'*On the faaarm, milking the cooow:*

There's Pa, on the tractor;

There's Maaa, feeding the chooks.'

We sounded terrible, and Sam couldn't even play. She strummed up and down on the strings, pretending she was a rock and roll star.

Sister Frances banged her ruler against the blackboard. 'Girls, settle!'

But we kept singing. I thought we were gonna get into the biggest trouble, especially when Sister Frances waved me up to the front of the room – but she smiled, and opened the top drawer of her desk. 'Don't let me see you wearing this again!' she said to me.

I'd forgotten all about the locket. I took it from her. 'Thanks,' I said. I sat down and opened it; my lucky four-leaf clover fell out. I'd already used up all 10 of the wishes, and even though my last three wishes were used up on the night of Dad's birthday when I was super-angry at him and wanted him to disappear, I looked at the photo in the locket of my parents, and I began to feel sad . . .

'Girls, settle!' Sister banged the ruler again. 'A bit of shush, please, or I'll keep the class back, for 10 minutes, *after* the final bell rings!'

Everyone shut up and went back to their desks.

'Whatcha got?' Sam asked me. 'A prize for being the biggest slurp-up?'

'Get lost,' I said. 'It's a locket: *dur*. Sister Frances took it ages ago, and just gave it back.'

'Show us,' Cas said, and leant over. 'Is that your dad? He looks like that Hollywood actor – you know: the one who's in that movie, about the bullfighter, and he's a total spunk.'

I snapped the locket shut and put it in my pocket. 'Don't make me puke,' I said. 'You're talking about *my dad*. And he's just moved out – so I don't really want to talk about him.'

'What?!' Cas asked. 'How come you didn't tell us?'

'Well, I just did, didn't I? And it's not that bad – it's better than how it was when my parents were fighting all the time. Now it's just my mum, my two sisters and me. Dad's moved into an apartment. He's seeing this other woman.'

'What an A-hole,' Sam said.

'I know,' I agreed. 'I thought he was the biggest creep. I cut him out of the photos around our house.'

'You what?!' Sam broke out laughing.

It didn't seem that funny to me though.

Cas looked shocked.

'But now I'm kinda feeling bad about that –' I said. ''cause, maybe, I reckon Dad's been an okay Dad to me, but maybe it's just that he's not been very good to Mum.' It felt good to share my life with Sam and Cas.

'That is so sad,' Cas said. 'I'm gonna write you a song, and make you all happy-smiley again.'

'Write *me* one too,' Sam said to her. 'Last night, my mum dropped me off at Dad's flat, and she deliberately backed into his letterbox.'

'Whoa!' I said, with a giggle. Now it was my turn to laugh. 'And I thought *my* parents were bad! It's kinda funny, don't you think?' I looked down at my lucky clover. Maybe some of my wishes were coming true: I *was* seeing the funny side of things, and really it wasn't so bad. Dad wasn't a creep – he'd just stuffed up in a big way. I remembered what'd happened by the horse shed that night, and he'd said, "not accepting change only makes life harder". I put the clover back in my locket and clipped the necklace around my neck, careful not to let Sister Frances see.

The bell rang. We grabbed our stuff and ran out of the room.

'Girls! Come back!' Sister Frances called out to us.

But we sprinted off down the corridor and skidded into the locker room.

'Stacks on!' Sam yelled, and pushed Debbie onto the floor.

Cas and I jumped on top.

'Get off!' Debbie yelled. 'I can't breathe!'

We screamed as more girls came over and stacked on.

'Girls!' Sister Frances was coming down the corridor.

We grabbed our bags and bolted out the back way to the oval.

'That was too funny!' Cas said. 'See ya later – I gotta go to rehearsal.' She waved as she ran off.

'Break a finger!' Sam yelled back to her, then grabbed my bag. 'Quick: here comes Sister Frances.'

We sprinted down the drive. Sam pushed and shoved to get in front. 'Ha! *Suffer*!' she said when she'd beaten me to the front gate.

'*Big poop*!' I said with a laugh, and backed away towards Amy.

'*See ya*!' she yelled back.

I waved: '*Yeah, see ya tonight*!'

We dropped Amy off at Lisa's and then headed to the concert. When we got there, we found the chapel packed. We ended up having to sit right up the front, where they'd put extra seats. I had a quick look around, but couldn't see Sam or Cas.

Father Curry shuffled across the altar, towards the microphone. Everyone shushed each other. Father said a quick mass, and then SS made a really long speech, and after that she handed out awards. When Sam won a medal for rowing, I clapped extra loudly: she'd come 'head of state' for her age group.

I whispered to Mum, 'That's Sam; she's one of my mates, and she's a wicked rower.'

Mum looked super-impressed – and I'd already told her about Cas's scholarship.

The lights faded. Someone coughed, and then it went dead quiet. When the spotlight was shone on the altar, we saw that SS had sat down and Cas was sitting on the top step. Cas was about four metres away from us, and her face was totally serious: I almost cracked up. With the light shining through her hair, she looked like she had a halo on.

She closed her eyes. Her fingers moved slowly and plucked at the strings. Then she leant forward and blew into the microphone. It sounded like the noise the wind made when it blew through the pine trees at Yarra Valley. Then she played fast and loud! Then she did this thing where she rapped her knuckles against the wood. Then she played faster and louder! Then she finished with the wind sound again.

Everyone clapped and stood up.

'Oh, she's fantastic!' Mum said.

We kept clapping.

Cas got up and bowed, then put her guitar under her arm and stepped down to her seat.

SS adjusted the height of the microphone and asked everyone to be seated. 'Supper is served in the music hall,' she announced. 'And girls, do enjoy the break.'

Heaps of girls jumped up and cheered. If the parents hadn't been there, everyone would have charged out the door like cattle in a muster. But some of the girls had brought their parents and grandparents, so it took us ages to get out.

I spotted Cas. She was standing by the music-hall stairwell. Heaps of people were crowded around her. She saw me through the crowd and excused herself so she could come over.

'Mum, this is Cas,' I said.

Mum shook her hand. 'That was beautiful,' she said. 'Veronica tells me you might be going to Italy.'

She crossed her fingers. 'The Australian Orchestra tells us who's going in September,' she said. 'I auditioned last week. There's two spots for guitar players, and if I get in, I get to go for two weeks just before Christmas. I've been to the Gold Coast twice, and that's it. So it'd be like *the* best Christmas present ever. And they pay for everything.'

'I wish you luck,' Mum replied. 'They'd be crazy if they don't choose you – you're extremely talented.'

'Thanks!' Cas said. 'If I don't get in, that's okay as well: a friend's in a band, and they need a guitar player, so I could do that. There's a couple of outdoor festivals over the summer, so that'd be pretty cool.' Then she introduced her parents and a group of boys to us. Her mum was tall, just like her.

'Congratulations,' Mum said to her mum, whose name was Anne.

'Thankyou,' Anne said. 'I like the idea of Italy better – rather than these festivals, where the kids get drunk.'

'Mum!' Cas rolled her eyes and turned away so she didn't have to hear it. 'And this is Tate,' she went on, 'and Nathan, and Chuck.'

I knew Tate was her boyfriend, and figured Nathan and Chuck were his friends. 'Hi,' I said, and quickly looked away. I didn't know what else to say, and they were staring at me, like they were waiting for me to say something. I fiddled with my locket. There was something familiar about Chuck but I couldn't quite place how I knew him . . .

'*Oi!*' Sam rushed over and barged in. She was super-excited about something.

'Show us ya medal!' Cas said to her. 'Did you know you were gonna get it?'

'No way!' she replied. 'I thought SS hated my guts – but she's changed my Junior Burger into a Big Mac!'

'For real?' Cas squealed. 'That is *so* cool. Where's your Mum?' She looked behind Sam to see whether anyone was behind her.

'Not here,' she said. 'She's got this exam, for one of her night-school subjects. Oi! *Donuts!*' Sam grabbed a handful of them as a waiter walked past carrying a platter of pink and chocolate ones. 'Grab a whole heap!' she said. 'Take them with us and let's go outside.'

'Hang on!' I said. 'I gotta tell Mum. I'll meet you out the front, on the steps.'

Mum and Cas's parents were talking to SS. Rather than go over to them, I waved and pointed towards the door to let Mum know I'd be outside. She waved back that it was okay for me to do that.

When I got outside, Sam and Cas were talking about their plans for Wilson's Prom. I sat down beside Sam. It was weird seeing Cas with her arm around Tate.

Chuck turned around and smiled at me. He had the most perfect teeth. 'Cas says you're a brain,' he said.

'Hardly,' I said, feeling weird.

'And that you've got horses.'

'Yeah – two: Eb and Maje.'

'My sister rides too,' he said. 'And she goes to pony club.'

'Which one?' I asked.

'It's North Eastern, or something like that.'

Sam was being a dick, flapping her hands behind Chuck's back. She pulled a stupid face to try and crack me up. I ignored her and kept a straight face.

'That's the one that's just near where I'm agisting my horses,' I said. 'I was gonna check it out, and if it was any good, I was gonna join.'

'Give me your number and I'll tell my sister to call you,' he said, and smiled. 'Hey, that's it! I know I've seen you before. I almost ran over you with my bike one day.'

'Oh, my God,' I said, remembering perfectly, that was the day when I found out Suze was going to live with her Nan. 'Yeah, sorry about that. I hope I didn't say anything rude? I was in a bad mood that day and I was running –'

'Veronica!' It was Mum, waving to me.

'Gotta go,' I said to Chuck, 'I promised my sister Penny that we'd be finished by 9.00 – I didn't realise what time it was and we're going to a gallery opening where she's exhibiting some art that she made.'

I turned around to hug Sam and Cas. 'See ya,' I said to them. 'Have *the* best-est time at the Prom . . .' And turning back to Chuck, 'Ah, nice meeting you.'

He got up. 'Yeah – you too. See ya.'

'Oh, and, um –' I almost fell over as I walked off – 'maybe Cas could give you my number . . . to give to your sister.'

'Sorted,' he said. 'It's North Eastern, for sure – so maybe you two can go for a ride.'

'Yeah – thanks.'

Mum had walked off ahead, so I caught up to her. On the way to the car, she stopped under a streetlight and searched through her handbag. 'I thought my keys were in here,' she said, but instead of keys, she pulled out a bunch of rocks.

'Mum,' I asked: 'rocks?'

She laughed. 'I've been collecting them for the mosaic.'

'I hope so,' I said. ''Cause, like, I don't think that's normal.' I'd seen the pile by the herb garden, and over the past few months it'd been getting bigger – so I knew she wasn't making it up; I was just glad she'd pulled the rocks out in front of me and not in front of my friends. 'I'll help you make the mosaic, if you want. We could do it over the holiday.'

'That'd be great,' she said. 'There's enough broken tiles and rocks now – you're a love.' She checked her coat pockets. 'Oh: here they are.'

When we got to the car, the central locking beeped as the doors unlocked.

'Hey, Mum,' I asked, 'do you reckon you'll ever get married again?'

She threw her head back and laughed, hard. 'Why? Would you like me to marry the coach of the Australian Olympic Eventing team?'

Wow. It *was* possible to love Veronica Bee. 'Yeah . . .'